SILENT CAME THE MONSTER

"A deeply compelling novel rich with historical detail
and surprising parallels to our modern world."

—HESTER YOUNG, author of *The Gates of
Evangeline* and *The Burning Island*

"Terrifying, delightful, thoughtful, and gripping."

—*BERKSHIRE EAGLE*

"Well drawn and believable . . . this combination
of historical events and thrilling suspense makes
for a taut, compelling read."

—*HISTORICAL NOVELS REVIEW*

"Chilling and entertaining."

—*SHREVEPORT TIMES*

SILENT

CAME

THE

MONSTER

BOOKS BY AMY HILL HEARTH

Nonfiction

Having Our Say: The Delany Sisters' First 100 Years

The Delany Sisters' Book of Everyday Wisdom

On My Own: Reflections on Life Without Bessie

In a World Gone Mad: A Heroic Story of Love, Faith, and Survival

Strong Medicine Speaks: A Native American Elder Has Her Say

Know Your Power: A Message to America's Daughters

Children's Nonfiction

The Delany Sisters Reach High

*Streetcar to Justice: How Elizabeth Jennings Won
the Right to Ride in New York*

Fiction

*Miss Dreamsville and the Collier County
Women's Literary Society*

Miss Dreamsville and the Lost Heiress of Collier County

*Silent Came the Monster: A Novel of the 1916 Jersey Shore
Shark Attacks*

A Novel of the 1916 Jersey Shore Shark Attacks

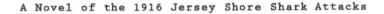

SILENT CAME THE MONSTER

New York Times bestselling author
AMY HILL HEARTH

BLACK STONE
PUBLISHING

Printed in the United States of America
Originally published in hardcover by Blackstone Publishing in 2023

First paperback edition: 2024
ISBN 979-8-212-87686-5
Fiction / Thrillers / Historical

Version 1

Blackstone Publishing
31 Mistletoe Rd.
Ashland, OR 97520

www.BlackstonePublishing.com

For Blair and all the other rescuers, lifeguards, and heroes who rush toward danger at their own peril. You represent the best of humankind.

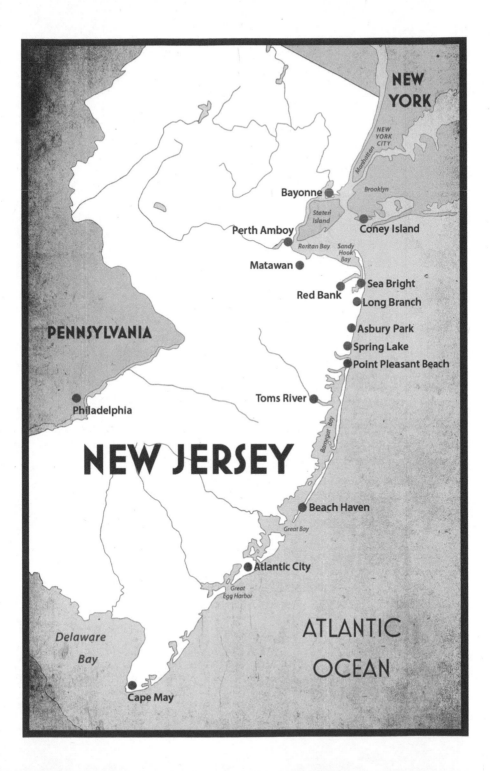

PROLOGUE

JUNE 17, 1880

The deckhand saw it first. *Sweet Jesus, what is that?* he asked himself. Before he could get a good look, the creature dove beneath the surface.

They were close to shore, less than a mile off Sea Bright, New Jersey. Propelled by a light but steady wind, they were heading in for the day with a full catch.

Maybe it's a whale, he thought. It was embarrassing that he knew so little, but this was only his third day as a deckhand. Two weeks before, he had graduated from the eighth grade. The summer of 1880 stretched out before him with visions of hammocks, fireworks, and girls. His father, however, had decided that a challenging job would toughen him up, and so the lad found himself aboard a wide-beamed nineteen-foot catboat, learning the ropes from an experienced captain willing to tolerate a novice assistant.

"Captain Longstreet," he yelled. "There's something out there!"

But when the skipper turned, there was nothing to see but the gray-blue waters of the Atlantic Ocean on a glorious summer day.

Then the creature surfaced off the starboard bow. This time the captain saw it and recoiled.

"What is it? A whale?" called the deckhand.

"It's a shark!" the captain shouted. "Big one! Never saw one like that 'round here! Now stay calm, boy!"

This was not the response the inexperienced deckhand was hoping for. He scanned the horizon intently. *Maybe it will just go away*, he thought.

But it appeared again behind the stern, the enormous dorsal fin protruding like the black sail of a pirate ship closing in. Instead of catching up, however, the shark hung back. Then it sped up and began to pace them, and the young deckhand saw that the shark was nearly the length of their fishing vessel.

It's not following us, the deckhand thought, his heart in his throat. *Surely, it can't be.*

Suddenly, the shark shot forward, its dorsal fin aimed directly at the boat. The deckhand screamed. The captain watched helplessly.

Just as they braced for impact, the shark simply disappeared. There was no sight of its dreadful dorsal fin at all.

It's gone! thought the deckhand, shaking with relief.

A few seconds later, it slammed the underside of the boat and tore right through the wood, sending chunks and splinters flying. Protruding through the bottom of the boat, stuck fast, was the massive head of the creature—its jaws wide, as if to bite the air.

Then the shark seemed to panic, thrashing wildly, flinging the captain overboard.

The deckhand grabbed ahold of the gunwale and held on.

The creature could not free itself. It shook the boat furiously, then spun the vessel back and forth in semicircles. Finally, it lifted the boat into the air, smashing it back down on the water's surface.

The deckhand hung on.

I must kill it, he thought. *I have to kill it.* But he could not reach anything that could be used as a weapon. At the same time, he wondered what to do about the captain, who was trying desperately to climb back into the boat.

"Don't give up, Captain!" the deckhand cried. He let go of the gunwale and reached for the captain's hand, gripped it tightly, and pulled him into the vessel.

At the same moment, the shark freed itself.

Water gushed through the hole where the shark's head had been. *We're going to sink!* the deckhand thought. He grabbed a tarpaulin and tried to stuff it into the hole, but the force of the water was too great.

The captain began to shout, and the deckhand's first thought was, *The monster is back!*

But that was not why the captain was yelling. He was calling to the captain of a much larger fishing boat that was arriving to help.

"Are you all right? My God, what was that thing?" shouted a crew member on the bigger boat, a two-masted schooner more than twice the size of the catboat. Seeing the extent of the damage, he shouted urgently to his own captain. A gangplank dropped into place, and three sturdy sailors scurried aboard the smaller boat. They shoved the young deckhand out of their way. Using their squall jackets, they managed to plug the hole.

This was only a temporary fix, however, and the men worked together, scrambling to locate material for a sturdier repair. There wasn't anything suitable on the smaller boat, but a piece of wood from a supply crate was located on the rescue boat and quickly nailed into place.

Now there was nothing to do but wait to see if the repair held. They used the time to bail water that had accumulated during the near-catastrophe.

The young deckhand scanned the sea for their attacker. There was no sign of it. He was starting to feel hopeful. *Is it possible we survived this?* But he was struck by the continued uneasiness of the seasoned crew that had rescued them.

"Tell me—what do you think it was?" one of the rescuers asked in a low voice, as if the sea beast might overhear and come back.

"We saw what was happening to you and couldn't believe our eyes," added another.

"My deckhand and me, well, 'tis a miracle we are still here," replied the captain, also speaking in a hushed voice. "I can scarcely believe it myself, but 'twas a man-eating shark, the kind with the white underbelly."

The first rescuer nodded his head. "That is what we thought too!" he said. "I've only ever seen one off the coast of Australia."

"I saw one off Nantucket, far out to sea, a long time ago," said another.

"Never heard of one here off the Jersey Coast," declared the captain of the damaged vessel. "And so close to shore! They are deep-sea creatures! But we can't be more than a half mile off Sea Bright!"

"Well, you know, it's still out thar somewhere," said the first rescuer. "We'd best all be going to our home ports. Where you headed?"

"Oceanic," said the captain. "Just got to cut through the inlet, then south a wee bit. It's not far, and the wind is picking up, so it won't take long at all."

"Do you want us to go with you?" asked the second rescuer.

"No thank you, she seems seaworthy," replied the captain. "But I thank you from the bottom of my heart for all you have done for me and my deckhand."

They all shook hands, and the rescuers went on their way.

All we need to do is get to the inlet, the deckhand thought, trying to remain focused. *Once we pass through the inlet, the docks at Oceanic aren't much farther.*

The wind was at their backs, the repair was holding, and soon they would be home. All seemed well.

The inlet, which separated Sea Bright from the barrier island known as Sandy Hook, was in sight. Beyond it, they glimpsed the tidal estuary that would carry them home. The estuary was flanked on the north side by a woodsy hillside known as the Atlantic Highlands—the highest elevation along the Eastern Seaboard south of Maine—and on the south side by lowlands and marsh, where the docks awaited. Within a few minutes, their ordeal would be over.

They were moving along at a steady clip, their confidence growing by the minute, when a familiar, horrible sight appeared behind them.

"It's back!" the deckhand screamed to the captain.

"No!" hollered the captain.

But it was. And this time it didn't just follow the boat. It caught up and swam along the starboard side.

"Try to hit it with something," cried the captain. "If it attacks the boat again, we'll sink for sure!"

The deckhand tossed an empty bucket, but it bounced off the shark's head, which it had raised slightly from the water.

"Go away!" yelled the deckhand as if it were a dog.

Maybe all it wants is the day's catch, he thought. He scooped up as many fish as he could and threw them toward the shark.

"You want the fish? Take them, and I hope you choke!" he shouted.

The shark slowed, opened its enormous jaws, and swallowed the fish. Then it caught up with the boat again.

The deckhand threw another armful. And another. *It's working! It may be eating all of the fish, but at least it's not attacking the boat.*

"Stop!" shouted the captain. "What are you doing?"

Horrified, he realized the captain was right. He wasn't distracting the shark. He was encouraging it. He threw an old lobster trap. The shark paused, lifted its massive head, and swallowed it.

For a moment, the deckhand lost all hope and stood frozen.

Then the captain called out, "It won't follow us through the inlet! We're almost there!"

Desperate, the deckhand rushed around the boat, collecting anything he could grab and heaving it overboard. He tossed cork life vests and a length of coiled rope, which caused the shark to slow down momentarily. It tore into the life vests but ignored the rope.

He found a hatchet, aimed for the creature's head, and flung it, but missed.

Next was a pair of boots. "How about these smelly old boots?" he shouted at the shark. "Take 'em! Go away!"

Again, the shark swallowed them.

But now they were in the inlet. Surely, as the captain had said, the shark would abandon the chase, preferring to remain in the open sea.

Yet it stayed with them.

"It's not giving up!" the deckhand wailed helplessly. There was nothing left to throw at the beast.

As the boat neared the docks at Oceanic, people hearing the commotion were stunned by an extraordinary sight: a small fishing vessel heading straight toward them at a brisk clip, and adjacent to it, an enormous dorsal fin protruding from the water, keeping pace.

"Look out!" the captain bellowed as people scattered.

To the deckhand, he shouted, "Hang on! We're going to hit the dock hard! Don't get thrown in the water! Be ready to jump on the dock and run for your life."

JULY 1-2, 1916

CHAPTER 1

"Hello! Could you tell me if I missed dinner?" a blond youth in a black woolen bathing costume, blotting his boyish face with a beach towel, called boldly to an exceptionally pretty debutante strolling the boardwalk.

"Not at all! You have plenty of time," she called back playfully.

"May I see you later?" he shouted.

"Not if you're still covered with sand," she replied and laughed. She smiled coquettishly, then turned and sashayed into the lobby of the majestic Engleside Hotel while he stared after her longingly, trying to imagine what she might look like in one of the daring new swim dresses.

As members of Philadelphia's high society, which comprised most of the guest population at the Engleside, the flirtatious pair, both younger than twenty, normally would not dare to interact so brazenly in public. But in the tiny seaside town of Beach Haven, New Jersey—a little slice of heaven compared to the suffocating, smelly streets of the city back home—everyone let their guard down, especially since it was the first of

July, a Saturday, and the beginning of the Independence Day celebrations.

The young man raced into one of the brightly painted beachside cabanas to change his clothes. He reappeared a few minutes later and dashed into the lobby in pursuit of his new friend.

The lifeguards were relieved that he had gone indoors. A competitive swimmer and a bit of a show-off, he was one of several young men who swam far out to sea, alone and for long stretches at a time. From where the lifeguards stood on the beach, it was difficult to see him past clusters of people splashing in knee-deep water. They knew there was little chance they could rescue him if he were afflicted with a muscle cramp, a jellyfish sting, or even simple fatigue.

The seasoned lifeguards, especially, groused about this new generation of men who actually went *swimming* in the ocean, as opposed to the good old days of the Victorian era when everyone went sea-bathing, an activity which largely consisted of wading, treading water, paddling about, and floating, often while clinging to ropes.

The lifeguards now turned their attention to a small group of boys who had just arrived with their families. Released from the stuffy confines of railcars or automobiles, they tore through the sand with nannies scampering after them. Pausing only to kick off their shoes, which flew haphazardly through the air, the boys hurtled themselves fully dressed into the surf, then ran back and forth in an impromptu game of tag with the waves, their arms outstretched and faces lifted to the sun, all the while screeching with joy.

The boys weren't easy for the lifeguards to monitor either, but at least their antics were amusing, unlike the ocean swimmer. Hotel guests also found the boys charming and paused on the boardwalk to watch. The sight of children in the surf, frolicking like dolphins, reminded adults of their own care-free younger days. This was part of the charm of returning year after year. Each new generation discovered and fell in love with the seashore while older family members observed, smiled, and reminisced. For the middle-aged and elderly, how comforting it was, in a chaotic world, to return to the seaside, where one could count on the certainty of salt-scented air, the soothing sound of breaking waves, and the hypnotic rhythm of low and high tides.

No one noticed the disturbance in the water—a ripple or strange current just beyond the safety ropes. A dark spot appeared, then vanished, like a shadow from a passing cloud.

It was time for the boys to come in and get dressed for dinner. Reluctantly, one by one, they responded to their nannies' pleas. Slowly, they left the blissful sea and trudged onto the sandy shore.

At last, the surf was empty. The lifeguards relaxed a bit. The activity had shifted almost entirely to the boardwalk, except for a few guests who relaxed on chairs placed in the sand. Inside the hotel, the newly arrived were settling into their suites, and everyone was preparing for the evening meal. Trunks were opened, gowns unfolded and pressed. Maids organized slippers and hatboxes. Dinner was a formal affair, and guests dressed accordingly. Some of the women were known to take more than two hours to prepare for their entrance at the dining room.

Among the late arrivals was a family which was new to the Engleside, the Vansants. The father, an esteemed physician, had made a last-minute decision that they would not vacation at their summer house in Cape May because of an outbreak of contagious disease there.

Charles, the only son in the family, was eager to take a quick swim in the ocean, although the dinner hour was growing near. His mother objected, saying there wasn't time, what with the unloading, unpacking, bathing, and dressing that needed to take place. But Charles insisted. He was, after all, a grown man, a stockbroker by profession who would turn twenty-four in August. He opened a leather bag, grabbed his bathing outfit, and hurried to a cabana to change his clothes.

The rest of the Vansants—his father, mother, and the one sister who had come along—stretched their legs on the boardwalk while servants unloaded their belongings and carried them inside. Dr. Vansant kept looking at his pocket watch, a little irritated at Charles for insisting on a quick swim. But as he watched his handsome, dark-haired son stride across the sand toward the water's edge, the father felt nothing but pride. Charles had excelled at sports as well as his studies in college and now excelled at his profession. He had been courting a young lady from a fine family, and a wedding seemed imminent.

A dog suddenly bounded across the sand and dropped a ball from its mouth in the path of Charles, who, delighted, stopped in his tracks. Charles had always liked dogs. He threw the ball, and the dog raced to catch it, then brought it back. A crowd grew on the boardwalk as people stopped to watch and cheer them on.

After a while, Charles coaxed the dog to follow him into the surf. The game of fetch continued in the water. As Charles swam farther out, the dog followed, and the game continued.

Then the dog appeared to tire. She turned abruptly and swam straight to shore. When she reached the sand, however, she showed no sign of fatigue. She didn't collapse or even lie down on the beach. She just sat there, facing the sea.

Charles called to her, but she refused to move. He swam for a few minutes without her, then started to head in.

"Look out!"

The words pierced the air, rising above the sound of the surf.

The lifeguards leaped to their feet, ready for action, but Charles Vansant was swimming calmly and steadily. They scanned the boardwalk. Who had shouted? What was wrong?

"Look out!"

This time, they saw the source of the warning, an older gentleman standing by himself on the boardwalk, pointing out to sea.

They glanced again at Charles. He was perhaps only two hundred feet from shore. He wasn't floundering. If anything, his swim stroke was measured and sure. Was someone else out there—someone who was drowning and needed rescue?

And then the lifeguards saw it. A triangular object. A fin of some sort, shockingly large, but attached to what, exactly? They had never seen anything like it but immediately realized what they must do: rescue an unaware swimmer from something menacing in the water.

They grabbed the gunwales on opposite sides of the lifeboat and ran as fast as they could while hauling the two-man rower through the sand and into the water. Sea spray flew from beneath their feet as they bounded through the shallow surf until the boat was free from drag. They leaped into the boat at the same time. Powered only by a double set of oars, the wooden craft surged over a large incoming wave. Their rowing was perfectly coordinated, just as they had trained.

From the boardwalk, the rescue boat, painted bright white, seemed to launch into the waves with the ferocity of a large predatory bird defending its offspring. Guests strolling the boardwalk stopped short and turned to look. Was a swimmer in trouble? Or was it simply a drill?

A young boy in his father's arms pointed and screamed, "It's going to get him!"

"What? What is going to get him? Who?" a woman cried as she stood on tiptoes, trying to get a better view.

Suddenly, everyone understood. The young man who had been playing with a dog was swimming toward shore. Behind him, something followed in the water. A large, triangular shape was closing in on the young man.

"It's a sea monster!" a man shouted.

The crowd began to chant, almost pleading with the lifeguards, "Go! Go! Go!"

The fin disappeared. Perhaps the mysterious creature was gone. Perhaps it was only an illusion, some trick of the sun on the water after all.

But then the fin protruded again from the water, this time closer to the young swimmer, and the chant from the boardwalk switched to "Swim! Swim! Swim!" as the crowd implored Charles to hurry.

Then the creature vanished again.

Charles might have heard the shouting. He trod water for a moment, looked around him, then cautiously resumed swimming to shore. He paused again, surprised by the approaching lifeboat. One of the lifeguards called to him, and he changed direction, swimming toward the boat.

"There! Look!" a woman shrieked.

The crowd gasped. Most had been focused on the lifeguard's outstretched hand and the proximity of the young swimmer to the boat. But behind the boat, the head of a great creature rose from the water.

"The monster!" shouted a man whose voice was choked with fear.

"Dear God, they are doomed! Hurry! Hurry!"

Then it disappeared again, slipping quickly back into the sea.

"Where did it go?" someone yelled.

"Is it gone?"

"What's happening?"

Charles screamed, a sound so loud and primal that people inside the hotel rushed to their windows. The cry was cut off when he was yanked beneath the water, straight down.

He popped up, his arms flailing as he half swam, half pawed the water, pushed by something which propelled him forward. In the commotion, he was no longer close to the lifeboat. He swam furiously for the beach, now only one hundred feet away.

As he broke through a wave cresting the beach, the lifeguards tried a different tactic. They beached the lifeboat and jumped into the surf, hoping to pull him to shore. They grabbed his arms and tugged, shocked by an unexpected and tremendous weight. Whatever had latched onto him was, they realized, still holding on.

Men watching from the boardwalk—many of them in their formal dinner clothes—saw the lifeguards struggling and ran down to the beach and into the water to help. The first to arrive grabbed ahold of the lifeguards, who were still hanging on to the young swimmer. They formed a human chain, working together like a bucket brigade in a fire. A fierce battle ensued—a horrific game of tug-of-war with a long line of men on one side and the sea monster on the other. In the middle was Charles Vansant, still fighting for his life while half drowning in a red-tinged sea.

Astonishingly, the monster held on. The rescuers managed to get Charles onto the beach, but still the creature would not let go. One of the lifeguards considered hitting it with an oar when, all of a sudden, it released its grasp. Using its huge, powerful tail, the monster flipped itself back into the surf and was gone.

CHAPTER 2

"Is this Dr. Edwin Halsey?" a tense voice inquired over the telephone.

"Yes, this is he."

"Sir, this is Constable Gilchrist, and I need your help."

"What's wrong?" Edwin asked.

"A young fellow has been attacked by a fish."

"A fish?" Edwin wondered if he'd heard correctly, and yet he shouldn't have been too surprised. The summer of 1916 was turning out to be an odd one, and it was only the first of July.

"Well, we're not sure what it was," replied Gilchrist.

"Where did this happen?" asked Edwin.

"In Beach Haven, right in front of the Engleside Hotel. The victim's name is Charles Vansant, and he's twenty-three years old. We're not sure he's going to make it. He's losing a lot of blood. We were thinking we could bring him up to the little hospital in Toms River. I called Monmouth Memorial in Long Branch, and they said you were already at Toms River, doing some kind of operation. Could you wait for us? You're this poor fellow's last hope."

"Of course I'll wait," said Edwin.

As he prepared for the arrival of the victim, however, Edwin grew uneasy. He explained what was happening to his new nurse, Miss Kelso.

"Beach Haven is a long way off," he said. "The constable said the patient was bleeding heavily. He won't make it here. It's just too far."

"Well, what can we do?" she asked.

Edwin thought for a moment. "Marnie," he called briskly to another nurse. "Call Constable Gilchrist at the Engleside in Beach Haven. Tell him I'm driving down there and they should prepare an operating room. Are you coming with me, Miss Kelso?" Edwin asked in a tone that sounded more like a command than a question.

"If you want me to," she replied timidly. "What if Marnie can't reach the constable? What if they've already put the patient in a car and are driving up here?"

"That's a chance we'll have to take," Edwin said impatiently. "There's only one decent road, so we'd likely cross paths with them."

"And then what?"

"Perform emergency surgery on the side of the road, if necessary," he said. "It wouldn't be the first time."

Miss Kelso, fresh out of nursing school, stared at him with round blue eyes, an expression that revealed her youth and inexperience. "Well, I don't know . . ."

"You don't know what?" asked Edwin.

"I don't know how to do that," she said. "Help in a situation like that, I mean. How do you . . . ?"

"I keep a complete set of surgical tools, chloroform, and a folding table in my automobile," he said. "Now are you coming with me or not?"

She hesitated before nodding.

He checked once more on his current patient, a farmer who had injured his hand while repairing a newfangled machine. The farmer was stable, and his care could now be turned over to the local doctor.

In the passenger seat of the Model T, Miss Kelso looked utterly miserable, her arms folded tightly across her chest, her mouth downturned. As Edwin sped up, the Model T began to bounce, and she grabbed the seat to hold on. "This is the main road?" she asked.

"Yes," said Edwin. "Miss Kelso, where did you say you are from?"

"Milwaukee," she said.

"Ah, you are a city girl and used to better roads," Edwin said.

"I didn't realize . . . I didn't understand that this would be part of the job," she said.

"I thought I made it clear that I'm often called away from Long Branch." He didn't bother to hide his annoyance.

Under ordinary circumstances, the drive south to the bridge that would take them to Beach Haven would have been a pleasant excursion. Each little town, decorated with bunting and flags for the upcoming Fourth of July holiday, was preparing for the busiest days of the year. Signs for fried flounder, fresh oysters, tomatoes, and blueberries were enticing reminders that Edwin hadn't eaten since morning.

"We're getting close to the bridge," he said.

"Bridge?"

"Why, yes, we have to cross a bridge. Didn't I say? Beach Haven is on an island. It's called Long Beach Island, and it's about eighteen miles long but very narrow. It's what they call a barrier island. Beach Haven is at the southern end."

She said nothing. Then: "What did you say was wrong with the patient? He was injured while swimming?"

"Uh, yes," said Edwin. "He was swimming in the sea."

"How did it happen?" she asked.

"I don't know," replied Edwin. "Now we are coming to the entrance to the bridge. It's quite new. I haven't been here since they built it."

When the narrow wooden vehicular bridge came into view, Miss Kelso screeched.

Edwin hit the brakes and pulled to the side of the road. "What's wrong?" he asked.

"That is not a bridge!" she cried.

"Why, of course it's a bridge," he said. "A modest one, perhaps, but it suits the purpose."

"It looks like it's made of matchsticks!"

"Miss Kelso, I am urgently needed in Beach Haven, but I can't make you go with me. If you're truly afraid, you could get out here and wait for me. Of course, I don't know how long it would be."

"Is that the ocean?" she asked suddenly.

"Why, no, that's a bay. See that strip of land in the distance? That's the island. I believe it's about two miles from here. The ocean is on the other side of it."

"So the bridge is about two miles long?"

"Approximately," said Edwin, tightening his grip on the steering wheel. "Miss Kelso, we are wasting time."

"Is that a railroad bridge?" she asked, pointing to a span to the south.

"Yes, that's been here a long while."

"Well, why don't we take the train?"

"Instead of driving? No, we don't have time," replied Edwin.

In truth, Edwin didn't relish the thought of driving across the new bridge either. It appeared to be five feet above the water and barely two lanes wide.

"Miss Kelso, please make up your mind!" he cried. "The patient awaits! You're either coming with me or not!"

"Okay," she said. "But—"

"But what?"

"I don't know how to swim."

Edwin sighed. "Don't be concerned, Miss Kelso. I have no intention of allowing us to end up in the water."

Considering the matter settled, Edwin drove across the bridge as fast as he dared, his eyes focused deliberately on the road.

But his efforts to ignore the bridge's meager dimensions were hampered as every minute or so, it became necessary to slow down and hug the edge to make room for a car to squeeze past from the other direction. Why were so many people leaving the island at the start of a holiday weekend? He glanced at Miss Kelso. Her eyes tightly closed, she gripped the seat, her lips moving in silent prayer.

Stifling the urge to join her, Edwin instead addressed his nurse in a dry tone. "Miss Kelso, if you are going to have a successful nursing career, you really must learn to be adaptable. You must—"

His admonition was interrupted when a sharp object ricocheted off the hood of the Model T. Then a barrage of similar objects rained down on the road before them. Miss Kelso screamed as he fought for control of the car.

Clamshells, he realized as he slowed down. He looked up. Seagulls were dropping them from great heights onto the rigid surface of the bridge in an attempt to crack open the hard shells.

"It's nothing!" Edwin yelled, but Miss Kelso kept screaming.

When he reached the island, Edwin wanted nothing more than to drop off Miss Kelso, but he didn't have time even for that. Instead, he drove straight to Beach Haven on the island's one primitive north–south road. Miss Kelso calmed down, and he began to hope she might even prove useful once they'd located the patient.

As he parked his vehicle near the Engleside, the hotel mentioned by the constable, Edwin realized immediately that something was very wrong. Guests were leaving in droves, not arriving as one would expect at the beginning of a long summer holiday. Trunks were being secured to vehicles by servants working at a frantic pace.

Miss Kelso was too mesmerized by the ornate building to notice the behavior of the crowd. "How beautiful," she murmured, staring up at the turret, which could be seen far out at sea.

Like every lifelong resident of the Jersey Shore, Edwin knew of the Engleside, a resort favored by well-to-do families from Philadelphia, only sixty or so miles away. Unlike some of the newer hotels, old-fashioned Victorian rules were still in place at the Engleside. Alcohol was not served, and guests dressed for dinner as if they were going to the opera. The hotel grounds included a private ocean beach and tennis courts.

How disconcerting, then, to encounter a scene where panicked guests rushed back and forth, waving their arms and calling to one another like lost children, as if they were doomed passengers on the ill-fated *Titanic* before it went down in the North Atlantic four years before, a ghastly event still in the forefront of everyone's mind.

As Edwin and Miss Kelso exited the vehicle and hurried toward the building, a gentleman with an ivory-handled cane stopped him. "Sir, let me warn you: If you are just arriving, you should turn around and leave! Trust me, you do not wish to stay here! Make haste! A sea monster has attacked a young man! He is in terrible condition!"

As he said the words *sea monster*, Miss Kelso spun around.

"Where are you going?" asked Edwin.

"I will be waiting in the car," she replied with a wave of the hand.

So much for having a nurse assist me, he grumbled to himself. *But maybe it is better this way. I won't have to worry about her.*

Edwin fought his way into the lobby of the lavish hotel like a salmon swimming upstream. Once inside, he couldn't get the attention of the staff. Desperate to locate the injured Mr. Vansant, he grabbed the arm of a passing bellhop and explained who he was and that he had been called to an emergency. The bellhop dropped the bags he was carrying, enraging the matron to whom the luggage presumably belonged, and quickly escorted Edwin through a long, dimly lit hallway.

The bellhop pointed to a corridor, then vanished. Edwin set out alone, following a sound he heard all too often. He hurried forward and came upon an alcove where two women sat together below a window with heavy drapes that were tightly drawn. They clung to each other, wailing.

"Pardon me, my name is Edwin Halsey, I am a surgeon, I am here to help," he said, speaking quickly.

The older of the two women, who wore the hat and jewels of a matron, slowly turned her head and looked up at him. "There is nothing that can be done," she shrieked.

The younger of the two, weeping so hard that her hairpins had fallen out, peered at Edwin through long, untidy tresses. She gestured toward a closed door.

Edwin knocked, but there was no response. He lifted his hand to knock again when the door slowly creaked open a few inches.

A tall, mustachioed man scowled at Edwin and said, "Please do not disturb us."

"Wait," said Edwin. "I am Dr. Halsey, the surgeon who was contacted by your constable, and I have come a long way."

After a pause, the door was opened wide, and Edwin was ushered in. There were four men in the room already. One man was slumped in a chair, his face in his hands. The others stood perfectly still in a semicircle, not looking at one another. Their demeanor confirmed to Edwin that the victim was dead.

The mustachioed man, who said he was the hotel manager, introduced Edwin to the others: Dr. Jeremy Sands, a local physician; Dr. William McBride, a retired public health official from Philadelphia who was a guest at the hotel; and, sitting in the chair, Dr. Maurice Vansant of Philadelphia.

"Dr. Vansant was the first doctor at the scene," the hotel manager said. "He is the father of the young man who was attacked by the fish."

Edwin's thoughts were scattered, and he tried to rein them in. This was every doctor's nightmare: to rush to the side of someone who was injured, only to discover a member of their own family. Edwin found it hard to think of the right words under such difficult circumstances. The best he could manage was, "I am sorry for your loss, Doctor."

Fortunately, the local physician, Dr. Sands, perceived Edwin's discomfort and spoke up.

"Would it be all right, Dr. Vansant, if Dr. Halsey were to examine your son?" he asked ever so slowly with a profoundly gentle manner that Edwin envied. "Dr. Halsey has lived at the shore all his life and is very highly regarded."

"Why, of course," Dr. Vansant replied, his voice hoarse and hollow. "By all means," he added. "I believe I will go sit with my wife and daughter." He stood to leave and lost his balance, collapsing into his chair. He rose again, and this time the hotel manager put his arm around the poor gentleman's shoulders to steady him.

When the door closed behind them, Edwin was free to make

his inquiries. "How long ago did the patient expire?" he asked, taking off his suit coat and rolling up his sleeves.

Dr. Sands looked at his pocket watch. "It's been one hour and forty minutes," he replied. "Unfortunately, there wasn't much we could do. He lost too much blood. He had a severe injury to his left thigh. Of course, we applied a tourniquet, but we didn't have chloroform or a bone saw to attempt an amputation. At first, we hoped he might hang on long enough to bring him to the hospital in Toms River, but it became clear he wouldn't survive the journey."

"Ah, I see," said Edwin. "I am the surgeon who was hoping to meet you in Toms River. So the young man died of shock brought on by blood loss caused by some kind of traumatic event."

"Yes," the other two doctors said in unison.

"Gentlemen," asked Edwin, "will you kindly show me the body?"

Dr. Sands gestured to an adjoining office. Edwin was surprised that the deceased lay in the next room on such a hot day. The body should have been moved immediately to a funeral parlor for embalming or, at least temporarily, to the hotel kitchen, where there was undoubtedly an icebox large enough for short-term storage.

There was no door to the adjoining office, and oddly, the hinges were half torn from the wall.

Dr. McBride followed Edwin's gaze. "We didn't have a proper examining table to lay him on," he explained. "We took down the door and used that instead. We were in such a desperate hurry, and we wanted to afford him and the family some privacy."

"And the light is better in here," Dr. Sands added, flipping on an overhead electric fixture. "We've got two lamps as well. They can be brought close. And a very powerful torchlight that belongs to the constable."

The door had been laid across two parallel desks. Upon this makeshift but adequate table was the distinct shape of a human form under a white sheet. The room reeked of blood.

"I've changed the sheets probably twenty times," Dr. Sands said apologetically. "I've never seen this much blood in my entire career, not ever."

He carefully rolled back the sheet, exposing the victim's body.

The upper torso, head, and arms of an athletic young man were undisturbed. There was a gash on the right thigh that would not have been life-threatening. The left thigh, however, was missing a massive amount of flesh in a crescent shape that went all the way to the bone. Indeed, it resembled a huge bite mark.

"Good Lord," Edwin said softly.

"I believe he was bitten twice," said Dr. Sands. "Right here and right there. Look at the teeth marks. What kind of fish has teeth like that?"

"A mackerel," Dr. McBride said authoritatively. "But several witnesses say it was a sea turtle."

"Gentlemen, this is a shark bite," Edwin said with conviction. "There is no question."

"Impossible!" Dr. Sands bellowed. "We don't have sharks like that here. *Anywhere* around here!"

Dr. McBride concurred. "There are no man-eating sharks off New Jersey, or New York for that matter!" he said. "It must be a large mackerel. And it must have been a *mistake*."

"A mistake?" asked Edwin.

"Well, it would not have been by *intention*. Surely, it was a mackerel or some other fish that simply misjudged. It probably thought our young victim here was, well, something else—a school of fish, perhaps."

"Has either of you ever seen a shark bite?" asked Edwin. "Well, I have! In Cuba during the Spanish-American War. I must insist, this looks similar to several shark bites I saw while I was down there."

"Similar?" asked Dr. Sands. "But not exactly?"

"No, not exactly," replied Edwin. "This one is actually much worse."

"Well, I may put 'fish bite' on the death certificate," said Dr. Sands. "Or perhaps 'bite from unknown source.' I hesitate to write 'sea turtle' or 'shark' or 'mackerel' or *anything* specific since we really don't know. And I'm going to say 'accidental bite.'"

Edwin felt dizzy, not from the sight of the wound or the smell, but from the frustration of arguing with these two men, who, although educated, were obviously ignorant or in denial. "What did the witnesses say?" asked Edwin. "There must have been many witnesses, yes?"

"Oh, indeed there were," replied Dr. McBride. "Many men tried to rescue him, poor lad."

"What did *they* say?" he asked again.

"The constable is talking to the witnesses now," replied Dr. Sands, "but my understanding is there's no consensus."

"Gentlemen, if this was a deliberate attack on a human being by a man-eating shark, the public has a right to know," said Edwin. "We can't hide that possibility."

"But we also must be *prudent*," Dr. Sands said hastily. "There is no point in causing unnecessary alarm."

"As a public health physician, I must say I agree with that sentiment," Dr. McBride said firmly. "We could cause a panic. We must act responsibly and with caution."

Edwin could no longer hide his disdain. *What are they afraid of?* he thought. *The possibility of being wrong—of looking foolish?* "Gentlemen," he said, "I will not be a part of willfully obfuscating the truth!"

"You do not have any solid evidence for your assertion, sir," replied Dr. Sands. "Please let me implore you not to be reckless."

"It is you who are being reckless!" said Edwin. Disgusted, he left the room and returned to the main part of the hotel.

The lobby had thinned out considerably. Across the expansive room, beyond mahogany furnishings and potted tropical plants, Edwin spotted the vaguely familiar face of Constable Gilchrist, who had telephoned him. They had met at least once before, although Edwin couldn't remember when or where. Probably after a drowning.

The constable was relieved to see Edwin. "I am very glad you are here, Dr. Halsey."

"I only wish I had been able to help," said Edwin. "But I did examine the body and offer my opinion."

"Well, thank you for that," said the constable. "Are you leaving?"

"Unless you need me for something else," replied Edwin.

"One of the lifeguards is feeling poorly," said the constable. "Could you take a look at him? His name is Sylvester Van Dorn. I believe he's in the kitchen, where they've been trying to give him tea and warm him up."

"Warm him up?" Edwin asked, alarmed.

"That's what they said."

"He may be suffering from shock," said Edwin. "It's at least ninety degrees outside, and the water is probably seventy. But you say he's cold? How long was he in the water? Never mind, I'll find him and look after him."

"Thank you," said the constable. "There are several other doctors around here, but I don't know if any of them have checked on Sylvester."

"I shall do so immediately," said Edwin. He thought briefly of Miss Kelso waiting in the car. She would simply have to wait awhile longer.

He found his way to the hotel kitchen and discovered that most of the staff had left. The remaining chefs, dishwashers, and servers were huddled in small groups. A few women were crying. Platters of food sat abandoned. Dinner had never been served.

A muscular lad with his feet soaking in a tin tub seemed a likely candidate for the lifeguard.

"Sylvester Van Dorn?" Edwin asked.

The lifeguard nodded.

My, how young he looks, Edwin thought.

He introduced himself and pulled up a chair. "The constable is a little concerned about you. How are you feeling?"

"I was shivering, but I'm much better now," replied Sylvester.

After checking the young man's vital signs, Edwin agreed.

"I think you're on the mend," said Edwin, "but I would like to keep an eye on you for a few minutes, just to be certain."

"I don't think it's necessary, sir, but thank you," Sylvester said politely.

"Is this your first summer as a lifeguard?"

"No, sir. My second." Suddenly, he lost his composure. "Oh, sir!" he cried. "It was so horrible! The evil creature would not let go! We pulled the young man all the way onto the beach—to dry land—and the monster was still hanging on to the poor fellow's leg!"

"What?" asked Edwin. "Are you saying the whole creature was on the sand?"

"No, not all of it. The front part, maybe more."

"You actually saw it?"

"Yes, sir, and I pray I never see such a sight again as long as I live."

"Well, what did it look like to you?"

"I don't know, sir. It happened so quickly, then it sort of flopped back into the sea."

"Could it have been a shark?"

Sylvester looked at Edwin in astonishment. "I don't see how that's possible, sir. We don't have sharks like that around here."

"Simply because no one has encountered one doesn't mean they don't exist."

"I suppose so," Sylvester responded cautiously. "But people have lived here a long time. Fishermen are out there every day. Why hasn't it happened before?"

"Maybe it did, but no one knows about it," replied Edwin. "Maybe it killed a person, but there were no witnesses. Or maybe someone had a close call but wasn't believed or didn't tell anyone because they feared ridicule."

"Well, sir, I don't know about any of that," Sylvester said slowly.

"There were plenty of other witnesses today," Edwin continued. "What did they think it was? Did anyone say?"

"One of the guests said it was like a creature in Scotland—Nessie, I think he called it. He said the Scottish monster is hundreds of years old, and he thought maybe it found its way here or it has a cousin. A couple of men who do a lot of sport fishing said it was a giant mackerel. But there were several who felt quite strongly that it was a very large sea turtle."

"Well, the authorities will be investigating," said Edwin. "Did Mr. Vansant say anything you could hear?"

"No, sir, he was in terrible shape. His left leg was nearly torn off. I wanted to make a tourniquet, and I shouted that I needed a strip of cloth, and one of the ladies tore the hem off her dress and gave it to me."

"So you applied the tourniquet?"

"No, a man who said he was a doctor applied the tourniquet. He came rushing down to the beach and pushed me aside. Then he asked if the young man could be carried into the hotel. The doctor was the young man's father, or so I've been told. If so, I think that's the saddest part right there—that his family saw it happen from up on the boardwalk and his own father tried to save him. I feel so sorry for them, and I feel like it's my fault."

"Why would you say that?"

"Because it happened while I was on duty."

"Trust me," said Edwin. "This is not your fault or anyone else's."

"Do you think it will come back—the monster, I mean?"

"I don't know," Edwin replied. But in truth he was filled with dread.

It's probably only a matter of time.

CHAPTER 3

On the drive home from Beach Haven, after they reached the mainland, Edwin and Miss Kelso were caught in a fierce, punishing coastal storm, the kind known locally as shipwreck weather. It was a fitting encore for a horrible day. Gusty winds and deafening cracks of thunder kept Edwin at the edge of his seat, hands clutched on the big wheel of the Model T. Miss Kelso shrank and jumped at each lightning bolt.

In several places, the roads were nearly washed out. Twice, he became stuck and had to climb out of the automobile and push it back onto solid ground. Once, he had to ask Miss Kelso to help.

The drive home in the dark took nearly four hours, plus an additional twenty-minute diversion because Miss Kelso asked to be dropped off not at Monmouth Memorial, where they had started out that morning, but at her boardinghouse in Eatontown—not that Edwin could blame her. As she left the car, her skirt muddied and her hat ruined from the rain, she announced that she was resigning.

He couldn't fault her for that either.

As he drove on to Red Bank, he felt so tired that he considered pulling over to rest, even though the storm showed no sign of abating. The day had not been an easy one, especially for a man who was no longer young.

Edwin was forty-nine years old—an age when younger men started asking vague questions about his "future plans," meaning, in this case, that they wanted Edwin's job as chief of surgery. *How dare they?* he asked himself often. *Why, I have only recently reached the zenith of my career, the intersection of experience and knowledge. I am at my peak. I have worked to get here! I deserve a chance to enjoy it! Who says it must be so fleeting?*

His indignation lasted until he remembered having the exact sentiment about old geezers when he was young.

And so he had been toying with the possibility of shaving his beard and adopting a more modern look. After all, the reason he'd started growing it years before was to make himself appear older and more distinguished. The facial hair was now, in fact, flecked with silver, a development that had not yet taken place in the hair on his head, which remained brown, or "chestnut," as his late wife, Charlotte, used to say.

Charlotte had insisted that he was very handsome and often praised his features, especially the strong jaw and cheekbones he had inherited from his father, along with what she called "the Halsey family's classic nose," whatever that meant. Edwin was not particularly interested in physical appearance, including his own.

But he did sometimes wonder how different he would look to Charlotte now. While trimming his beard, he had noticed in the mirror that his gray eyes, which she had called "twinkly," had become slightly hooded and small bags had begun to form underneath. Another odd development was that the corners of his mouth tended to turn downward.

His firm belief in regular exercise as advantageous to one's health had kept him in good physical form, however. He took brisk walks frequently, and in the carriage house on his property, he kept a small gymnasium, which he used three times a week. These efforts were not for vanity, but to maintain his endurance as a surgeon. The hours standing on his feet, working in total concentration while trying to save a stranger's life or limb, were grueling, even when he was young.

Edwin knew that, even if he were to surrender his surgical tools, retirement was unlikely. There weren't enough diagnostic physicians in the area, and his home office was well equipped. The people of Red Bank, where there was no hospital, would continue to need his services.

Perhaps what he needed to give up were excursions like the one to Beach Haven. It was not a day he would ever wish to repeat. The death of young Charles Vansant was a terrible tragedy, and it would weigh heavily on Edwin's mind for a long time to come.

When he reached home at last, it was a quarter past midnight. His clothing and shoes were so filthy that he stripped to his underclothes in the alcove by the back door. Then he pulled on an old robe that hung on a peg alongside other articles of clothing that were destined to become rags. At least he would be decent enough to walk through the house.

He planned to take a hot bath and go to bed immediately, but he couldn't relax until he confirmed that his daughter Julia had returned home safely from her evening with Mortimer Weeks, the wealthy and—in Edwin's opinion—vacuous man who had been courting her. Edwin was not impressed by Mortimer's connections, which included being related to President Wilson's second wife. Edwin was not interested in social status, but evidently Julia was. Edwin's greater objection, however, was the age difference.

Mortimer was a very immature—again, Edwin's opinion—thirty-two, and Julia was not yet twenty.

Mortimer was good-looking in a dramatic sort of way, a bit like the hero of a stage play. His hair was dark, almost black, and his eyes were an unusual shade of brown, almost amber. He was a bit of a dandy, very aware of his effect on women, and not at all hesitant to use it.

Not especially tall or athletic, he made up for his deficits by wearing extravagantly tailored clothing, especially hats. He owned an extensive collection of cuff links, a detail which Edwin would never have noticed except for Mortimer's habit of fidgeting with them constantly like a parrot preening its feathers. He wasn't just annoying, however. He was unreliable, a trait which Edwin found inexcusable. Most egregious of all, Mortimer didn't really have a profession; he "dabbled in finance," whatever that meant.

Whenever Julia had been out and about with Mortimer, she arrived home past her curfew or just in the nick of time. Edwin took it as a personal affront and had spoken to Mortimer several times, letting him know he was displeased. Edwin doubted that even a good-for-nothing like Mortimer would want to stay out late on a miserable night like this but decided to be certain that Julia was home and asleep in her bed.

He knocked on her bedroom door. Alarmingly, there was no response. He knocked again, this time calling her name. Still no reply. He opened the door and peered in. There was no lump indicating a human in the bed, so he flipped on the overhead electric light.

Julia was not there.

Fear gripped his heart. *Still out on a night like this?* he fretted. *She could be injured or dead.* His experiences as a doctor often made him assume the worst.

The storm had not let up. An old shutter came loose and

slammed the side of the house like a metronome. Surprisingly, the electricity had not gone out, but Edwin figured that was only a matter of time, so he lit the candles on the old candelabra in the main hallway downstairs.

He considered what to do about Julia. *Should I telephone the police?* he wondered. *What if it turns out she's fine and just out canoodling with Mortimer? If that's the case, getting the police involved could prove embarrassing, perhaps even scandalous.*

A tremendous clap of thunder made him jump and propelled him straight to the telephone. This was no time to worry about reputation.

"My daughter is out in this storm, and I am frightfully concerned about her," Edwin told the desk sergeant when he finally got through.

"How old is she?"

"Nineteen."

"When did you expect her back?"

"Hours ago," said Edwin. "I was detained, answering a medical emergency."

"Oh, is that you, Dr. Halsey?"

"Yes. I'm so sorry, did I fail to identify myself? I guess I am quite upset."

"Dr. Halsey, I'm not sure how much we can do at the moment. We're barely keeping up with calls where we know someone is in imminent danger."

"Oh, of course," said Edwin.

"I'll tell everyone to be on the lookout for her. Try not to worry too much, Doc. She's probably just holed up somewhere safe, waiting for the storm to end."

"I'm sure you're right," said Edwin. He thanked the desk sergeant and hung up, feeling a little foolish. Still, he worried, and since waiting patiently was not high on Edwin's list of natural-born abilities, he made an impulsive decision. He would get dressed and look for her himself.

Just as he was ready to leave, the front door, buffeted by a huge gust of wind, was flung wide open. There she stood, like an Old Testament apparition, her hair blowing in all directions, leaves and debris swirling about her and into the house.

"Hello, Father," she called to Edwin. "What a night!"

"For heaven's sake, close the door!" Edwin shouted crossly. He rushed toward her and pulled her by the arm out of the doorway and into the foyer. Together, they pushed the door shut against the wind.

Edwin stepped back and took a good look at her. She was so drenched from the storm that her clothing stuck to her in ways that were not entirely modest. He frowned. Then he noticed a pool of rainwater forming at her bare feet.

"Good Lord," he cried, "where are your shoes?"

She held up her new satin pumps, the ones he thought were too expensive but let her keep anyway. "I took them off so I wouldn't ruin them."

"Where is Mortimer?" Edwin demanded. "Please don't tell me he dropped you off without escorting you to the door!"

"Oh, *Father!*" Julia replied with a sigh. She put her hand to her forehead like an actress in a silent film, one of her favorite new types of entertainment. "You are *so* old-fashioned. So very *last century*. But I'm sorry I worried you. Truly, I am."

The electric lights flickered.

"Where in God's name have you been?" asked Edwin.

"We had dinner in Deal with Mortimer's cousins," she replied. "I told you that's where I'd be! Weren't you listening? On the way home, we got stuck in a rut near the new army base. Thankfully, some soldiers came and pushed us out. It was a grand adventure!"

Grand adventure. Oh, how the words grated on Edwin's nerves. "Young lady, go upstairs straightaway," he said, employing his most serious, fatherly tone. "Get out of those clothes and take a hot bath *immediately.* Then put on your winter robe and slippers. I shall meet you in the kitchen. I am going to make you some hot soup!"

"*Hot soup?*" Julia laughed hysterically.

It crossed Edwin's mind that she might have consumed alcohol.

"Well, something warm," he replied. "I don't care what it is. But you will drink it and stay up until your hair has dried completely."

"But, Father, look at *you*," she said, suddenly noticing his wet hair. "What has happened?"

"I got caught in the storm too," he replied, again remembering the sea monster and poor young Vansant. "I had an emergency in Beach Haven."

"All the way down *there*?" she asked. "That's not that far north of Atlantic City! Why you, Father?"

"Because the original plan was to meet the patient in Toms River, but it didn't work out," he said, without providing any detail. He had perfected the art of telling Julia his whereabouts without revealing any disturbing information. Protecting Julia from the grim realities of medicine was an old habit, one he might as well give up, seeing as she was studying to become a nurse.

"You must be exhausted, Father," said Julia.

"Yes," he said. "It was a remarkably bad day."

"Did your new nurse go with you to Beach Haven? How is she working out?"

"Well, it turns out she is afraid of water," said Edwin. "Also bridges, at least the kind we have here. She has decided to go home to Milwaukee."

"Already?" Julia asked mischievously.

"Go! Take your bath!" he insisted. "I will get out of my wet clothes too and meet you in the kitchen."

By the time she came down and joined him, Edwin had heated up chicken broth that he found in the icebox. It was nearly two in the morning.

Looking at her across the table, her face freshly scrubbed, Edwin was reminded of just how much Julia resembled Charlotte, the mother she had barely known. The tip of Julia's slightly upturned nose, which came to a point that Julia hated but Edwin—and Mortimer, for that matter—thought was rather cute, was identical to her late mother's. The tiny overbite with otherwise perfect teeth was also like Charlotte's, but the color of Julia's eyes, slate gray, was from Edwin, as was the chestnut color of her hair.

Edwin had been rehearsing the scolding he planned to give her, but he was too tired, and perhaps too sentimental, to be angry. Besides, there was something unexpectedly nice about sitting together at the kitchen table, sipping soup. He was reminded of all the times she'd had croup or some other malady as a little girl and how he stayed up with her all night, coaxing her to eat or drink to regain her strength.

Julia, however, did not seem the least bit nostalgic and slurped the rest of her soup. "Good night, Father!" she said and burped.

As she went into the hallway, Edwin called after her, "Young lady, I'm still upset with you."

"Stop worrying so much, Father!" she called cheerfully, her footsteps sounding up the stairs.

Oh, to be young and carefree! He couldn't help but smile, just a little.

But sentimentality was no match for his anxiety. His concerns about her came rushing back, always in the same order.

She had become very unreliable since meeting Mortimer. Edwin believed the relationship was a mistake, but at the same time, he didn't want to curtail her happiness. She had lost her mother so young and had been an unusual child, precocious, lively, and questioning. She had floundered at secretarial school but excelled after enrolling in the nursing school at Monmouth Memorial. But now that, too, was slipping away.

Edwin was too agitated to sleep. He decided to pour himself a small glass of Laird's apple brandy and read for a while in the parlor, in his favorite chair, which Julia rightfully believed was embarrassingly decrepit but which he would not give up.

His mind was too troubled to read, however, and he found himself talking to the photograph of his late wife. "Oh, Charlotte," he implored, "what am I to do about our Julia?"

Edwin fell asleep in his chair, still uneasy about Mortimer. The next thing he knew, he awakened from a vivid nightmare in which he was trying to save the leg of a young soldier injured in the Spanish-American War. In the dream, he was removing shrapnel from the soldier's wounds when, inexplicably, the shrapnel turned into shark teeth.

In that hazy place between sleep and wakefulness, he listened to sounds coming from—well, he wasn't sure. He listened carefully. Was he in Cuba? Tampa? Or at home in New Jersey, years after the war? Then he heard some gentle cursing and realized, with great relief bordering on joy, that it was Hannah, his longtime housekeeper, who often muttered and mumbled while clunking around in the kitchen making breakfast. That meant it was six o'clock. More importantly, it meant he was in present-day Red Bank, New Jersey.

When neither Edwin nor Julia came down for breakfast, Hannah shouted, "Good morning!" up the stairs in her Irish brogue.

"In here," said Edwin.

Hannah appeared in the doorway. "Are you all right, Dr. Halsey?"

"Yes, I believe so. Just tired. I had a very difficult call in Beach Haven yesterday and then drove home in the storm."

"Beach Haven!" Hannah exclaimed. "That's a long way from here!"

"Yes," he replied. Edwin started to stand up and was dismayed at the soreness in his back and legs. *That's what I get for sleeping in a chair at my age*, he thought. But then he recalled the long drive to Beach Haven and back. His mind turned to young Charles Vansant, the upsetting scene at the resort hotel, and the horrendous wound to the young man's leg. He thought of the shattered Vansant family, the heroic lifeguard, and the overwhelmed constable.

And then a thought came roaring back: *the sea monster.*

"Hannah, what is on my calendar for the day?" he asked. "When is my first patient arriving?"

"It's Sunday, Dr. Halsey," replied Hannah.

"Oh, of course. Church at ten. On call at the hospital for emergencies in the afternoon and evening. But don't I have some kind of meeting?"

"No, that's tomorrow," she replied. "With the governor and a few others at three o'clock. To discuss the epidemic."

"Oh," he said. "I wish I didn't need to go. He already knows how I feel. If he's still considering an emergency proclamation to close the roads coming into the state, I'm all for it."

"Close the roads?" asked Hannah.

"Not to all traffic," replied Edwin. "To any vehicle with a child under sixteen. Newark is already doing it."

"That seems quite drastic," said Hannah. "Families won't be able to visit each other."

"Well, would that be so terrible, just in the short term?" he asked, annoyed. "It's only a precaution. We don't know what's causing the epidemic, and this would keep children safe. Why can't people understand such things?"

"Because not everyone had your schooling," replied Hannah. "But even a doctor needs a day of rest once in a while," she added. "Forgive me for saying this, but you look terrible."

"I feel terrible."

"Mercy, is that mud on your forehead?"

"Could be."

"I think you should stay home today and rest," she said firmly. "Not even church," she added.

"I'm supposed to help with Communion. They'll wonder what happened to me."

"Well, I'll call them and say you had an emergency," Hannah said flatly.

"Why, Hannah," he couldn't help but tease her, "that would be a lie!"

"It is not a lie," she said indignantly. "*You* are the emergency."

Edwin laughed. He'd known Hannah for almost thirty years, ever since the malignant diphtheria epidemic in the Limerick section of Long Branch, home to recent emigrants from Ireland. She was like an aunt or much-older sister to him, and there was no sense in arguing with her.

"You win," he said.

"Where is Julia?" she asked.

"Still asleep," he replied.

Hannah scowled. She didn't like Mortimer Weeks either.

Deciding to let Julia sleep in, Edwin went upstairs to take a bath and dress for the day. He then ate breakfast while Hannah filled him in on the latest news of her grandnephew who had joined the British army and was fighting in the war that was tearing Europe apart.

He returned to his armchair and waited for Hannah to leave. As soon as the kitchen door shut behind her, and despite his agreement to rest for the day, he got to work. There was much to be done.

Although the telephone operator, at Edwin's insistence, tried again and again, no one answered at the front desk of the Engleside Hotel in Beach Haven. Finally, after more than an hour, someone picked up. A man's voice, barely audible, said in a monotone that neither the owner nor the manager was available and hung up.

Edwin had better luck with Constable Gilchrist.

"There's been no sign of the fish," the constable reported.

"Shark," Edwin corrected him. "I'm quite certain it was a shark."

"Well, that's yet to be determined," said the constable. "We're still calling it a fish."

"But it's not . . . Oh, never mind," said Edwin. "There's something I'd like to ask you. When you interviewed witnesses yesterday, what did they say about the size of the creature?"

"Oh, there was no consensus at all. Some folks said ten feet; one lady said eight or nine feet. Others said twelve feet, maybe fourteen."

"I see," said Edwin. "I suppose that's not surprising."

"Yes, considering how unexpected it was and how quickly it happened," said the constable. "Plus, people saw it from different vantage points. So basically, the witnesses were just guessing."

"How are the Vansants? Did they leave yet?" asked Edwin.

"Yes, Dr. and Mrs. Vansant and their daughter left for Philadelphia about an hour ago with the body. The hotel manager and I saw them off."

"What else is happening?"

"The hotel manager is enclosing the swimming area with steel netting. They're working on it now. The beach is closed until then."

"Did you notify the other hotels?" asked Edwin. "And the other beach towns?"

"Well, no," he hedged. "That's not my job. I don't want to step on anyone's toes, so I'm awaiting instructions."

Edwin groaned. The constable was afraid to act in a timely fashion. *Afraid of what exactly?* Edwin thought. *Being reprimanded?*

Delay, denial, fear of all the wrong things—job security, reputation, and social niceties—placed ahead of saving human lives. Edwin didn't say any of this to the constable because there was no point and there wasn't time. It was the Sunday of the Fourth of July holiday, the busiest weekend of the year at the shore. The beaches would soon be packed. He'd have to take matters into his own hands.

There was no time to lose. Edwin dressed quickly and was preparing to leave the house just as Julia came downstairs.

"Where are you going, Father?" she asked. "It's not time for church yet."

Edwin told her they would talk later, then walked a few blocks to the telegraph office. While he couldn't go to every single location along the shore and warn people, he could send a telegram to every police chief.

"Extremely dangerous situation," Edwin dictated to the telegraph operator, whose eyes grew wide as Edwin spoke. "This is an alert from Dr. Edwin Halsey of Red Bank, New Jersey. Large, aggressive shark deliberately attacked and killed swimmer in Beach Haven, Long Beach Island, on July 1. Shark not captured or killed. Close beaches immediately."

Did he have the authority to send those telegrams? *Probably not*, Edwin thought. *But I'll never forgive myself if something else happens and I didn't try.*

CHAPTER 4

On the same day as the Beach Haven attack but much farther north, Miss Margaret Atkins rose early, unable to sleep because of the oppressive heat. She could not recall Matawan, her hometown, ever being this hot.

Might as well get up rather than toss and turn in bed, she thought. She brushed her hair, pinned it to her head in a loose Gibson-girl braid, and tied it with a blue ribbon. She dressed in the loosest cotton housedress she owned. No corset today. A camisole would have to do. No silk hose either. And definitely no extra petticoat.

Someone knocked at the front door. No one was expected, and it was much too early in the day for calling hours.

Her mother, trying to hold back a full-blown headache, was irritated. "Margaret," she called, "please go see whoever in the world that is."

Margaret cracked open the door. Standing perfectly still and very straight, holding a bouquet of wildflowers, was her longtime sweetheart, Watson Stanley Fisher, known to all as Stanley. His presence, as well as his formal demeanor, surprised her.

"Why, Stanley," she said. "I thought I would be seeing you tonight."

He thrust the flowers at her. "Let's go down to the creek," he said. "I want to take you out in the canoe."

"Stanley, it's half past six in the morning!"

"It's the coolest part of the day," he said. "And it's so beautiful down at the creek at this hour."

"Well, I'll have to change my clothes first," said Margaret. "And I haven't eaten any breakfast."

"Oh, I packed breakfast for us." He gestured to a small picnic basket on the bench beside the front door.

"Good heavens, Stanley, you've thought of everything!" Margaret was puzzled by this early morning visit, though. She rarely saw Stanley before he went to work, yet here he was—and with a picnic basket and flowers, no less.

He waited on the front porch while she got ready. She changed quickly into a blue gingham dress with a white bib, then stuffed her hair under her new broad-brim straw hat.

Still not exactly practical for going out in a canoe, she thought forlornly. If only it was acceptable for a proper young lady to wear pants.

She took a quick look in the mirror and wondered if it were true, as people often said, that she looked like "America's sweetheart," the film star Mary Pickford. She could detect some similarities such as a heart-shaped face, diminutive figure, and dark-blond hair, although Margaret, unlike Miss Pickford, rarely wore her tresses in voluminous ringlets.

"Mother, I'm going out for a little while with Stanley," she said, without mentioning the creek.

"What? At this hour?"

"He wants to spend a little time together before he goes to work," replied Margaret. "Can I borrow your parasol?"

"Oh, honestly, what a silly thing to do," her mother grumbled. "Going for a walk at six thirty in the morning!"

Margaret ignored her mother's comments. She found Stanley sitting on the white wicker furniture in the shade of the overgrown rose of Sharon bushes. She was struck by how serious he looked.

"Stanley, is everything all right?"

He grinned, but to her, it seemed forced. "Of course," he said.

Maybe he's just worn out from the heat like everyone else, she thought. She opened her parasol and took his arm.

"I hope you like what I made," he said.

"You made something?"

"Yes, I baked some muffins."

"Stanley, you're worrying me. I don't remember you ever baking anything."

He laughed. "Give a fella credit for trying," he said. Now he sounded like his old self.

As they walked toward the creek, Margaret wanted to ask more questions but thought better of it. She wasn't fully awake, anyway.

"The tide is coming in, so you may need to take your boots off," he said. "Either that or I'll pick you up and put you in the canoe."

"I don't mind going barefoot," she said. "Although, come to think of it, I wouldn't mind being carried either."

"Why, Miss Atkins, are you flirting with me?" he asked playfully.

"Possibly," she replied, doing her best to look demure.

They walked down the path to the spot where Stanley's friend Rusty kept a canoe that anyone was allowed to borrow. Stanley handed Margaret the picnic basket and dragged the canoe toward the water.

She liked to watch him when he was preoccupied and unaware. She had always admired his profile, especially his strong jaw. His hair, light brown most of the year, acquired strands of blond from the summer sun. His eyes were blue, but a darker shade than hers. When doing close work indoors, he sometimes wore wire-rimmed glasses. His manner was welcoming and friendly, and he instantly put people at ease with his boyish grin. He was sometimes mischievous but never mean, and she always knew when he was about to tease her because the corners of his mouth would curl up ever so slightly.

Moving the canoe was not difficult for him. He was six feet two inches tall and weighed more than two hundred pounds—nearly double her weight and a foot taller. He moved with the ease and grace of an athlete. His favorite sport was baseball, and even in the winter, except for the coldest days, Stanley could often be found playing a spirited game with his friends or teaching younger boys how to catch or hit the ball.

He took off his shoes and socks and rolled up his pant legs. The tide was rising swiftly, and he pushed the canoe partway into the water with little effort.

"Okay, now," he said. "Do you want to climb in? Or do you want me to pick you up? Don't forget the picnic basket!"

"I believe I can get in all by myself," said Margaret in a mocking tone. It wasn't easy, however, considering that she had to gather her skirt with one hand while balancing the picnic basket in the other. She almost fell over. "I'm so elegant!" she said, laughing.

"Shh! You'll scare all the birds," said Stanley, and sure enough, two herons nearby took to the air.

He waited for her to get situated, then climbed in himself.

"Do you want me to paddle?" she asked.

"Absolutely not," he replied. "I'll do the paddling. You relax and eat your breakfast."

She ate two of the muffins and tried to hide the fact that they were slightly bitter. She declared them excellent, anyway; it was delightful to be out on the water nibbling a muffin her beau had made for her.

Stanley paddled on one side, then the other, keeping a smooth momentum as they headed against the incoming tide to a bend in the creek, their favorite location. From here, they could see egrets, red-winged blackbirds, maybe even a bald eagle if they were lucky. He set the paddle down and dropped the anchor over the side.

They listened to the sounds of the creek. The water, always moving, gurgled a song of the ages. Sea oats, rustled ever so gently by an invisible breeze, whispered a harmony.

"Margaret Atkins, will you marry me?" asked Stanley out of the blue. He didn't sound like his normal self at all. For a second, she thought it might be some kind of joke, although that wouldn't be like Stanley.

He reached into his vest pocket and produced a ring box, which he flipped open and held out to her. "I guess I should get down on one knee, but I'd probably flip the canoe."

She had been hoping he would ask one day, but the time and place caught her completely off guard.

"Why, yes, of course," she said, barely getting the words out.

Stanley reached for her left hand and tried to slip the engagement ring on her finger, but his hands trembled slightly. After the third try, she started to giggle. Then he laughed too.

"Oh, this is terrible!" he said. "I'm bungling it."

"It's all right," she said, although she was a little worried the ring might be too small. "Here, try again."

This time the ring slipped right onto her finger. "A perfect fit!" she declared. "Stanley, it's lovely."

"You like it?"

"I do!"

"Well, that's the point of it all—saying 'I do'!" he joked. "I hope you don't mind my asking you like this. I was going to wait until the heat spell ended and take you out for a proper dinner somewhere nice. But when I got up early this morning, I decided that today was the day."

"Well, this way you truly surprised me," said Margaret. "Besides, you could have asked me any old way, and I would have said yes."

He grinned but then grew serious. "I was thinking I should come by the house tonight and ask your father for your hand in marriage," he said. "But your mother's still feeling poorly. Maybe I need to wait."

"I see what you mean," said Margaret. "We haven't had any visitors in days. And Mother certainly isn't up to any type of celebration."

"You do think your father will give his permission, though?"

Margaret knew he was being a little playful. Father loved Stanley. Mother did too.

"Well, I certainly hope so," Margaret replied. "And if he doesn't, I just might marry you anyway."

They both laughed. Then Stanley said, "I guess we ought to keep it a secret for now. Your parents should be the first to know."

"When do we tell your parents?" she asked.

"Right after we tell yours," he replied. "But remember, my parents are leaving Tuesday on their trip. I'm hoping this all comes together before they leave. If not, we'll have to hold off until they get back. Don't you think?"

"I suppose so," she said. "But what should I do about the ring? Take it off? Hide it? Oh, I hate waiting."

"Well, look at it this way, Miss Atkins," Stanley said, pretending to be formal. "I've been wanting to ask you to get married since we were, oh, sixteen. I suppose we can wait a little longer to announce our engagement. I don't want to do anything improper and upset your parents. I wouldn't want to get off on the wrong foot."

They lingered for a while. Finally, Stanley said they had to head back. He needed to get to work, and she needed to get home before her mother became worried. Margaret felt a little sad and said so.

"You don't want to go back?" he asked.

"No," she replied. "I wish we could spend the whole day together."

"Me too," he said. "But remember, we have our whole lives ahead of us."

JULY 3-4, 1916

CHAPTER 5

"Let me take you to Cliffwood Beach this afternoon, Mother," Margaret pleaded. "I bet it's ten degrees cooler there. It's so stuffy here in Matawan, and all that fresh air will do you good. You could soak your feet in the water."

But her mother, lying flat on her back in bed, turned her head and scowled. "There is no way this side of glory that you will get me to any beach. Not with a sea monster out there!"

"Oh, Mother, you're not really worried about that, are you?" asked Margaret. "That's a long way from here. Cliffwood Beach must be sixty or seventy miles from Beach Haven."

"It's just horrible," her mother mumbled. "Like we didn't have enough to fret about in this wicked world, now we have a sea monster."

"You worry too much, Mother."

"It's just so shocking. Perhaps it's some kind of mistake. Like maybe someone is covering up a murder or something like that."

"What? Mother, that doesn't even make sense."

"It's just hard to believe, that's all. Never heard of such a thing."

"All right, well, maybe we'll go to the beach another time," said Margaret.

"You seem awfully chipper, considering this heat," said her mother.

"Well, it may be hot, but have you noticed the beautiful, bright blue sky we've had lately? Not hazy at all! It's so lovely."

Her mother smiled wanly. "Margaret, you are such a dear creature. I'm glad you know how to enjoy the simple things in life."

The real cause of Margaret's cheerfulness was, of course, her secret engagement to Stanley two days earlier. Keeping quiet was harder than she had imagined. The worst part was not being able to wear the ring, which she had hidden in the back of a drawer in her wardrobe.

Stanley was right, however. With her mother in this condition, it wouldn't be proper for them to celebrate or make an announcement. Perhaps her mother would improve in a few days.

Margaret kissed her mother on the forehead and got dressed to go out. As a third-grade teacher, Margaret ordinarily would have summer off, but she'd agreed to tutor students aged six to fourteen who had fallen behind for various reasons, usually illness. Summer school was their chance to catch up.

They met at Old Broad Street School three mornings each week. Margaret was allowed to organize it any way she wished. Currently, the little ones focused on arithmetic. The older children worked on their Independence Day essays, "What America Means to Me."

When Margaret returned home at lunch, her mother seemed worse. She had run out of her pills and asked Margaret to go to the pharmacy for her.

Margaret didn't mind. Unfortunately, she arrived at the shop at a busy time. Four or five customers were ahead of her, but she could pass the time by sampling the latest soaps, creams, lotions, and scented waters.

Near the front of the store, by the door where a bell jangled each time someone walked in or out, three old men were talking loudly. They were often there, the same three, always gossiping. There was a joke in town that anyone who wished to find out what was really going on in Matawan didn't need to attend meetings at the town hall. All they had to do was cross paths with Captain Thomas Cottrell, Robert Kerfoot, and William Bingley on any random day.

Margaret didn't usually mind their attempts to outdo each other, but today it was simply too hot to listen to their silliness.

"I'll tell you what I think," Mr. Kerfoot announced in a booming voice. "I think the Germans did it."

"Did what?" asked Captain Cottrell.

"Caught the sea monster and then set it loose off Beach Haven, or pretended to. The whole thing sounds like a hoax to me."

"Why would they do that?" asked Mr. Bingley.

"Because they're taunting us, that's why. They know that President Wilson is spending time here at the shore this summer. They want to upset him."

"Well, Bob, that doesn't make total sense," argued Mr. Bingley.

"They're a sneaky bunch, those Germans—a devious people capable of anything!"

Captain Cottrell objected. "Now wait a minute. There are plenty of normal German people. Sam's lady friend, for example."

"Sam has a lady friend?" asked Mr. Bingley.

"Are you talking about the woman who cleans his house?" cried Mr. Kerfoot. "She's not his lady friend!"

"All right, well, he may be exaggerating a little," Captain Cottrell admitted.

"Exaggerating a *lot*," Mr. Bingley said with a laugh.

"C'mon, fellas, let me get back to my point about the sea monster," Mr. Kerfoot whined. "As I was saying, I think the

Germans are trying to distract President Wilson. And all the while, they're preparing to invade."

"Oh, baloney," Captain Cottrell grumbled.

"What makes you such an expert?" Mr. Kerfoot demanded.

"Well, in case you've forgotten, I spent my whole life at sea! And you spent your life in a barnyard!"

"So what do you think, Cottrell?" asked Mr. Bingley.

"I doubt the Germans have anything to do with it at all," he replied. "Everyone knows that U-boat *Deutschland* is prowling off the coast, but I think it's a coincidence."

"So what do you think it was, then?" asked Mr. Kerfoot.

"Well, I've seen sea turtles that weighed more than five hundred pounds, so that's my guess."

"But sea turtles don't attack people!" cried Mr. Bingley.

"That's true," said Captain Cottrell. "Maybe it was a near-sighted sea turtle."

"What?" asked Mr. Bingley. "You must be joking."

"I was just speculatin'," said Captain Cottrell. "Now, getting back to your idea, Kerfoot. The only way I can see the Germans causing this is by accident—I mean, unintentionally. Suppose there's some kind of sea monster that stays to itself, that we never see, but the Germans disturbed it with their U-boat?"

"That makes sense," said Mr. Bingley. "Who knows what might be in the ocean? I bet we don't know half of what's out there."

"Oh, less than that," Captain Cottrell said with certainty. "I bet we know only five percent of what lives in the ocean."

A man browsing the tobacco products seemed to enjoy the discussion. "I heard there's a doctor who believes it was a shark," he said.

"Well, that's the most ridiculous idea of all," said Captain Cottrell. "We don't have man-eating sharks at the shore or anywhere near here! And what would a doctor know about it, anyway?"

"I have no idea. I'm just telling you something I heard from my brother-in-law. He's a constable in Ship Bottom."

At last, Margaret's order was ready, and she was called to the counter. She wanted to scoop up her purchase, make a beeline for the door, and not hear another word about the sea monster. Usually, these same men were discussing the war or the epidemic. Margaret was weary of it all.

One comment about the sea monster stayed with her, however. *I bet we know only five percent of what lives in the ocean*, Captain Cottrell had said. She dwelled on the remark for the rest of the day.

The ocean frightened her; it always had. There were too many unknowns. She was perfectly content to float in a canoe on the creek with Stanley, and once had even gone sailing with her father on Raritan Bay, yet she had no desire to experience the open sea. She had always felt that way, but the story of the *Titanic* had magnified her fears, as did the sinking of the *Lusitania*.

There were several women in town whose husbands had been lost at sea, and Margaret knew that women whose men made a living on the high seas spent much of their lives alone at home waiting, watching, and worrying.

Margaret had no desire to be among them. And yet she had fallen in love with Stanley, who had always seemed destined for a career at sea.

Stanley's father was a retired sea captain. It was assumed, as though it were the natural order of things, like leaves turning gold and crimson in the fall, that Stanley would follow in his father's footsteps. All of the men in his family had been sea captains going back generations.

From an early age, however, Stanley had doubts. This was clear from Margaret's first memories of him in grammar school. He simply showed no enthusiasm for what most boys thought an exciting future was. Several boys envied Stanley openly, saying they wished they were going to sea one day, and Stanley simply shrugged.

When Margaret turned sixteen, her father finally permitted Stanley, who was only a few months older than her, to make social calls to see her. These visits mainly consisted of her and Stanley sitting on the porch swing while her mother peered at them from behind the Irish lace curtains in the front parlor, but at least they finally had an opportunity to talk, and sometimes Stanley confided to Margaret that he was conflicted about his future.

Margaret did not want him to go to sea, but she did not say so. She didn't think she had a right to. It seemed like a problem that needed to be sorted between Stanley and his father, and intuitively, she knew to stay out of it. As she became more attached to Stanley, she hoped that somehow it would work out. She did not ever want to be in a position to give Stanley an ultimatum.

Stanley's confusion made her realize her good fortune in knowing that she wanted to become a teacher one day, a goal from which she never once wavered. In the summer during high school, she ran an informal "play school" at the library for children on the cusp of learning to read and, as such, became known throughout Matawan as Miss Margaret.

Meanwhile, the more rock solid her path was, the more confused Stanley's became. In Margaret's final year of college, during one of her usual weekend trips home, Stanley was in the midst of a major disagreement with his father. Finally, Margaret asked him why, exactly, he objected to becoming a sea captain.

"Because I know what it can do to a family," he had said. "My mother was so unhappy when Father was gone for long stretches at sea. If you and I are married one day, it's not something I would do to you."

She was surprised but thrilled. This was the first time either of them had said anything about marriage. At the same time, he had expressed a type of unselfish concern for her and her happiness that was so genuine she was left speechless.

Margaret thought the dilemma was close to settled. When she returned the following weekend from college, however, she was shocked to learn from Stanley that he had relented, at least partially, to his father's pressure. His father had asked, "Won't you at least try it?"

Stanley decided this was a fair request. He agreed to serve a four-month apprenticeship at sea, and his father promptly set it up. This had all happened in a matter of a few days.

Margaret was upset throughout his absence and gradually resigned herself to the fact that this would probably be his career. She concluded that she could accept being a sea captain's wife if it meant being married to Stanley. Her bigger fear, however, was for Stanley himself. If this was not what he truly wanted, would he be unhappy, or could he adjust?

The problem resolved itself, however, when Stanley returned from his apprenticeship at sea and announced, "Well, I tried it, and I didn't like it. I want to work and live on the land."

His father thought he meant farming, but Stanley devised another plan. On his own, he arranged for a second apprenticeship, this time with a tailor. As soon as he completed his course of study, Stanley opened his own shop just off Main Street, selling men's suits, specializing in a new style known as the Cecil, which cost between sixteen and thirty-eight dollars, depending on the fabric.

It had been five months since Stanley started his new business. His relationship with his father was still strained, but he had hope that, over time, he and his father would come to an understanding.

As she hurried home from the drugstore, Margaret was reminded of how well things were working out. Stanley was not going to sea. She was glad she had been patient and let him decide for himself. Their life together seemed assured, and the future beckoned. Nothing would stand in their way.

CHAPTER 6

Edwin was frustrated that the local newspapers did not refer to the creature as a shark. Instead, they used the term *sea monster*. Most peculiar of all was coverage in the *New York Times*, which published a small story on an inside page near the back with the headline, "Man Dies After Attack By Fish."

Not the clear message Edwin hoped for. In fact, it raised more questions than it answered. And the location of the story within the newspaper meant most readers wouldn't notice it.

He did not have time to ruminate about it for long, however, because an entirely different problem commanded his attention: six new patients with infantile paralysis had arrived overnight at Monmouth Memorial, where they were immediately placed in isolation in a separate building and their parents sent home with quarantine orders.

It was not known what caused the disease or how it spread or why it affected children and not adults. There was no proven treatment, only comfort care. As was typical of the disease, the patients brought to Monmouth Memorial were under five years of age.

Infantile paralysis, also called poliomyelitis, was as mysterious as it was devastating. While there had been previous outbreaks, such as one in 1907, the current epidemic of "the child plague," as some called it, spread faster with a significantly higher fatality rate than in the past.

If we keep going like this, the 1916 epidemic of infantile paralysis will be the worst ever, Edwin thought glumly.

The first sign was typically a fever, followed by a severe headache. Then the child might become stiff in the limbs, a condition which could progress to paralysis. Worst of all was when the disease spread to the lungs. If that occurred, the child usually died. Those who survived often had permanent damage that impeded their ability to use their legs.

The first cases had appeared in an immigrant neighborhood in Brooklyn earlier in the year, and "polio," as some newspapers had dubbed it, quickly reached neighboring states, especially New Jersey. By June, the number of cases was rising sharply. In the first few days of July, it was clear that a full-fledged epidemic had taken hold throughout the Northeast and beyond.

Edwin had considered skipping an advisory meeting with the governor, but the growing caseload changed his mind. He spent the morning at the hospital, discussing the new cases with his colleagues while, at the same time, trying to avoid Julia or any of her nursing-school friends or instructors. He was still upset with his daughter—in fact, more so. After their recent kerfuffle, she had again gone out with Mortimer and returned quite late.

Just one year before, Julia had been the most promising nursing student in her class. Now Edwin doubted that she was even keeping up. He could ask the nursing director but wasn't sure he wanted to hear the answer. Whereas everyone used to speak to him of her intelligence and dedication, no one brought up her name anymore. Her waning interest in becoming a nurse coincided with her growing entanglement with Mortimer. Edwin spent the half-hour drive to the meeting fuming, oblivious to his surroundings.

Edwin knew he had arrived at the right place, however, when he encountered a roadblock where security guards asked for his name, then allowed him to pass, instructing him to turn right onto a broad private drive lined on either side with maple trees. The governor was visiting his sister at her home in Middletown, and she had graciously agreed to host the meeting. The house was spectacular and reminded him of a Scottish castle he had toured during a medical conference in Edinburgh years before.

A man in a servant's uniform opened the massive front door and ushered Edwin down a hallway to a formal dining room where, the servant indicated, the meeting would be held. The room featured a table, at least twenty feet long, that appeared to Edwin's inexpert eye to be made of mahogany.

As head of the committee, Edwin was seated at one end—a place of honor. Alas, this meant that his back was to those who entered the room, while the *real* head of the table, the governor, was situated at the opposite end, facing the door. Behind the governor, a collection of antique swords dangled high above the mantel of a hearth made of native stone. Physicians representing different parts of the state trickled in and were seated along the sides of the table in the order in which they arrived.

There was only one woman in the entire group, Miss Ophelia Jennings, the governor's secretary. She sat to his right, prepared to take notes. Once they were all assembled, the governor spoke. There was no need for an introduction, but he provided one anyway.

Finally—*Finally!* Edwin thought—they got to the heart of it. Miss Jennings announced the time and date and called upon Edwin to make opening comments.

Edwin was tempted to say, *We are here to discuss that which we have already discussed, ad nauseam and in perpetuity.* Instead, he maintained his civility. "Gentlemen," he began, "as you know, the infantile paralysis epidemic is especially bad this year. The disease is being studied by numerous eminent scientists, but even they are uncertain how this dreaded disease is spread or contracted. We must be aggressive and deploy all the techniques we have used to halt or at least mitigate typhoid, scarlet fever, even smallpox. That is, we must keep the sick isolated from others. As I have stated before, I believe strongly that we should monitor our state borders. For the next three weeks—to be extended if necessary—we should turn back those persons who have with them a child age sixteen or younger. This should apply to all those who arrive by boat, rail, or automobile. This recommendation needs only a declaration of emergency by the governor. You may recall, gentlemen, this decision was tabled from our last meeting. It is now time to move forward. In fact, it is past time. The number of cases is rising. Some towns and cities are guarding their borders already."

"I am in support," declared Dr. Kantor of Camden.

No one else said a word. Instead, all heads pivoted in unison, as if choreographed, to gauge the governor's reaction.

"Can you guarantee that closing the border will work, Dr. Halsey?" asked the governor.

"No, sir, I cannot," replied Edwin.

"If you're not certain, I don't see the point," the governor said dismissively.

Edwin's shirt collar suddenly felt too tight, and a rivulet of sweat trickled down the back of his neck. "But it is our best option, sir," he said. "If it doesn't work, no one will be harmed. But it might help a great deal. It is only logical, sir."

"Dr. Halsey, you are a man of science," said the governor. "There are other considerations."

"And what would they be?" asked Edwin, knowing the answer but forcing the governor to say it for the record.

"The business community, the tourist industry—they are heartily opposed to closing state borders, even for a brief time," the governor replied impatiently. "The season is short, and this is their only opportunity to make money. The entire economy will suffer. And you're asking me to turn away the tourists?"

"Only the ones with children sixteen and under."

"Well, that's the majority of those who come," noted the governor.

"Sir, how can we put a price on the life or well-being of a child?" asked Edwin. "We need bold action. That is what will be best for *all*. And business owners will be grateful in the long run. If the Jersey Shore became known as the place where children are infected with infantile paralysis, that could damage tourism for many years—not just this year."

The governor paused. "Let's adjourn and discuss this again next time."

"Putting it off again will not help; it will only hurt," said Edwin, speaking quickly.

But the governor was already rising from his chair. The others took his lead.

"Wait, gentlemen," Edwin called suddenly. "Please, before you leave, there is another public health threat that we must discuss." Edwin glanced at the governor's secretary, who nodded.

"We have not formally adjourned," Miss Jennings told the governor. "If Dr. Halsey has something else to bring up, he really must be allowed to do so."

The governor sighed and sat back down, as did Edwin's medical colleagues. No one bothered to hide their annoyance.

Edwin cleared his throat, determined to proceed. "You may have read about this in the local papers," he said, trying to ease into the topic. "A young man in Beach Haven was attacked by something in the water Saturday afternoon. I was called to assist. Unfortunately, I arrived too late, and the young man died, but I did examine the body. Gentlemen, I believe he was attacked by a shark, and I fear that it will strike again."

Guffaws and snickers erupted throughout the room.

Edwin slapped his hand twice on the table. "Gentlemen, I insist upon being heard!"

They quieted down.

"Please go on," the governor murmured.

"Gentlemen," Edwin continued, "some of you may recall that I volunteered as a surgeon during the Spanish-American War. In Cuba, I saw what man-eating sharks can do to the human body. The attack in Beach Haven was even worse."

This roused the governor. "We do *not* have man-eating sharks at the Jersey Shore!" he snapped. "WE DO NOT! Frankly, Dr. Halsey, I realize you are renowned in this state and were a fixture long before my time as governor, but I am starting to resent your interference. You are an alarmist!"

"Well, sir, with all due respect," said Edwin, "I saw the bite mark on the young man's leg. The entire thigh was ripped away in one bite. There were witnesses, sir. Multiple witnesses. The incident was entirely unprovoked. No one was trying to capture or injure the shark; it deliberately hunted and tried to eat a human being as if he were a seal. I'm very concerned. This type of shark is relentless, and I strongly suspect it will strike again."

There were murmurs among Edwin's colleagues.

A doctor from Cape May leaned forward in his chair. "He was injured so badly he could not be saved?"

"That is correct. By the time he was on dry land, it was already too late. He'd lost too much blood. He received medical attention immediately from his father, who is a doctor, and two other physicians. When I arrived, he was dead. This was a *massive* injury. Even an immediate amputation might not have saved him."

Now Edwin's colleagues were listening.

But the governor was not. "What do you expect us to do?" he asked Edwin. "Close all the beaches? It must have been a freak incident. Surely, you aren't suggesting it will happen again."

"Governor," Miss Jennings said. "Did you read the papers I put out for you this morning? This is a big story! Some of the resort hotels are putting wire netting in the water to protect swimmers. And they've hired men to go out in boats and patrol the waters for the sea monster."

The governor was taken aback and agreed to look into the matter further. As they adjourned, Edwin was hopeful. Perhaps he had gotten through to the governor and the other physicians.

One of Edwin's colleagues, however, surprised him as they walked to their automobiles. "You know what I think, Halsey?" he asked. "I think you're making a fool of yourself. Mark my words, this so-called shark is a hoax. The whole thing sounds to me like it was staged."

"But, my dear sir," replied Edwin, stung by the condescending words, "I saw the bite marks on the body of the young victim. You did not. Why would I participate in a hoax?"

The other doctor didn't answer. With a superior smirk, he simply turned and walked away.

CHAPTER 7

Independence Day began badly even before Edwin left for the hospital. He still had not cleared the air with Julia.

He didn't want to be angry at her, not this morning, especially. They both had a long day ahead at the hospital. The biggest holiday of the summer always brought flocks of tourists, a portion of whom inevitably needed urgent medical attention.

As they sat together tensely at the kitchen table, sipping coffee, Edwin searched his mind for a neutral topic and settled on the lavish setting of his meeting with the governor the day before.

"It was held at his sister's mansion in Middletown," he said and described the palatial home.

"That sounds lovely," said Julia in a polite tone.

"Would you like some more coffee?" he asked.

"No, thank you," she replied.

"You're going to need it with the day we have ahead of us at the hospital," he commented lightly.

She cleared her throat. "Oh, I meant to tell you," she said

casually, pushing a wayward strand of hair from her eyes. "I'm not going in today."

"What?" he asked, stunned. "Are you sick?"

"No, no. I have other plans."

Edwin stared at her in astonishment. "Other plans?"

She looked away.

"What other plans could you possibly have?" he persisted. "This is the busiest day of the year at the hospital!"

"I'm going to a party in Spring Lake," she said nonchalantly.

Edwin groaned. "Young lady, you need to get your priorities in order."

"It's fine, Father. I made arrangements with another girl to take my shift."

"You should never interfere with the scheduling of the nursing staff!"

"I'm sure they'll manage without me," she snapped. "I'm not even a nurse yet!"

"That hardly matters! They are counting on you to work alongside one of the experienced nurses!"

"I'm sorry, Father, but I've made up my mind. It's all arranged."

Edwin squeezed his eyes shut, trying to rein in his temper. When he opened them again, she was staring defiantly at him, twirling a lock of her hair. "Julia," he said slowly, "I want you to promise me something. Since you insist on going to Spring Lake, I implore you, please stay out of the ocean. No sea-bathing. The shark is still out there."

"Oh, Father," she groaned. "What are the chances of the shark attacking someone in Spring Lake? That's *miles* from Beach Haven. Really, you worry too much."

"It is bad enough that you're neglecting your duties at the hospital," he cried. "Now you are willfully ignoring my concerns about your safety! Really, Julia, this is too much. I expected more from you."

"When did you become so judgmental, Father?"

Judgmental? Edwin's jaw dropped at the accusation.

"And when did *you* become so completely irresponsible?" he asked, his voice shaking. "Oh, wait, no need to answer. I know! It's when you met *Mortimer!*"

Julia glared at him and tossed her napkin on the table. "I hate it when you're sarcastic!" she yelled. And then she burst into tears.

"Oh, now, now," he murmured, searching his pocket for a handkerchief to give her.

She blotted her tears with the hanky and handed it back. "Father, we all swap shifts at the hospital. Do you recall Lucy Cole?"

His mind drew a blank.

"Lucy Cole went to a wedding, and I took her shift. It was no problem at all."

"But this is a holiday! Everyone will be needed!"

"Well, maybe the tourists will stay away on account of the shark," she said and took another sip of her coffee.

"Even if half the tourists stay home, we'll *still* be inundated!" he cried. "I am shocked that you would shirk your duties like this! For shame."

"Father, what has happened to you? You used to be such a nice man. And now you've become so unfeeling, so coldhearted. I'm not the only one who says so! Everyone talks about it at the hospital."

"They gossip that I've become coldhearted with my daughter?"

"With the patients," she replied. "With everyone."

This shocked Edwin. He knew his reputation had changed over the years, but he hadn't suspected this. Perhaps it had happened so gradually that he hadn't been aware. *Have I grown tired of my profession?* he thought, aghast.

With his anger deflated for the moment, Edwin found

himself struggling for words. "Well," he said slowly, "I admit, I might be less patient and perhaps less compassionate than I used to be. It is a tendency that may have simply grown with age. Or maybe it has happened incrementally since your mother died . . . and the others."

Julia studied his face. "Father," she said, folding her arms across her chest. "It's been *eighteen years* since Mother died. And 'the others,' as you put it. I think we should call them by name, Father."

Edwin stood up from the kitchen table. With his back to Julia, he took his time getting a drink of water from the tap. He watched through the kitchen window a gold finch hopping from branch to branch in the lilac tree that Charlotte had planted a few weeks before she died.

Julia persisted. "The others had names, Father! I'll list them for you: Matilda. Edwin Jr. Agatha. Martin. Genevieve. Five of your children, gone at the same time as Mother. Leaving only you and me."

Edwin turned toward her, more furious than sad. "As if I need to be reminded," he said bitterly. "What kind of person do you think I am?"

"I'm not trying to upset you, Father, but I think a part of you, quite frankly, died when they did. And to be honest, I feel cheated. I grew up without a mother or siblings. And with a father who is still grieving. I think the old, compassionate you is still there somewhere. It's just the melancholia has grabbed ahold of you, and you can't detach yourself from it."

"Thank you for your diagnosis," Edwin said sharply.

"Oh, not more sarcasm!" Julia shrieked. She leaped up from her chair and stomped from the room, slamming the door for good measure.

Edwin finished his coffee and left for the hospital without

saying goodbye. He did, however, leave a note. *Let's continue our discussion later when we've both calmed down*, he wrote. *Please do consider my request to stay out of the sea.*

The drive from Red Bank to the hospital in Long Branch was just six miles, but the roadways were packed. Edwin dodged pedestrians, automobiles, and the occasional horse-drawn vehicle, including one mule-drawn farm wagon with a load of tomatoes. As he drove past the tiny station in Little Silver, passengers were exiting a packed train that had pulled in from New York.

Edwin was disappointed at the size of the crowds. *Surely, they all know about the epidemic*, he thought. The shark was another matter. The fatal attack in Beach Haven had occurred just three days earlier. It was possible that some visitors had not heard about it.

Still, it was difficult for Edwin to understand people who knew of the risks and didn't care. As a doctor, he had a different perspective. He had seen what infantile paralysis could do to a child. He had observed the devastation of a rogue shark's bite.

Then he thought of what Julia had said about his being judgmental. *Life is hard for most people*, he mused. *Spending a day or two at the seaside may be one of the few joys they have.*

Perhaps, he realized in a thought that cheered him greatly, *many of these people will not go in the water at all. Perhaps they know about the shark and plan to picnic on the beach or simply stroll the boardwalk.*

There was much to do besides sea-bathe. There were restaurants and shops and live musical performances. The fiddle player from the Pinelands of South Jersey, who strolled back and forth in front of the Peninsula Hotel, would surely be there. The old drummer from the Grand Army of the Republic, who told war stories near the public water fountains, never missed the Fourth of July. There would be portrait painters and photographers, wood-carvers and quilt-makers.

And if tourists weren't aware of the fatal shark attack, he hoped they would soon find out. In the local paper that morning, he'd read that some municipalities and resort hotels claimed they would restrict or prohibit swimming. He worried, however, that it had not been a uniform decision, which could lead to confusion. He wondered, also, how well these new temporary rules would be advertised and enforced. He knew that determined people could find a way around rules. In fact, some people seemed to enjoy the challenge.

As soon as he parked and walked into the emergency room, he learned that, prohibition or not, mobs of tourists were indeed going into the water, at least in Long Branch and nearby beaches. The staff was already treating patients who had nearly drowned.

One of the patients, whose name was Jack, had been brought to the hospital from a beach two miles south of Long Branch. He told Edwin that, yes, he'd heard of the sea monster, but he was completely unconcerned. "That wouldn't happen to me," he said with a certainty that took Edwin's breath away. Knowing about the creature, Jack went into the water although, as he told Edwin, he had no idea how to swim. The lifeguard who pulled him from the surf told him he'd been caught in an undertow, but Jack did not know what that meant and asked Edwin to explain. Jack had been staying at a hotel that kept the beach open and provided each guest with a printed notice informing them that they could "swim at their own risk" without providing any detail.

As the day progressed and Edwin queried other patients, he learned that some hotels had placed new signs with the words *caution* or *danger* by the water, which, although vague, was still better than nothing. Several of the big resorts had added steel netting in the water, as had been done at the Engleside, but no one knew if this actually worked.

One young fellow who nearly drowned off Avon-by-the-Sea admitted to Edwin that he had been trying to impress a lady friend. "We weren't supposed to swim, but I wanted her to know I'm not afraid of the sea monster," he boasted.

After a few hours of stories like this one, Edwin needed a break and went outside, intending to buy an Italian ice from a vendor. The streets and sidewalks around the hospital were practically vibrating from the heat, however, so he retreated back inside. The only place where he thought he might be left alone for a few minutes was the fourth-floor doctors' lounge. He took the stairs to avoid the slow and crowded elevator.

There was, at least, a comfortable place to sit in the doctors' lounge. A pile of disheveled newspapers, both tabloids and broadsheets, beckoned from a table, and Edwin couldn't resist perusing them.

Three days had passed since Charles Vansant's death in Beach Haven, and authorities, as quoted in these papers, were still arguing over what exactly caused the young swimmer's death.

Edwin was dismayed. *Do I have to get more involved in this?* he wondered. *I sent all those telegrams to police chiefs. I told the governor and all those doctors at the meeting in Middletown.* He needed to call the newspapers himself and vowed to do so on his next break.

A sea turtle remained the favorite theory among those asked to comment. In second place was a giant mackerel. The problem with both of those suggestions, from Edwin's view, was the implication that neither of those creatures would have bitten Mr. Vansant *on purpose.* This was precisely the point made by one of the doctors in Beach Haven, and to Edwin, it was worri-some, for a large but confused sea creature was a very different situation from a man-eating shark hunting human beings. The latter was much more likely to repeat its actions.

The gist of several newspaper stories was, "Not likely a shark, because we don't have that kind of shark here." Edwin could not understand this line of thinking. Was it a lack of imagina-tion or a failure to be logical? Just because they hadn't seen it for themselves, it couldn't exist?

We don't have that kind of shark here. Edwin wondered how to counter that statement since clearly it wasn't true, yet it was repeated by authorities, almost reflexively, as a fact.

When people say something often enough, Edwin thought, *they start to believe it.*

Denial was so rampant that even a superintendent of the Coast Guard ridiculed the possibility. "Sharks are as timid as rabbits," he told a Philadelphia newspaper.

Edwin wondered about the influence of a wealthy eccentric named Hermann Oelrichs. He hadn't thought about Oelrichs in years. Oelrichs, the owner or part-owner of a shipping empire, was one of the best long-distance swimmers in the world and had become famous for swimming with sharks in and around New York harbor. He and his antics had been a favorite of the tabloid press for a generation.

That Oelrichs fellow was on a one-man mission to convince people there are no man-eating sharks around here, Edwin mused, vaguely recalling that the wealthy eccentric had even offered a huge reward to try to prove his point.

Edwin didn't know if the reward had ever been collected. Impulsively, he went to the hospital's medical research library. Although it was a holiday, the library was always open to doctors. There was not a huge collection of topics outside of medicine, but Edwin recalled some general-interest volumes in the reference section. He thumbed through them and had no luck until he found an encyclopedia of internationally known businessmen.

Oelrichs, it turned out, had died about fifteen years earlier. He was especially famous, the entry noted, for a five-hundred-dollar reward in the *New York Sun* to anyone who had ever been "deliberately attacked by a shark on the East Coast of the US north of Cape Hatteras, NC." The reward had been publicized relentlessly for more than a decade, starting circa 1890 and continuing until his death. And in all that time, no one collected.

Surely, this has a role to play in the mind of the public, Edwin thought.

But Edwin had no more time to reflect upon the shark. He had been gone from the emergency room for as long as he should. If this was like every other Fourth of July, activity at the hospital would become increasingly frenetic as the day wore on. This was true ever since Long Branch had become a popular resort in the 1880s—a result of steamboat travel between New York City and the northern New Jersey Shore.

As a boy, Edwin had witnessed Long Branch metamorphose from a sleepy seaside village to its current state, which, from the viewpoint of the local populace, including Edwin, was positively overrun with New Yorkers—most of them rich and more than a few overbearing. Enormous hotels and palatial estates were constructed. The *New York Times* published a front-page column filled with juicy gossip from Long Branch during the summer months. Among the contributors paid by the item was Stephen Crane, then an Asbury Park schoolboy on a bicycle but later the author of *The Red Badge of Courage*, one of Edwin's favorite books. Former president Ulysses S. Grant started a tradition in which US presidents came for the summer. Winslow Homer came to paint, and Lillie Langtry to sing. Mark Twain visited, made witty pronouncements, and held court.

Although it was exciting to be the center of national and even international attention each summer, a backlash grew. Longtime residents resented the loss of peace and quiet. The only inhabitants for many thousands of years were Lenape Indians. In the mid-1600s, Dutch and English colonists arrived, some of whom intermarried with the Lenape, and most lived as farmers and fishermen. Big cities flourished north—Newark and New York City—and west—Philadelphia. The Jersey Shore had been sparsely populated and off the beaten path, and local folk liked it that way. One of the small towns had posted an official sign that read, WELCOME! NOTHING MUCH HAS EVER HAPPENED HERE, AND WE HOPE NOTHING EVER WILL.

Well, these days, there was no peace anywhere near Long Branch, especially on the busiest day of the year for the small city and subsequently for Monmouth Memorial Hospital. In addition to the drownings and near-drownings, there were food poisonings, severe sunburns, jellyfish stings, and mishaps with folding chairs and sun umbrellas. After dark, patients with firecracker injuries to eyes and hands streamed in.

At nine o'clock, just as the sun was setting, an event was held which never failed to unnerve every doctor and nurse at the hospital: the annual firing of an old cannon by Union Army veterans, specifically, the Fourteenth New Jersey Volunteers, now all quite elderly. Although the cannon was aimed out to sea, the potential for disaster was real, and the ancient warriors in blue refused to listen to reason. Thankfully, once again, the event went off without a hitch.

Edwin agreed to stay until midnight, filling in for a young doctor whose wife was about to give birth. Edwin didn't mind.

After all, no one was at home waiting for him. Julia was at the party in Spring Lake, and even Hannah was out and about with her sister. He had used his dinner break to telephone as many newspapers as he could and shared with reporters his belief that the sea monster was a shark that would strike again. The fact that swimmers were not being kept out of the water was, he added, deeply disappointing and disturbing.

In the late hours, the liberal consumption of alcohol led, as per usual, to falls and fights between menfolk of all ages, and Edwin did his share of stitching wounds and setting bones. By the time he could finally go home, there had been two gunshot victims, one that occurred at close range during a card game and would likely prove fatal in the next day or two. The other involved a reveler shot in the knee, apparently by accident.

But to Edwin's great relief, there were no reports of shark attacks anywhere along the shore.

CHAPTER 8

"Hey, mister, you want to buy a paper?" called a newsboy. "This edition's all about the Beach Haven sea monster!"

"No, thank you," said Stanley. He glanced at Margaret. "Unless, of course, the lady here would like a copy."

"Um, no thank you," Margaret said quickly. "I don't want to hear another word about it."

"Neither do I," agreed Stanley.

They were at the Matawan train station to wave goodbye to Stanley's parents, who were leaving for a trip to Minnesota. That his parents were actually on board the train, en route to the Midwest, was surprising.

"I can't believe they're really going," said Margaret as the conductor called out a final boarding announcement.

"I know what you mean," said Stanley. "I hope they can work things out."

The trip was the first sign of a possible truce between the Fishers and their daughter, Betty, who was Stanley's only sibling. A year earlier, Betty had married a man from Minnesota and moved there with him—a shock to her parents, who had expected her to marry someone known to them and stay in Matawan to take care of them in their old age.

A year older than Stanley, Betty had, for a long time, pushed the limits set by her parents. She had decided against becoming a teacher, one of the few possibilities open to her, and found employment with the telephone company, a job which displeased her father. When she started traveling to New York City to attend job-related training sessions, he insisted on escorting her and spent the day waiting to accompany her home.

Unbeknownst to Captain Fisher, Betty met a man she liked, anyway. She did not bring her beau home for inspection by the Fisher family, as was customary. When Betty finally did bring her sweetheart to meet her parents, it was to announce their engagement.

The result was a spectacular argument and estrangement. Later that same day, the couple eloped and were married by a justice of the peace in Atlantic City. A week later, they sent a letter stating what they had done and that they would be settling in Minnesota.

Mrs. Fisher was heartbroken. Captain Fisher was enraged. For several months, there was no communication—until Betty wrote and invited them to visit.

Captain Fisher refused, insisting that he was not going anywhere. He claimed that his sea legs would become more arthritic on a long train ride and that it would be hard on his heart to be at an elevation above sea level.

Finally, Mrs. Fisher had enough. On Easter Sunday, after the dishes were cleared and coffee had been served, she made an announcement. "I am going to visit Betty in Minnesota in July"— then she turned to her husband and added—"whether you come with me or not."

Margaret, who had come over for dessert, had never heard a woman confront her husband like that. Certainly, her own mother had never done so. Margaret glanced nervously at Stanley, who was trying to suppress a grin.

"Sounds good, Ma," said Stanley.

His father glared at him.

To everyone's surprise, the old sea captain, after harrumphing and scowling for a few minutes, quietly agreed to go. His love for his daughter, and also his wife, had overcome and conquered his pride.

The journey was planned entirely by Mrs. Fisher. They would leave on the morning of the Fourth of July and return two weeks later on July 18. When Margaret and Stanley saw them off, they anticipated that his father might change his mind at the last minute and were relieved when the train pulled from the station with both his mother and father waving from a window.

"I hope they have a good time and your father and Betty don't argue," said Margaret.

"I asked Ma to send a postcard to let me know how it's going," Stanley said with a chuckle. "I'm keeping my fingers crossed."

Just after ten o'clock, Margaret and Stanley met at the sycamore in front of the church to watch the parade. The procession began with a six-member brass band that performed John Philip Sousa marches. The musicians were followed by a man on stilts in an Uncle Sam costume and a troupe of children, most of whom Margaret knew by name, who marched and waved flags.

A blushing girl dressed as the Statue of Liberty smiled shyly and waved tepidly to the crowd. She was followed by a slightly built boy of about thirteen dressed as an American patriot. The boy's ensemble included an antique musket, which he struggled to carry across his shoulder. Behind him was a cluster of elderly men in Union Army uniforms, the last of the Matawan veterans of the Civil War, a number which dwindled with every passing year, and for whom the crowd went wild with cheers and applause.

Then came a man and woman leading a black stallion that had won national prizes and been the star of many newspaper front pages until the arrival of the headline-grabbing Jersey Shore sea monster.

Coming in last was a mule-pulled farm wagon bearing a sign that read The Bounty of America. As if to prove the point of overabundance, the wagon was weighed down by haphazard piles of melons and baskets of Jersey tomatoes and succulent peaches, the latter of which sometimes came loose individually and tumbled off the back of the wagon to the delight of the hopeful children who followed behind.

The residents of Matawan were proud of their town's role in the Revolutionary War. There had even been a skirmish at the Burrowes Mansion, a town landmark on Main Street, which was attacked by the British in an attempt to capture the owner's son, a major in General George Washington's army. Matawan was also the home of Philip Freneau, known as the "Poet of the Revolution" for his ballads and other writings in support of the cause of freedom.

In honor of those men and others, each Fourth of July, the parade ended in front of Matawan's town hall, where the mayor read the Declaration of Independence while the flag was raised, followed by the ringing of the church bells, which was Margaret's favorite part of the whole day. Then the celebration took on a more festive tone with horseshoe pitching, egg-and-spoon races, and everyone's favorite, the pie-eating contest.

Margaret and Stanley drifted from one activity to the next, cheering on the participants, until it was time for the annual picnic and barbecue sponsored by the Rotary Club.

Surrounded by American flags and bunting, with the focus of the day on American independence from the British, perhaps it was inevitable that someone at the Rotary picnic would bring up the subject of the current war in Europe. Suddenly, the easy banter in the crowd became confrontational.

"Why should we help them out?" groused a man Margaret recognized as the father of one of her students. He stood up from his table to make sure he was heard. "We broke free of them in 1776!"

Someone else agreed heartily. "Hear! Hear!" he shouted. "It's their war. They've been fighting each other forever! Why should we get involved in their old battles?"

"They are our friends, and we must help them," a man with thick glasses called out. "We must intervene to save them!"

"Why should American boys be sent over there and killed?" cried a woman wearing a hat with red, white, and blue flowers. "I don't want my son to go!"

From the next table, a man called out, "If we *don't* help our friends, it will be too late for us. The Germans will come after us next!"

Then a young farmer stood and announced, "I'm willing to go! If our country joins the war, I'll be the first to sign up. Who else is with me?"

A few hands went up. One of them was Stanley's.

Later, when they were alone, Margaret told him she was terrified of the idea of him joining the war effort.

"I know," he said softly. "I can't say I like the idea myself. But if the time comes, I'll do my part."

JULY 5, 1916

CHAPTER 9

Several days a week, regardless of the weather, Edwin went on a brisk morning jaunt, varying the route around Red Bank. On the morning after his late night at the hospital in Long Branch, he needed exercise and a little time alone to think.

He was about to exit from the back door, as was his habit, when something caught his eye. Hanging on a peg in the alcove by the back door was a woman's bathing costume—a risqué one at that. And it was dripping water on the tile floor.

Julia. His jaw tightened. What time had she come in? How had he forgotten to check her room? Where had she gotten that tawdry bathing getup? And the biggest question of all, where had she been swimming?

Edwin tried to calm himself. It was possible she had not been in the ocean but in one of the private saltwater swimming pools that were all the rage. He must give her the benefit of the doubt for that much, at least. But why was it soaking wet at half past five in the morning? Obviously, she had slipped in through the back door in the early hours of the morning.

Now what? he thought. He could go upstairs and announce that he was going to disown her. He could wait in the kitchen, drink coffee, and stew in his anger until she showed up for breakfast. Or he could go for his walk.

He chose the last. He trekked farther than usual and, with each footstep, felt slightly better. He reflected on the changes to Red Bank. Since it was not directly on the ocean but on a tidal river, Red Bank had escaped the wilder fate of Long Branch. Red Bank still felt like a small town and had even rallied after a colossal fire in 1882 destroyed much of the downtown. Rebuilding a large swath in a short time resulted in a pleasing uniformity of architectural style.

On this morning, the streets of Red Bank were exceptionally quiet, as if the whole town, including the buildings, was hungover. The docks on the Navesink River were empty. But even here in Red Bank, evidence of excessive drinking and merrymaking abounded. On some streets, debris made the town look like a miniature Long Branch.

Edwin noticed a single empty brown paper bag and began filling it with detritus, avoiding unidentifiable or clearly disgusting items since he had not brought gloves. He made a mental note to ask the town to dispatch street cleaners at an earlier hour after next year's celebration.

There was a surprising amount of paper which, he soon realized, were multiple copies of the same flyer, a large number of which had blown down a side street toward the river. The flyer featured a crude illustration which caught his eye: an image of a large shark. Within the outline of the shark were letters spelling out the word *Deutschland*, which was Germany's endonym. *Deutschland* was also the name of a German submarine that was very publicly prowling the eastern coast of the United States that summer, supposedly traveling as a merchant, not a naval vessel.

But who really knew what the Germans were up to? Perhaps the *Deutschland* was a decoy, and there were more of these newfangled underwater boats quietly scoping out the East Coast of America.

Edwin read the rest of the flyer as he walked:

LONG BRANCH PROMENADE, NEAR THE STATUE OF NEPTUNE

NOON, JULY 5

COME HEAR THE REAL STORY ABOUT THE "SHARK."

Good Lord, what is this? Edwin thought. He looked at his watch. Perhaps he would find the time to attend the strange gathering. He resumed walking, now eager to get back to the house, dispose of everything but the flyer, and get on with his day. But as he rounded the corner to his home, he came face-to-face with Mortimer, Julia's paramour.

"What are you doing here?" Edwin demanded. His tone was rude, but he didn't care.

"I'm waiting for Julia," replied Mortimer.

"Waiting for Julia? Didn't you just drop her off?"

Mortimer looked at his feet. "Well, we did come in a tad late, I'm afraid. I apologize. I just thought I'd take her to breakfast."

"I don't think so," Edwin snapped. "Why are you standing here like this? Where is your automobile?"

Mortimer didn't reply.

"Answer me," Edwin growled.

"I was—well, we ran out of gasoline."

"*What?*"

"Last night. So we walked the rest of the way here."

Edwin sighed. "Leave," he said through clenched teeth. "You and I need to have a long talk, but not right now." Edwin turned his back on Mortimer and went into the house. He marched up the stairs just as Julia, in a robe, came out of her room.

"Oh, good morning, Father," she said guiltily.

He stared at her, flummoxed for a moment. "What have you done to your hair?" he cried once he found his voice. Her chestnut locks had been chopped off just above her shoulders.

"Do you like it, Father?" she asked lightly, ignoring his shocked reaction. "There was a girl at the party from New York, and her hair was cut like this, and I told her how much I liked it. And she said she would cut it for me right then and there if I wanted her to. And I thought, why not?"

"Never mind that," Edwin said with a frown. "I know how late you were out, and I know you were with Mortimer and you ran out of gasoline. I have just one question for you, and you had better be honest with me. Where did you go swimming?"

Julia hesitated. "At Spring Lake," she replied evasively.

"Yes, I know you went to Spring Lake, but did you swim in the ocean? Or the lake? Or someone's swimming pool?"

"What difference does it make?" she asked in a grumpy voice. "Why are you still going on about that shark? Mortimer says there's nothing to be afraid of."

"Ha!" Edwin shouted. "That means you were in the ocean. You foolish girl!"

"I was not in the ocean! I was in a pool several blocks inland!"

"I certainly hope so!" Edwin snapped. He retreated to his room and dressed for work quickly, determined to leave the house as soon as possible. It was too early to go to the hospital, so he headed for a favorite destination: Bob's Diner in Long Branch. This was where he had gone often for solace after a brutal day at the hospital or in those excruciating days and weeks after Charlotte's and the children's deaths, when going home was painful. Some men needed a tavern and a drink; Edwin preferred a diner and a big breakfast, served at all hours.

Two fried eggs, rye toast with butter, potatoes, and an

orange. This was the most food he'd consumed all at once in several days, and afterward he felt ready to face the day. His patients counted on him to give his professional best. He would not disappoint them, despite everything else going on in his life. He paid quickly, left a generous gratuity, and hurried on his way.

One of Edwin's favorite patients, Maybelle Taylor, was his first patient of the day. The matriarch of a large family, Mrs. Taylor paid Edwin not in cash but with fruit and vegetables she had grown and canned herself.

She suffered from rheumatism and, that morning, had received a letter from an elderly aunt in Georgia, who had prescribed beets.

"What do you think about that, Dr. Halsey? Should I eat beets every day? Do you think it will help?"

"I think you should give it a try," Edwin replied. "How about every other day? And skip the citrus fruit—oranges, limes, lemons—because there's some evidence they increase inflammation."

He liked talking to Maybelle Taylor and hearing the news about her extended family. Their friendly chat as he examined her was a reminder that there were aspects of his work he still enjoyed. With his longtime patients, like Mrs. Taylor, he was less brusque and more patient. *At least*, he thought, *I'm not cold-hearted to everyone, as Julia claims.*

But then Mrs. Taylor inadvertently spoiled the moment. "My son told me you've been in the newspaper talking about that shark," she said. "That poor young man!"

Edwin nodded. He had forgotten to check the morning newspapers to see if he'd been quoted. "Yes, it's very sad," he said, then added, "I'm trying to let everyone know. I don't like talking to reporters, but I feel I must. Just promise me that you won't go ocean swimming or even wading right now."

She laughed. "Don't worry about me, Dr. Halsey," she said

playfully. "Since that happened, I wouldn't put my big toe in the sea, not even if you paid me a million dollars, not until I'm pretty sure it's dead or gone on its way."

"Well, then you are smarter than most everyone else around here," he said with a smile.

He saw five more patients after Maybelle Taylor, but no one else mentioned the shark. One was an elderly man who had lost a leg in the Civil War and still had phantom pain. This fellow was notoriously talkative, and Edwin had been certain the topic would come up, yet it didn't.

When it was close to noon, Edwin had second thoughts about going to the boardwalk to listen to the speaker who claimed to know the "real" story of the shark, as the flyer had put it. Did he really want to hear a bunch of nonsense stirring people up? Perhaps it would be better to not know what was said. But in the end, his curiosity won out.

The boardwalk was only a few blocks from the hospital, and as he approached the section where the statue of Neptune stood, Edwin felt an uncomfortable tightness in his throat and abdomen. A large, restless crowd had gathered already.

A man with a curious accent was addressing the group in an animated tone. "Do not be fooled!" he shouted. "There is no sea monster other than the *German government*!"

There were murmurs in the crowd. Some people, Edwin noted, nodded in agreement.

The speaker continued. "Is it not suspicious that a German U-boat, *Deutschland*, is known to be cruising along our coastline at the very moment we have the son of a prominent Philadelphia family massacred in the sea at Beach Haven?"

"It's just a merchant vessel," shouted a man from the middle of the crowd. "It's going to Baltimore with a load of dyes, that's all. And we need those dyes in manufacturing!"

"Ha!" yelled the speaker. "It's only pretending to be a cargo vessel. They're spies!"

Edwin glanced around him. The crowd was practically drooling with paranoia and rage. While it was well-known that the *Deutschland*, under the auspices of the North German Lloyd Steamship Company, was traveling northward along the Atlantic Coast of the US that summer, tying it to the shark attack was an extraordinary leap.

"The Germans are trying to provoke us," the speaker continued. "They will stop at nothing. They are a diabolical people! They are spying, they are tormenting us, and they are capable of *anything*! They used a U-boat to send a torpedo to sink the *Lusitania* last year, killing over one thousand innocent civilians, including one hundred and twenty-three American citizens! These are the fiendish people who invented bombs the size of a cigar that detonate on ships far out to sea! They have used poison gas as a killing agent on the battlefield! This is what they are doing to our friends on the battlefield! We must *join* the war effort and *stop them* or we are doomed! Once they win over there, they will come here. In fact, the presence of the *Deutschland* should make us realize they are already here!"

Ah, Edwin thought. *Well, there it is.* The speaker was a proponent of joining the war effort and was shamelessly exploiting the fear surrounding the shark attack for his own cause.

"Who are you and where are you from?" Edwin shouted.

The speaker smiled calmly, displaying a broad, even smile with a gold front tooth. "My name is Chester Morton, and I'm from Altoona, Pennsylvania," he called out.

"Who do you work for?" Edwin hollered.

"I work for no one but myself," he replied.

Edwin pushed his way closer to the stage. "What in the

world could the *Deutschland* have to do with the shark attack in Beach Haven?"

"I am glad you asked that question!" the speaker replied. "They could have captured the monster and brought it here, off Beach Haven, known to be a place where influential Philadelphians vacation, and let it go, having starved the monster first so it would attack and kill. This is a way to terrorize us, to distract us, to catch us off our guard! They know perfectly well that President Wilson is summering here at the shore. The Germans are a clever lot and devious! They must be stopped, and the only way to do that is to join the British and fight the Germans and win. If we wait until the British have lost, the Germans will be unstoppable."

A few people booed, and Edwin started to move away. Chester Morton was not a man to take seriously. Then the speaker stepped aside, and another man took his place. Edwin froze. He recognized the new speaker as a well-respected local civic leader, one who was not known to have controversial views.

"Now listen," the new speaker shouted to the crowd. "What Mr. Morton said may sound fantastical, but we live in fantastical times. Even if you don't believe it was intentional, mark my words, the German U-boat is responsible for the sea monster attack. That U-boat should not be out there, off our shores! Perhaps the swimmer was hit by the U-boat's propeller, and there was no sea monster at all. Or, if there *was* a sea monster, it might have been led astray or confused by the underwater ship and followed it from the deepest part of the sea. Could all the bombing in the North Sea have chased a sea monster across the Atlantic? What about American bombing practice along the coast of North Carolina? Could that be driving a man-eating creature northward?"

"Or maybe it's just a coincidence!" Edwin shouted. "Perhaps

a fatal shark attack was bound to happen now that there is a fad of ocean swimming! Maybe we never knew of the danger until now! Or maybe it is related to the heat spell! That is more logical because—"

"NO!" shouted the speaker, cutting Edwin off. "It is the fault of the Germans! One way or another, it is their doing! Perhaps, with all the ships sunk in the North Sea and the deaths of thousands of sailors, sharks have developed a taste for human flesh!"

The crowd gasped. They seemed more confused and upset than when Edwin had first arrived.

"May I speak to the crowd?" Edwin yelled.

But the event had boiled over into chaos. One man shoved another, and two women screamed at them to stop. A policeman standing nearby blew his whistle. Several more officers arrived and set about dispersing the crowd.

Edwin watched as people scattered. He was frustrated that a sizable part of the crowd had been unable to see what was obvious to him: that they were being manipulated. *The rally was about the war, not the shark*, he thought, *yet some simple-minded people didn't grasp that fact at all.*

Then Edwin had a jolt of insight. He was indeed—as Julia had put it—judgmental. He cringed and tried to think about the crowd's reactions from a more charitable viewpoint as he walked back to the hospital. The world was becoming more unfamiliar and more terrifying, and he knew from his experience with epidemics that it is the nature of human beings to, when fearful, look for answers. Of course people were deeply disturbed by the war in Europe—he was too. For the first time in human history, a war was being waged from the air as well as land and sea, with unprecedented levels of carnage. No one had ever before employed lethal poisonous gas on a large scale as a weapon on the battlefield, but the Germans had done so.

The arrival along the Jersey Coast of a man-eating shark, which people had been told could not happen, was one more event that made people deeply unsettled. Under the circumstances, even wild theories seemed plausible. That the attack was random made people desperate to explain it away.

Had the attack by the shark in Beach Haven not been so brutal or if the description of the creature's behavior not been so appalling or if he had not seen similar shark bites during the Spanish-American War, Edwin supposed that he, too, might have been as perplexed as many persons in the crowd seemed to be. He, too, might have been hoping for an alternative explanation. But he knew the truth and could not run from it. His personal experience with sharks would not allow him to ignore the danger.

JULY 6, 1916

CHAPTER 10

It was two days after the Fourth of July, but at the Essex & Sussex Hotel in Spring Lake, fifty miles north of Beach Haven, festivities would continue all week long. Bell captain Charles Bruder, knowing that he had several more grueling days of work before he would get a day off, decided to take a break and enjoy a quick midafternoon swim in the sea.

Usually, Bruder swam in the morning. But one of the perquisites of being in charge of fifty-two hotel attendants was being allowed to take a half hour off now and then, as long as the hotel was, at that moment, running smoothly.

Bruder was a favorite of the guests, and as he made his way to a beach cabana to change into a bathing outfit, he was greeted warmly. Staff members were generally ignored, but Bruder was special. He was so congenial that he was treated almost like family by the guests who came year after year.

He loved the job. He loved the people and the atmosphere of the busy, grand hotel. And when the season ended in the fall, he used the money he had made to travel. Twenty-eight years old, a former soldier in the Swiss Army, he was an adventurer at heart. He was fascinated by America and determined to see as much of the country as he could, particularly its beaches.

Bruder had spent the previous winter in California. He'd wanted to swim in the Pacific Ocean but at first was alarmed by the presence of sharks. Reassured by those who lived in the vicinity that he was in no danger, he tentatively entered the water, sharks or not. Nothing happened, and after a while he grew confident that sharks posed no threat to swimmers.

He returned to the Jersey Shore in late spring, and when news came of the sea monster attack in Beach Haven on July 1, Bruder was puzzled. Based on his own experience, he rejected the idea that it might have been a man-eating shark and even suspected that the whole thing might be a hoax.

As he left the cabana, he paused to chat with the lifeguards on duty. One of the guards noted that the beach was packed but fewer people were in the water than usual. He asked Bruder if he had any concerns after the Beach Haven incident five days before.

"Not at all," replied Bruder. "I swam with sharks in California, and I don't think they know what really happened to that poor man. And even if there is a sea monster, Beach Haven is a long way from here. I'm not worried. The risk is minimal, and the day is hot."

Bruder continued on his way, nodding politely to the menfolk and discreetly keeping his eyes off the ladies in their swim dresses. He appreciated the new fashion that made it respectable for grown women to show their legs at the beach. What a sight! Bruder tried not to stare, but when one long-legged beauty dashed across the sand in front of him, he was so distracted that he stumbled and nearly fell. He hoped no one noticed.

The ladies held hands and squealed whenever a wave came

too close or was more powerful than they expected. The men, meanwhile, entertained themselves by leaping into breaking waves. No one went farther out than that—until Bruder did. Strong and sure, he swam out alone, just beyond the roped-in section of the water.

He didn't mind being by himself. In fact, it was kind of nice to be away from people for a few minutes. Here, he could relax. The water felt delicious on his bare arms and legs. He swam a few yards, then rolled onto his back and floated. The sky was a soft shade of blue. He searched for clouds, but there were none.

On the beach, the lifeguards were watching Bruder closely. He seemed fine. He was perhaps only twenty or so yards beyond the safety ropes. They knew his work break was not long and that he would come in soon. Momentarily, they looked away, discussing their work hours for the coming week.

Then came a scream.

It came from Bruder.

But where was he? He seemed to have been shoved or thrown from where he'd been floating, as if struck by an automobile and flung aside. How had he moved so quickly? No one could swim that fast.

Oddly, Bruder then waved to the lifeguards. He seemed to be all right. He appeared to be treading water. Perhaps something had simply startled him, but the lifeguards couldn't be sure. They raced to their rescue boat, pushed it into the surf, hopped in, and began to row.

Bruder screamed a second time. Now the lifeguards knew for certain that something was terribly wrong. They pulled on the oars with all their might, at the same time shouting, "Out of the water!" at the few people who, uncomprehending or immobilized by fear, were not fleeing of their own accord. Like their brother lifeguards in Beach Haven, they headed toward danger.

On the beach, there was confusion.

"Is someone drowning?" asked a man who was among the last of the guests to leave the water.

"There was a man swimming alone," a woman remarked.

"I thought I heard a shout," said someone else.

"I heard something too, more like a scream, but I thought it was someone being silly."

"Yes, I heard that too. It sounded like a person who was knocked down by a wave, something like that."

"Well, don't worry, the lifeguards are very skillful. See how quickly they launched their boat. I'm sure they will rescue the swimmer."

"What are they doing now?"

"They seem to be rowing in circles. They must be looking for him!"

A woman in street clothes, her shoes in her hand, joined the informal group at the water's edge. "Something is just completely amiss here," she said breathlessly. "Look, look!" she cried and pointed, suddenly agitated. "There's a man in a red canoe, and it has flipped over!"

"That's not a canoe!"

"My God, is that blood in the water?"

Even as the awful truth dawned on those closest to the water, a large portion of the crowd on the beach was completely unaware that something was wrong. Hundreds of guests milled about, greeting one another and making plans for billiards or croquet. Others settled onto blankets with large umbrellas protecting them from the sun. Many had not heard Bruder's screams at all, and the lifeguards' sudden activity was easily explained by the fact that drills were a daily event.

Then the head of a great creature surfaced with Bruder in its mouth, flinging him from side to side like a rag doll. The screams of dozens of men and women—the ones closest to the water—sliced through the air.

All heads turned. All activity stopped. Conversations ended midsentence.

Had a meteor landed at their feet or the sun fallen from the sky, the eight hundred souls on the beach at one of the most glamorous seaside resorts in America could not have been more shocked. A sea monster? With a man in its mouth?

Suddenly, the creature released its grip and disappeared beneath the surface, leaving Bruder to flail and splash in the water. Now all attention was on the lifeguards. Amazingly, they seemed undeterred by the sight of the monster. They called to Bruder; they were so close. If only they could get him into the boat.

Bruder tried to paddle his arms as the lifeguards, calling encouragement, rowed frantically to meet him. Approaching, they saw that Bruder's right leg had been bitten off above the knee. There was not much time to save him before he would bleed to death. Yet it seemed possible; they were mere yards away.

They were close enough to grab him, reaching out, when, with no warning at all, he was yanked under the water. The creature had attacked him again.

But seconds later, Bruder popped back to the surface. He raised his arms, and this time the lifeguards were able to pull him over the gunwale and into the boat.

They were appalled by what they saw. Bruder's left leg had been bitten off too. A large piece of flesh was missing from his torso as well. As they laid him on a blanket and tried to stop the bleeding, Bruder lifted his head and spoke a few words, then fell silent.

The lifeguards glanced at one another. They had not clearly seen the horrible creature. It had all happened so fast. But Bruder, who had swum with sharks off the coast of California, had identified the culprit. The monster, he said, was a shark.

CHAPTER 11

At half past two, Edwin received a telephone call from an old friend and colleague, Dr. James McCarthy in Spring Lake.

"Edwin," he said, "it has happened here."

It has happened here.

From the mournful tone of Dr. McCarthy's voice and his terse words, Edwin knew the meaning immediately. The shark had attacked again.

And it had occurred at the oceanfront town of Spring Lake, where Julia might or might not have been sea-bathing two days earlier, on the Fourth of July.

Dr. McCarthy had trouble catching his breath. A bell captain at the Essex & Sussex Hotel, he said, was taking a break from his duties and enjoying a brief afternoon swim when he was attacked by the sea monster in front of hundreds of witnesses. His name was Charles Bruder.

He was already dead.

"I saw in the newspaper that you examined the body of the poor fellow down in Beach Haven," Dr. McCarthy said, his voice shaky. "Please come immediately. I need you to see this and help me figure out what to do. I'll be on the beach directly across from the Essex & Sussex."

Of all places, the Essex & Sussex Hotel! thought Edwin. He had just read in the newspaper that former President Taft had given a speech at the Essex & Sussex on the Fourth of July, and that every room in the hotel was reserved for the week. A massive colonial revival building with columns that reached five stories high, the Essex & Sussex was a famous summer destination for the well-heeled throughout the United States and abroad.

Edwin didn't hesitate. "I will be there as quickly as I can," he said. He grabbed his medical bag and hurried to his Model T. As he drove, he was preoccupied with the distance and direction the shark had traveled. Spring Lake was fifty miles due north of Beach Haven. *The shark is moving up the coast*, he thought.

When he arrived at Spring Lake, the scene was similar to Beach Haven five days earlier, except this time the body was still lying on the beach. Clotheslines draped with bedsheets shielded the body from view.

Edwin was distracted by the peculiar sight of two dozen well-dressed women lying prone or perched haphazardly on the sand, attended to by family members and hotel staff.

Dr. McCarthy spotted Edwin and plodded through the sand as quickly as he could. "Lord be praised, you're here," he cried, throwing an arm around Edwin's shoulders. "'Tis an awful situation, and it is beyond anything in my experience."

Edwin started to ask him about the incapacitated women, but Dr. McCarthy anticipated the question.

"Don't be concerned about them," he said, following Edwin's gaze. "They will be fine. There are many more who have been brought inside the hotel already. They witnessed the incident and either fainted or vomited or both."

Before Edwin saw the body, Dr. McCarthy stopped abruptly and cautioned him. "Listen, my friend, you must prepare yourself. I know you were a surgeon in the Spanish-American War, but even so, this may come as a shock. It certainly has to me."

A constable allowed them to pass through the impromptu screening. There, sprawled on the sand, were the mutilated remains of Charles Bruder.

Dr. McCarthy provided the background information. "Twenty-eight years old, athletic, strong swimmer, former soldier in the Swiss Army, well-liked by staff and guests."

Edwin knelt by the body. There was no question in his mind that a shark had done this horrific damage. The bite marks appeared to be the same size and shape as the fatal wound he had examined on young Mr. Vansant. And this time, importantly, the victim himself, Mr. Bruder, identified the culprit as a shark.

"This is a disaster," Edwin said to Dr. McCarthy. "But we need to find answers. You can have the body removed to a funeral parlor, if the constable agrees. But tell them I will look at the wounds more closely later. In the meantime, I'll go into the hotel and make sure they contact the proper authorities."

In the lobby, Edwin encountered the same frantic atmosphere he had seen at the Engleside. The genteel class, especially women, were ordinarily protected from exposure to the realities of life, and in this case, they'd had front-row seats to a slaughter.

Poor Mr. Bruder, Edwin thought. *Was it not terrible enough to be killed in such a gruesome way, but to have become a spectacle as well, and one that would be a devastating memory for all those present?*

Many of the women wept openly. An elegant older lady in magnificent but dated Victorian finery roamed the lobby, collecting donations for Bruder's mother in Switzerland and for his funeral expenses. Men handed her money. One gave his pocket watch. "Sell it for his mother," he insisted.

To Edwin, who overheard, these acts of generosity seemed remarkable until he recalled what Dr. McCarthy had mentioned. The victim was well-liked and had been known for years by the guests, many of whom returned each summer.

Edwin bypassed the clusters of people checking out of the hotel. At the front desk, however, he was overheard telling a clerk that he wished to consult with the manager and that he was a doctor, which caused several men nearby to plead with him to check on their wives. Edwin was torn until another gentleman spoke up and said he, too, was a physician, and offered to see to the ladies, freeing Edwin to pursue his grim task.

He located the administrative section of the hotel without much difficulty. Unlike the labyrinthine hallways of the Engleside, the Essex & Sussex was laid out more sensibly, with detailed maps of the building posted at every fire exit.

The hotel manager, a man of about forty-five, overly tanned, with wavy, dark hair that was just beginning to thin in front, was on the telephone, his demeanor urgent. He did not sit, but paced back and forth, holding the telephone, drawing heavily on a cigarette when he was not speaking. He was jacketless, and the sleeves of his shirt were rolled up. He was irritated with the person on the other end of the telephone and shouted, "It's not my fault!" before hanging up.

He waved at Edwin, still lingering by the open door, to enter and sit down. He did not introduce himself, but Edwin had noted the name on the door read Donald W. Jaynes.

"And you are?" he asked distractedly.

"Dr. Edwin Halsey."

"What may I do for you, Dr. Halsey? Oh, if you have come to help with the ladies who fainted, thank you, and I will direct you to the hotel nurse, who is organizing their care."

"No, no," Edwin said quickly. "I'm here to discuss the

actions you are going to take, or perhaps have already taken, to protect the public. I examined Mr. Bruder's body a few minutes ago. Last Saturday, I examined the body of Mr. Vansant in Beach Haven. Who have you spoken to? Have you notified the Coast Guard?"

"I was in the process of doing that," replied Mr. Jaynes. "Who else should I contact?"

"Well, the governor, although I can do that for you if you provide access to a telephone."

"We did notify him," he replied. Then he rattled off a list that included mayors and police chiefs of nearby towns.

"Excellent," said Edwin.

"What a terrible thing," Mr. Jaynes commented sadly. "A hideous accident."

"Accident?" asked Edwin. "This was not an accident."

"Why, of course it was!"

"My dear Mr. Jaynes, a man-eating shark hunted down and killed a poor fellow in Beach Haven just five days ago. That the shark attacked again along the coast is not surprising. It is hardly an *accident*. The question I have for you is, why was the beach open at all?"

Mr. Jaynes extinguished his cigarette and folded his arms across his chest. He was still standing, hovering above his desk. "We warned people and let them choose for themselves."

"Hmm, when it comes to public health, I must say that doesn't work," said Edwin. "There are times when people need to be protected from themselves."

"That's a rather condescending view, isn't it?"

"You would not think so if you were in my shoes," replied Edwin. "There are always those individuals who lack common sense or are in denial or want to show how tough they are. Now tell me, how did you warn your guests? I saw no signs."

"When they checked into the hotel, they were told. Most of them knew, anyway."

"Surely, the victim, Mr. Bruder, knew about the previous attack?"

"Yes, he did. As a matter of fact, he had been saying the whole brouhaha in Beach Haven was exaggerated. You see, Bruder went to California during the off-season. He said he often swam with sharks out there and that he wasn't afraid of them, that they had never hurt him."

"Well, that is very sad indeed," said Edwin. "My understanding is there are many types of sharks, and it can be difficult to tell one kind from another. The poor man! How tragic."

"I agree," said Mr. Jaynes. "But again, it was his choice. He knew about it. He talked about it. We all did. It's been in the papers. But this is a free country. People have a right to make their own decisions. We did our part. We put up steel netting in the water and made sure guests knew to be careful."

"*Careful?*" asked Edwin. "You make it sound like there were jellyfish in the vicinity. This is an aggressive man-eating shark, sir!"

"We do not know that."

"Mr. Bruder said it was a shark!"

"Perhaps he was wrong," the manager said with a small shrug. "Who knows? Again, it was his choice to take the risk."

"Now just a minute," Edwin protested. "I agree—he was fully informed. But what about your guests? Did they have the information they needed to make a good choice? I think not! Besides, the victim's choice also endangered the lifeguards who tried to save him!"

"That's their job!"

"Mr. Jaynes," Edwin said firmly, "there is an enormous difference between what took place in Beach Haven and what happened here. You had advance notice. In Beach Haven, they did not. This beach should have been closed."

"Nothing is conclusive about Beach Haven," Mr. Jaynes said. "In fact, nothing is conclusive here!"

"What more evidence do you need, other than two dead bodies?" shouted Edwin.

"A dead shark! And only if it has human remains in it, frankly. Otherwise, as far as I'm concerned, we don't really know what took place. I've been here ten years, and I can assure you this is the first time anything like this has happened. The whole thing may be staged, for all I know. It could be a hoax. It's also possible it has something to do with the German U-boat that's out there. Don't you think it's strange that it's only happened at two of the most beautiful and expensive resort hotels on the Atlantic Coast—the Engleside and now the Essex & Sussex? Why hasn't it happened at public beaches? Perhaps this is some kind of socialist plot."

"*Socialist plot?*" Edwin snapped. "Do you realize how ridiculous that sounds? If you say that to the newspapers, you will look foolish."

"I have no intention of talking to the papers," Mr. Jaynes replied.

"Well, you can be certain that I will." Edwin stomped from the hotel manager's office and drove to the town's only funeral parlor. He performed a thorough examination of the body, which somehow looked even more grotesque under the glare of electric lights.

Then he drove straight home. He telephoned every newspaper that he had called two days earlier, plus a few more. Some of the reporters had not even heard of the new attack yet, so his message came across as especially powerful and dire. He made his points as clearly as he could. There were now two deaths. He was the only doctor who had examined both bodies. The shape of the bite marks was very similar. In the attack in front of the Essex & Sussex Hotel, the victim had identified the monster as a shark.

"Make no mistake," he told reporters again and again. "No one should be swimming or even wading until the shark is killed or we are fully confident that it has gone on its way."

CHAPTER 12

Arm in arm, Margaret and Stanley were out for an evening stroll through town, chatting about where they would live after they got married. Margaret thought they might rent a small apartment in downtown Matawan. Stanley said he had another idea, but he was interrupted by a disturbance taking place two blocks away at the train station.

From what they could see, passengers exiting a northbound train were shouting.

"I wonder what that's all about," said Margaret.

They paused for a moment to look, then continued on their way. Stanley described a farmhouse on the western edge of town that he had his eye on. It was in deplorable shape, but he figured that if his friends and his father offered to help, it would take about six months to a year to fix up.

"Is there room for a little garden?" asked Margaret, already picturing the vegetables and flowers she would nurture there.

Before Stanley could answer, a man rushed up behind them, talking frantically. They had never laid eyes on him before, but he was so agitated that they paused out of concern.

"You would not believe what happened in Spring Lake," he cried.

"Are you all right, sir?" asked Stanley, stepping in front of Margaret.

The man ignored the question and spoke extremely fast. "I was at the Essex & Sussex Hotel," he said breathlessly. "I was taking my mother out to lunch. I saw the whole thing! It was horrible!" He described a bloody, vicious attack by the sea monster in such graphic terms that Stanley pulled Margaret away.

"I'm sorry, sir, but you shouldn't be talking about such things in front of a lady!" said Stanley. To Margaret, he murmured, "Let's get away from here."

They walked a half block away. When they looked back, the man was gone.

"How peculiar," said Stanley.

"Was he saying there's been a second attack by the sea monster?" asked Margaret.

"I think so," replied Stanley. "This time in Spring Lake."

"Stanley, do you think the sea monster is a shark or something else? Could it be some kind of little game the Germans are playing—you know, with that U-boat offshore? Why doesn't our navy chase the U-boat away, anyway?"

"Because if we did, it would be an act of war, and that might be what the Germans want," he said. "Actually, it would be worse than an act of war, because technically the *Deutschland* is a private vessel. It's not operating as a part of their military."

"But that seems like a sham, doesn't it?"

"Agreed," he said, "but if their goal is to unnerve us, it's working."

"What about the sea monster?" she asked.

"I don't think it's related," he replied, "unless it's accidentally connected in some way. Like maybe they disturbed something we didn't even know was out there. Maybe mankind was not meant to be in a boat that travels underwater."

"Now you sound like Miss Thomas at the post office," said Margaret. "My father said Miss Thomas was the last person in Matawan to get electricity. She thought the electrical current would flow straight through the wall plugs and right out onto the floor of her house."

Stanley laughed and put his arm around Margaret's shoulders. They were walking in the direction of Mrs. Stoddard's Ice Cream and Confectionary Parlor, their original plan. "Still feel like having a sundae?"

"Not anymore. That man really rattled me."

"Well, there's not a thing we can do about any of it, so let me at least buy you a piece of chocolate," Stanley said, smoothing a lock of her hair.

She made an effort to smile. "I don't think I could ever turn down a piece of chocolate," she said playfully.

Stanley grinned. "Yeah, I have noticed that about you over the years. Chocolate *über alles*."

"*Über alles?*"

"Above all," said Stanley. "It's a German expression I learned from a customer."

"You have a German customer?"

"As a matter of fact, I do," he replied. "There are plenty of normal German people around here. All over the US, in fact. Just because someone speaks German as their first language doesn't mean they're the enemy."

"But in the newspaper, they said they could be spies."

"What are the chances of my customer being a spy?" Stanley

asked. "If it'll make you happy, I'll keep my eye on him, though. I wouldn't want any of my customers doing any nefarious deeds."

"Ha!" she said. "Now you're making fun of me."

"I wouldn't dare!"

"Stanley, stop being silly and listen to me," she cried. "The war worries me. I think American boys are going to be sent over there to fight, and I don't want you to go. I just have this feeling you wouldn't come back to me."

"Why do you say that?"

"Because I know you. You'd probably do something heroic and sacrifice yourself for someone else."

"You think so?" he asked.

"Yes, I do," she replied. "And you know what? I'm just like every woman in the world who faces this situation. I don't want you to go! I want you here with me! I couldn't bear it if something happened to you."

JULY 7, 1916

CHAPTER 13

Reporters seemed to be listening to Edwin. Most newspapers were now calling it a shark rather than a fish or sea monster. The headline in the *Philadelphia Inquirer* was:

Shark kills another bather, in front of New Jersey Hotel

But as he pored through more newspaper accounts, he saw there were some holdouts. Some of the greatest scientific minds of the era, among them the director of the American Museum of Natural History in New York City, insisted that it couldn't possibly be a shark, yet offered no explanation for their opinion. Even worse, the director of the US Bureau of Fisheries, to Edwin's great dismay, claimed the culprit was a broadbill swordfish.

A swordfish? Edwin thought. *Well, that is a new one!*

Another official declared that no shark along the Jersey

Coast was capable of biting clean through a human bone, as had happened to poor Bruder, and therefore the monster—in this dubious exercise of logic—must be a giant sea turtle.

Oh, not the giant sea turtle theory again!

The problem with all this speculation was that it created mistrust. When that happened, there was always a segment of the population, Edwin knew, that would become disgusted and disregard all warnings. From his experience with epidemics, he understood the fine line between educating the public and scaring everyone half to death.

With two attacks just five days apart, the populace of the East Coast of the United States was now aware, watchful—and confused. There was a scare on a beach in Maryland. Then another at Coney Island in Brooklyn, where a woman claimed she'd been stalked by the "Jersey shark," as the New York papers were starting to call it. The woman admitted later that she might have spooked herself.

Business owners at the shore feared a mass exodus, perhaps permanently, of summer tourists. Meanwhile, the shark seemed to have disappeared again. Up and down the coast, men were heading out to sea in shooting parties to search for it. Hundreds, perhaps thousands, of harmless sharks and other sea creatures were shot in the process. From reading the papers, Edwin detected an unsavory competitiveness between some of the men in these shooting parties. It sounded as if most of them wouldn't know the difference between a shark and a porpoise, and many seemed to be motivated by self-interest—specifically, the desire to become a hero in the eyes of the world.

Edwin had no interest in the hunters, but he was very curious about the commercial fishermen. For some reason, fishermen had not been talking to the press. Had they been overlooked? Or were they just edgy about being interviewed? Fishermen were a notoriously clannish group.

And yet, he thought, *their perspective might be the most important of all*. After seeing his last patient in the afternoon, Edwin drove to Point Pleasant, the home port for a large commercial fishing fleet. His plan was to wait for the fishing boats to return to the docks with their day's catch. Hopefully, he would find a way to engage in conversation with a seasoned crew member or two. At least, it would be a pleasant outing, and perhaps he would treat himself to fried flounder for dinner.

The sea was calm as, one by one, the boats passed through the inlet and pulled up to the docks. Impatient seagulls circled and demanded a share of the spoils. Fishermen laughed and complied, tossing menhaden fish to the gulls. Patterns of light, created by passing clouds, flickered across the water as the waning rays of sun welcomed the boats home. The rough-hewn wooden docks creaked and groaned underfoot, reminding Edwin that he was not on solid ground, either physically or figuratively.

Edwin was used to being in charge, but he was out of his element. *I should wait for them to approach me*, he told himself. He leaned against the sagging wall of a bait shop and tried his best not to look eager.

Sure enough, an older man with a severely bent back sauntered in his direction. He had come in on a boat called *Jake's Bounty*.

"What're ya doing down here on the docks wearing clothes like that?"

"I'm a doctor," replied Edwin.

"What, did somebody get hurt?" the man asked.

"No," Edwin said simply.

"Well, are you looking for somebody?"

"Not specifically. But I'm hoping that one of you fellows can help me out."

"Help you out?"

"I'd like to talk to anyone with knowledge or insight about

the shark that killed two men this week," said Edwin. "I examined both of the victims' bodies, and I'm trying to gather as much information as possible."

"Are you sure you ain't a newspaperman?"

Edwin took his hospital identification from his vest pocket. "That says Monmouth Memorial Hospital, Dr. Edwin Halsey."

"I can read," the man snapped.

"I'm sorry, I didn't mean to imply—"

The man interrupted. "Never mind." He stepped closer, sizing Edwin up, as if he were a horse at Monmouth Park racetrack and the man was considering placing a bet. "Why do you care so much about that shark?"

"Because it's a killer, and I don't want it to attack anyone else," said Edwin.

The man responded with a full belly laugh that revealed no teeth. Edwin studied the man's face, noting deep lines, crevices really, on the forehead and around his eyes.

"I beg your pardon," Edwin said slowly, "but I don't understand what is funny."

"Listen, mister," the man answered flatly. "It was a fluke. Do ya know what a fluke is?"

"Of course," Edwin replied. "It's the lobe of a whale's tail. I've lived here at the shore all my life, except when I was in Cuba during the Spanish-American War."

"Ah, you were in Cuba?" the man asked. "I love Cuba."

At last, Edwin thought, *I have said something he liked.* "Have you ever seen or heard of a man-eating shark around here or is this the first time?"

The man paused. He rubbed his bent back and winced. "If you're talking about the beast, the answer is no. I ain't seen it. But others have."

"The beast?" asked Edwin.

"That's what we call it."

"What makes you think it's the same shark?"

"Oh, it's the same one."

"How can you be so sure?"

"Because of the way it behaves," the man replied. "It's not just aggressive. It's stealthy. And it's a maniac."

Edwin thought for a moment. "There haven't been reports of fatal shark attacks in recent memory."

The man howled with laughter. "People get killed by the beast, you just don't know about it," he said. "Fishermen drown. Swimmers get caught up in riptides and sucked out to sea. Folks just disappear and the police think they've run away. At least half the time, it's the beast that got 'em."

"You're making this up," said Edwin.

"No, I'm not!"

"Well, why haven't any of you told anyone? Why hasn't it been in the newspapers so that people could be warned?"

"Well, those that have seen it don't like to talk about it."

"Why is that?"

"Who would believe one of us?" he answered and shrugged.

"Some years back, there was a reward," said Edwin. "You must have known about it. Why didn't any of you try to collect the money?"

"Didn't have proof," he replied with another quick shrug of his shoulders. "But we know what we've seen. Every couple of years, someone will whisper, 'I saw the beast,' and we know exactly what they mean."

"I still think you're pulling my leg," said Edwin.

The man looked out at the water. "The beast is out there," he answered simply.

"Is there anyone who's seen it who will talk to me?" asked Edwin.

"What about Old Timer?" asked a young fisherman who had been inching closer and closer, drawn in by the topic. "Old Timer has seen everything. You should talk to him."

"What is Old Timer's real name?" Edwin asked, taking out his notebook.

"Don't know," replied the first man. "Never heard him called anything but Old Timer."

"Do you know where I can find him?" asked Edwin.

"He lives at a boardinghouse, but he might not talk to you."

The rest of the crew gathered around Edwin, their guard lowered after seeing two of their shipmates talking to him.

"Has this been an especially bad year for sharks?" Edwin asked. "I've been hearing there are far more than usual. Do you agree?"

"Last year was a shark year, not this year," replied one fisherman, and the others nodded.

"What makes you say that?" asked Edwin. "Were there attacks last year?"

"I don't know about attacks," the man replied. "But I do know that most of us saw a lot more sharks last year than this year. Folks is just noticing them more this year, on account of what's happened."

"Could there be more than one man-eating shark out there?" Edwin asked.

They were in complete agreement that it was one shark, but they differed on the type.

"It's a bull shark," a short, stout fisherman declared.

"No, it's a great white," countered a tall sailor whose left arm featured a crude tattoo of a mermaid.

"Now wait a minute," said Edwin. "Tell me why you think it's a great white."

"Only a great white will lift its head out of the water," replied the tattooed fisherman.

"Yeah, but the fellas who were fishing from the *Emma Ruth* said the shark was dark brown or gray," argued another.

"Great whites are white on the belly," replied the tattooed man. "And the captain said the belly was white."

"It ain't normal, coming into shore like this," another man said. "It must be sick."

"There's a lot we don't know about sharks," said the tattooed man. "I think there are hundreds of types."

"Does everyone here call it the beast?" asked Edwin.

They nodded.

"Yeah, and it very well might be a demon," one man said. "It's been around for a long time."

"How long?"

"Who knows?" he replied. "Maybe forever."

"Do you really think it might be some kind of creature with special powers?" asked Edwin.

"It might," replied the tattooed fellow. "If you'd spent time at sea, you would know that anything is possible. There are things you just don't question."

"You know that story from the Bible, Jonah and the whale?" asked someone with a wide scar on the left side of his face.

"Yes, of course," replied Edwin.

"Well, maybe it weren't no whale," he said. "Could have been a *shark*, a great white, like the beast."

"May I have your names?" Edwin asked, eager to follow up on these sightings.

At that, a few men glanced back at their boat filled with fish that needed to be off-loaded.

"Gotta get back to work," said the tattooed man, leaving abruptly.

The others shrugged and, one by one, walked away.

"They ain't going to give you their names," said the first

fisherman, the only one who remained. "I'll take you to meet Old Timer if you want. You got an automobile?"

"Yes," replied Edwin, "I sure do."

Another fisherman, sixteen years old at most, was walking past carrying equipment and paused. "You don't need to drive anywhere."

"Isn't Old Timer over at Sharp's boardinghouse?" the first man asked in surprise.

"No, he left there," the young fisherman said. "He's been sleeping under the boardwalk in Asbury."

"What's he doing up there?"

"Don't know, but he just came back yesterday or the day before. I saw him hanging out at Bill's Tavern. He's been drinking again."

Edwin was disappointed to hear this news. Interviewing an inebriated person did not hold much promise. Still, he'd come this far. He knew the location of the tavern, so he thanked his new acquaintances and went on his way.

Bill's was nearly empty when Edwin pushed through the weathered front doors. The commingled smells of salt, fried fish, spilled beer, and sweat permeated the air.

The bartender called a greeting to him, however, and Edwin felt obliged to linger. He ordered a draft beer and sat at the bar, where his gaze was drawn to a piece of driftwood on which someone had painted the Fisherman's Prayer: *Oh, Lord, thy sea is so vast, and my boat is so small.*

Quite grim for a bar, he thought, *but then, this is no ordinary bar.* No doubt, it was a place of comfort and refuge. In an hour or so, he would be elbow to elbow with men like the ones he'd just spoken to, stalwart souls who had spent the day tangling with the sea.

"Pardon me," Edwin said finally to the lone barman. "Would you happen to know where I can find someone called Old Timer?"

The bartender gestured to a poorly lit area of the tavern along an outer wall. "Over thar."

Edwin squinted and saw the silhouette of a person sitting alone at a table for four.

If this strange fellow had any information that could help, Edwin wanted to hear it. He made his way across the sticky wooden floor and paused opposite the solitary person.

As his eyes grew more accustomed to the gloom, Edwin realized he was in the presence of an old man, at least sixty-five, who was suffering from several maladies. Among them was a palsy of some sort, which Edwin detected when the old man lifted a beer glass to his mouth. When he finally looked at Edwin, his gaze was harsh and unsparing.

Edwin introduced himself and slowly sat down in the opposing chair. He placed his business card on the table and pushed it close to the old man.

"The crew of *Jake's Bounty* suggested I speak to you."

He nodded, then picked up Edwin's card and put it in his pocket without examining it.

"I'm investigating the shark attacks—one in Beach Haven on July first and the other in Spring Lake yesterday. Are you aware of them?"

He nodded again.

"The crew from *Jake's Bounty* told me there's a shark they call the beast, and I understand you've seen it," said Edwin.

To Edwin's surprise, the old man flinched.

Edwin persisted. "Do you think it's a great white shark or something else?"

The old man slurped some of his beer and then took an unusually long time to swallow. Momentarily, Edwin could think only of the man's health.

"I'm a doctor of medicine," he said. "If you don't mind my asking, how long has it been since you've had a medical examination?"

The old man scowled. "Never have, and never will," he replied in a granular voice.

"Well, if you change your mind, please come see me. I have an office at my home in Red Bank, but I could also meet you at the hospital in Long Branch. Anyway, about the shark . . ." Edwin said, trying to get back on track. "Some think it's a great white. Some think it's sick or confused or maybe lost."

"Lost? Oh, hell no," the old man said with conviction. "This is where it lives."

The man sounded so sure that Edwin was taken aback. "Would you mind telling me where and when you saw it?"

He hesitated. "I don't want anyone bothering me about it. If I tell you, you've got to promise you won't tell nobody."

Edwin agreed.

"I've seen the beast twice in my life. Once, at Ocean Grove when I was about ten years old. Another time, maybe twenty years back, I seen it off Ship Bottom. I still go out if the weather ain't too bad. Can't do much real fishing these days. Too damn old."

"Did it try to attack you either of those times?"

"No," he replied, "but I got a good look, especially the second time. Darn thing lifted its head right out of the water. It was like looking into the face of evil. I'll tell you what the Lenape say. When they see the beast, they know that *Matanto*, or Death Spirit, has arrived."

Edwin paused, taking this in. "Who told you that?" he asked

finally. "There aren't any Lenape Indians around here, not for hundreds of years."

Old Timer laughed. "You're wrong about that," he said. "They're still here. They just don't tell anyone who they are, 'cause if they do, the government takes their property away and sends them to a reservation out in Oklahoma." Old Timer saw Edwin's surprise and said, "Yes, sir, the government is still doing that."

"So they—the Lenape—say that the Death Spirit arrives with the beast," said Edwin, prompting Old Timer to say more. "And you, yourself, saw the beast twice. Were you with anyone when you saw it?"

"The first time, yes. I was with my grandfather. He said to me, 'Don't tell no one.' He said people would treat me funny if they knew I seen it."

"What makes you think it was one creature, all those years apart?" asked Edwin.

"Oh, it was the same."

"But what makes you so sure?"

"Can't explain it. I just know."

"Why do you think you escaped it?"

Old Timer shrugged.

Edwin brought the conversation back to the present. "Do you think the beast is the creature that killed the swimmers?"

"Yep."

"Do you think there's any way we can catch the beast?"

Old Timer chortled. "Why would you try?" he asked. "Look, I've got nothing more to say."

Edwin leaned back in his chair and finished his beer in one long gulp. "Well, I thank you for your time," he said. Then he drove home, more confounded than ever.

CHAPTER 14

Meanwhile, in Matawan, the sea monster was the talk of the town again, and some people were even beginning to believe it might be a shark, bizarre as that seemed. The second fatal attack had unfolded just as the frantic man from the train had told Margaret and Stanley.

"Surely, it will just go out to sea, whatever it is," said Margaret's father. Her mother still insisted that it was a hoax.

A different concern suddenly moved to the forefront, however, as the number of cases of infantile paralysis grew rapidly. Margaret's father came home for lunch with news that a ten-month-old baby, the son of a floor manager at the basket factory he owned, had died of infantile paralysis.

"We've never had so many cases," said her father. "The talk is that the governor will start closing our borders."

"How in the world will they do that?" asked Margaret.

"I guess constables and deputies will be stationed at every road into the state—you're right, not an easy thing to do. If there's a child sixteen or under, the vehicle will have to turn around."

"Why would anyone want to come to the shore this summer, anyway?" Margaret's mother asked crossly. "There's a sea monster out there! And an epidemic!"

"Well, actually, my dear, the epidemic is worse in the city and people are trying to escape it by coming here," said Margaret's father. "Reverend Rutledge knows a family from New York who leased a house in Avon-by-the-Sea for the *sole purpose* of getting their children away from the epidemic."

"What about people arriving by ferry? I assume they'll have to go back if they have children with them?" asked Margaret.

"Hoboken is doing that already," he replied.

"Did you hear about the woman from Newark who went to Highlands on the train with three children?" asked Margaret. "This happened yesterday. They put her and the children on the next train and sent them right back. She was very upset, but she was told that Newarkers were barred from entering the borough. I didn't know they could do that!"

"Well, it's very confusing as to who can do what," her father noted grimly. "Every little town has its own laws. People are frightened. It's a sad situation."

"You can say that again!" cried her mother, tossing a napkin down on the table. She pushed back her chair and slouched from the room. They could hear her trudging slowly up the stairs.

"I should have known better than to bring it up," Margaret's father whispered. "She can't stand any talk of an epidemic."

Twenty years had passed since Margaret's only siblings, twin boys, died during a measles epidemic when Margaret was four. Her mother rarely spoke of it, but sorrow hung in the air around her like the clinging scent of smoke.

"Should I follow her?" Margaret asked.

"Let's give her a few minutes to herself," he replied.

"At least I'll put her food in the icebox," Margaret decided.

"Thank you, dear." Her father looked tired. His sky-blue eyes, which she had inherited, were bloodshot. Margaret knew he was upset with himself for having been thoughtless. Her mother would never get over the loss of the boys.

"Father," Margaret said, "there is something I'd like to ask you. There's a possibility that the opening of school will be delayed this fall if the epidemic doesn't slow down. What do you think?"

"Delay the opening of school?" he asked.

"Yes, but only if there are no other options."

"Well, I certainly hope it doesn't come to that," he said. "But if the number of cases keeps growing, I don't think there will be any choice."

"If only we knew how it spreads," Margaret said anxiously. "Or if they could come up with a way to treat it. It's no wonder people are up in arms about it." She sighed, thinking of a colleague she had run into a few days earlier. The poor woman was worried sick for her three young children, all of whom were under six years old, the age most likely to become infected with the disease.

Margaret's father needed to get back to work.

"I'll look after Mother," Margaret told him as she saw him off. "Don't worry."

After her father left, she felt the full weight of responsibility for comforting her mother. "Would you like anything, Mother?" she called up the stairs. When there was no answer, Margaret waited a few minutes and tried again.

"Mother, may I get you some iced tea? Do you want me to read to you?"

Still no answer. Margaret climbed the stairs, preoccupied by her own private worry. *When Stanley and I get married,* she thought uneasily, *who is going to look after Mother? Could Sally, the housemaid, work more hours? Could Father afford it? Would Sally agree to it?*

And then the worst question of all: *Would Mother decline without me living here?*

Her mother looked pitiful, curled up on the four-poster bed, lying on the quilt with the log cabin pattern made by a great-aunt long ago.

"Let me go to the store for you, Mother," Margaret urged. "I'll get you anything you want. Would you like ice cream? It would be melted by the time I got back, though. How about a slice of German chocolate cake from Mrs. Stoddard's shop? Or I could go to the library and get you a new book. I'll read it aloud if your head hurts too much."

"No, just sit with me, dear," said her mother. With her back to Margaret and her face in a pillow, Margaret could barely hear her.

"Mother, it is much hotter up here right now than downstairs," said Margaret. "At least come back downstairs with me."

"No, thank you," she answered. "But I think I will take you up on a new book from the library."

Margaret was elated. "Oh, *good*, Mother," she said with relief. "I'll be back as soon as I can."

But the trip to the library did not turn out as planned. Before she could get to the entrance to the building, she had to navigate past a group of people in the midst of an animated discussion on the sidewalk, and Mr. Smith, who owned a poultry farm, recognized her.

"Miss Atkins," he all but shouted. "We heard they are postponing the start of school from September to October, maybe even November! You're a teacher. What do you know about it?"

Margaret was taken aback by his tone. "I don't believe any

decision has been made, Mr. Smith," she replied firmly. "That is my understanding."

"But how likely is it to happen?" he demanded.

"I don't know," replied Margaret.

"Well, tell them they shouldn't postpone!" Mr. Smith insisted. "The children getting sick are not even school age! Why should all of the children have their schooling interrupted?"

An older lady who worked as a seamstress at Cartan's Department Store spoke up. "Dr. Brewster told the *Journal* that the paralysis could spread between older children in the classroom and then be brought home to their younger siblings. That could be disastrous!"

"Could?" asked Mr. Smith. "Not much certainty, is there?"

"All the more reason to be *more* prudent, not less," the seamstress insisted. "There seems to be some link between the disease and warm weather, and Lord knows this is one hot summer, so maybe delaying the start of school would be wise."

"Aw, for pity's sake, why do people choose to live in fear?" he asked.

"Perhaps it's better to be safe than sorry," said Margaret in a calming tone. "Now pardon me, but I must get home to my mother." She had not even gone inside the library. She just wanted to get away.

As she separated herself from the crowd, a man she didn't know spoke chilling words. "The family of the baby that died last night live next door to an Italian family that just moved here. Before they got here, no one was sick. Now they're all under quarantine and scared for their children's lives."

Margaret turned. "What a terrible thing to say," she cried, but she wasn't even sure he heard her. She tried to speak again and was flatly ignored as several men began talking loudly. As she walked home, she was so upset and distracted that she came close to stepping in front of an automobile turning onto a side road. The driver honked the horn and rudely shook his fist, an act of hostility she had never experienced before.

Everyone is unnerved this summer, she thought. *Everyone is on edge. It feels like the world is closing in on us.*

JULY 8, 1916

CHAPTER 15

Edwin sat up late, sipping brandy and puzzling over the things said by the Point Pleasant fishermen late Friday afternoon. It was past midnight now, but he doubted he could sleep.

As a medical doctor, Edwin immediately wanted to reject the idea of a mythological sea creature. Having grown up by the sea, however, he'd heard more than a few strange tales and had even seen a few things himself. In his gut, he respected these men who, after all, spent their lives at sea. If anyone was an expert, it was them. He could not dismiss it as some sort of joke either, especially after observing Old Timer's reflexive cringe when Edwin broached the topic.

Who am I, he wondered, *to declare whether something is real or not?*

Perhaps the answer would come in time, but worrying half the night would not solve the mystery. He had trudged halfway up the stairs, leaning on the banister more than usual, when the telephone rang. He panicked, thinking of Julia.

Then he recalled that for once—*for once!*—she had come

home more or less on time and gone to bed. So what was this about, then? *Please, God, not the shark. Any type of emergency— just not the shark.* He could handle a burst appendix or an arm crushed in a late-night automobile accident. He could not handle another exsanguinated sea-bather.

It was nothing of the sort, however. The call came from— of all people—an aide to Woodrow Wilson, president of the United States. Following a long tradition begun by Ulysses S. Grant, President Wilson had decided to spend the summer at the Jersey Shore. Edwin had been selected by Monmouth Memorial Hospital's board of directors to serve as the president's local medical liaison—a role he'd assumed was mostly a formality.

For a few days, the newspapers had been reporting that Wilson was in West Long Branch at a borrowed estate called Shadow Lawn, which was being considered for a formal rental arrangement later in the summer.

Edwin gasped when he realized who it was. "What is the emergency?" he cried. "Do you need me at Shadow Lawn? I shall come at once!"

"No, no, that isn't necessary, Dr. Halsey," replied the aide. "The president apologizes for the short notice, but he would like to see you first thing in the morning for a consultation. Not at Shadow Lawn. At the offices he's thinking of renting at the Asbury Park Trust Company building."

They settled on quarter past seven for the appointment. After they hung up, Edwin wandered restlessly around the first floor of the house, straightening pictures on the walls in the parlor, organizing bookshelves in the library, and pacing in the main hallway.

What if he's truly ill? Edwin thought. *What if the aide didn't want to say what was wrong with him over the telephone?* And to his immediate shame, he wondered, *What if he dies on my watch?*

Edwin had become acquainted with Wilson about fifteen years earlier, when Wilson, a college professor, was president of Princeton University. Later, Wilson ran successfully for governor of New Jersey. During his tenure, Wilson appointed Edwin as the chairman of several health committees, and the two men maintained a professional relationship.

In 1912 Wilson was elected president of the country, and Edwin neither saw nor heard anything from him after that. Now Wilson was running for reelection on the Democratic ticket using the slogan, "He Kept Us Out of War," and had decided to plan his campaign at the Jersey Shore.

Edwin was not a fan of the president. After winning the highest office in the land, Wilson, long associated with the northern state of New Jersey, suddenly revealed that his true sympathies were with the South, where he was born and raised. Five decades after the Civil War ended, Wilson surrounded himself with Southerners and instituted directives that revealed his true self, including segregation among employees of the federal government.

He didn't seem so bad when he was at Princeton or when he was governor, Edwin mused about Wilson. Much as he disliked the man, however, Edwin would never let his personal views interfere with providing medical care to whoever needed it. He would treat him like any patient in need of help.

Edwin decided he should try to get some sleep, even if it was just for an hour or two. By four thirty, however, having tossed and turned restlessly, he got up and made coffee. For an hour, he read medical journals. Finally, he could stand it no longer and decided to drive to Asbury Park and arrive ahead of the president. Only a few milk wagons were on the road, so the trip went quickly. When Edwin pulled up, however, he was surprised to learn that the president was already there.

Wilson's armed men escorted Edwin to the fifth floor of the building and down a wood-paneled hallway. The office that Wilson was considering for a formal rental arrangement later that summer was easy to pick out, since four additional armed men stood outside the closed doors.

The double doors were opened on either side by two members of the security force. Upon seeing Edwin, the president smiled and stood up behind an antique library desk. He dismissed his security men and aides as he waved Edwin in.

"Dr. Halsey, it is good to see you," Wilson said warmly, "although I seem to have chosen the wrong summer for the shore."

Edwin was not sure what he meant. Certainly, he could not be referring to the shark.

But that was it precisely.

"This is not a medical visit," Wilson announced. "I've seen your name in the papers, and I need someone knowledgeable about the shark, er, *problem*. I hope you don't mind. I know we'll be seeing each other at the dinner party tonight, but Mrs. Wilson won't want us to talk about the shark."

Dinner party?

The president saw that Edwin was caught by surprise. "Surely, you're still coming tonight," he said petulantly. "Your daughter will be there, I understand, with Mortimer Weeks. He's my wife's grandnephew, you know. And my secretary of the treasury, William McAdoo, will be there too, with his wife, my daughter Eleanor. They summer in Spring Lake—you knew that, I assume? They own that big place at the corner of Passaic and First Avenues. Anyway, I think it will be a very pleasant evening. The owners of the house have given us free rein. It's a tryout, of sorts. They're hoping we choose Shadow Lawn."

His verbosity gave Edwin a chance to compose himself. "Of course!" he said, feigning enthusiasm.

The truth was that Edwin had completely forgotten. Julia had been chatting about it for weeks, but Edwin had barely paid attention.

The president began peppering Edwin with questions about the shark. Was it one or two or more? Edwin told him he believed it was one. He kept his promise to Old Timer and the other fishermen who had confided in him, however, and kept silent about what they had said.

"Why do you think these attacks are happening?" asked the president.

"I have no idea," replied Edwin. "No one really knows. Sharks have not been studied enough for us to have many answers."

"What do you think about these conspiracy theories?" the president asked, his voice lowered. "You know—the ones about the Germans being behind it?"

"I think they're silly," replied Edwin.

The president frowned. "Yes, I agree it seems outrageous, but I will confess that it does concern me a bit," he admitted. "Perhaps the Germans are trying to distract us in some way, so they can gather information or plan an attack. Meanwhile, their U-boat *Deutschland* is right off our coast! It's no secret. It's in all the papers! It's due to arrive in Baltimore tomorrow. And the British are livid, not that I blame them. But as long as we're neutral and the U-boat is a merchant vessel, there's not much I can do. Still, I believe the Germans are taunting us! And if I send the navy after them, even just to shoo them away, it would be interpreted as an act of war, which may be what they want!"

"I think it is all coincidence," Edwin said quickly. "The most likely explanation is that it's a quirk of nature. A rogue shark, an aggressive type we don't usually see at the Jersey Shore."

The president sighed. "You are probably right," he said. "I knew you would be calm under the circumstances. Everyone else

I've spoken to is in a complete state of panic. There are concerns about the economy. But my understanding is that many of the hotels are acting responsibly, and the tourists are still coming. Have you seen these?" He handed Edwin several newspapers from a stack on his desk. The front page of the one on top read:

Asbury Park Bathing Grounds all to be surrounded by wire
Will assure absolute safety to bathers

Edwin had not seen this story. "Well, I'm glad to see the newspapers are getting the word out," he said. "But I hope they're not being too reassuring. How do we know the wire will hold back the shark? What if it can get through or around it? Personally, I believe all beaches should be closed."

"Yes, I know you are of that opinion," the president said with a frown. "But that would be up to the state, not the federal government. Not a thing I can do about that, except to put some pressure on Trenton."

"Well, I do hope you'll do that," said Edwin. "There could be more attacks."

"How did you get to be such an expert on sharks?"

"I'm not an expert," replied Edwin. "I just learned a bit about them when I was in the Spanish-American War."

"Ah, I see," said the president.

The conversation stalled, and Edwin studied the president's face and hands, searching for signs of illness. "Are you getting enough rest?" he asked.

"It is a bit hard to sleep," the president admitted. "The war, the epidemic. And now this shark problem! What a summer!"

Edwin commiserated with him. "Yes, it's been very odd. And we will have a full moon with an extreme high tide next week, which won't help."

"What?" asked the president. "You believe in that hogwash about full moons?"

"Oh, growing up at the shore, you pay attention to the cycles of the moon and how they impact the tides," Edwin said.

"You don't believe in werewolves or anything like that?"

"No, no, nothing like that," Edwin said quickly, wishing he hadn't broached the subject. People who lived inland never understood. "Astronomy was one of my favorite subjects in college," he added, hoping that would be a soothing response.

They said their adieus until the dinner party, which, Edwin wrote down carefully in his notebook, was to begin at eight o'clock—not that he had any interest in going, except perhaps for the chance to share a civilized meal at the same table with his daughter.

As he left Asbury Park, the sun had already burned through the early morning haze on the sea. Another relentlessly scorching day was on its way. Edwin, although a regular churchgoer, had not had his heart in worship for years, but he found himself pleading with God.

Please, Lord, he prayed, *let the people be safe today.*

CHAPTER 16

Ben Everingham, a local farmer, was happy to make a few extra bucks as a hired hand serving on shark patrol, as some of the towns and big hotels had started calling it.

This will be the easiest money I've ever made, Ben thought gleefully. He was among those who believed it was a hoax.

His assignment was to keep watch from a rowboat just offshore at the Asbury Avenue beach, one of four public beaches in the city. He was supposed to bring a rifle with him, but he didn't want to take the chance that his favorite gun might rust from exposure to salt water.

Hundreds of people splashed in the surf, and since it was a Saturday, many more would no doubt be arriving. He didn't envy the lifeguards stationed on the beach, whose job was to keep all the visitors—many of them hapless city folk—from drowning.

For an hour, Ben rowed back and forth just inside the swimmers' safety ropes. He had read that steel netting enclosed the swimming area, but he saw no sign of it. *Perhaps the netting is below the surface,* he thought. *Anyway, what a silly waste of money.*

The job was more tedious than he expected. Several times, he considered tying the boat to the safety ropes and taking a nap.

As his second hour on duty began, he drank water from a flask, wishing he had accepted his wife's offer to pack him an apple and a ham sandwich.

And that's when he saw it.

Fifty feet away, heading straight for him and his little rowboat, was the tall, dark dorsal fin of a very large shark.

He had no way to defend himself. He had no axe or gun, and it was moving faster than he could row to shore.

He grabbed an oar and held it like a spear. He'd have just one chance. As it closed in on him, the shark lifted its head, its jaws wide open—a sight so horrible he almost dropped the oar.

He struck it hard, right in its face.

The shark seemed stunned. Ben stabbed it a second time, screaming in panic. Both man and shark froze for a long moment.

Then the shark whipped around and went out to sea.

CHAPTER 17

Edwin used the time driving to the hospital in Long Branch to steel himself for new cases of infantile paralysis. Indeed, there were six, and only one, a boy of four years, seemed likely to survive.

I cannot wait for this summer to end, he thought. The epidemic would probably wane in the fall. No one knew why, but there seemed to be a connection.

Was it possible that with cooler weather, the shark problem, as the president had called it, might also resolve itself? Perhaps the shark would vanish as quickly as it had appeared. Maybe its sudden arrival had something to do with currents or ocean temperature. But even if the shark was still lurking, fewer people would be swimming in the sea.

Edwin had been at the hospital only an hour when he was called to the telephone for an emergency. He thought it might be Hannah, phoning to let him know that a very ill patient was en route to the hospital. It was, however, an aide to President Wilson, the same man who had called the night before. Edwin's heart skipped a beat. His first thought, once again, was for the president's health.

"The president has asked me to inform you that there has been a close call with the shark at one of the beaches here in Asbury Park," said the aide.

Edwin swallowed hard. "What about the steel netting?"

"There are four beaches in Asbury Park," replied the aide. "We have just learned that they've only completed the job at one."

Edwin was too stunned to say anything.

The aide added, "There were hundreds of people swimming in the surf. It's a Saturday in July, you know."

"You said it was a close call," Edwin said, finally finding his voice. "No one was hurt?"

"Everyone is all right, but it was very close," replied the aide. "A fellow named Everingham was patrolling in a rowboat. He hadn't brought a gun, so he whacked the shark in the head with his oar."

"What?" asked Edwin. "And that worked?"

"Yes, but he was very lucky."

"I should say so," said Edwin, imagining the scene. "Have they closed all the beaches?"

"Yes, sir," replied the aide. "According to my notes, the municipal officials immediately closed the Asbury Avenue and Seventh Avenue beaches. The Fourth Avenue beach, the one with steel nets in place, was allowed to stay open, although few people went in."

When Edwin hung up the phone, he felt unwell and sat down for a few minutes. This was devastating news. The beaches had been open even though steel netting was in place at only one. The fellow on "patrol" had not been prepared properly.

And of course, worst of all, the shark had once again been hunting humans along the beaches of the Jersey Shore, continuing in a northward direction.

From a scientific standpoint, the shark was likely hungry and searching for food, and it just so happened that humans were in its path. It was becoming harder, however, for Edwin to react dispassionately.

Even I am beginning to think of it as a beast.

CHAPTER 18

Edwin was late. *Very* late. Guests were seated for dinner when he arrived at Shadow Lawn. He had missed formal introductions to the First Lady of the United States; Mr. and Mrs. McAdoo; and the parents of Julia's paramour, Mr. and Mrs. Weeks.

He was escorted hurriedly to his place at the table, where the guests had begun a first course of oysters on the half shell. He tried to catch Julia's eye, but she avoided his gaze and instead stared at her plate. It was then that Edwin realized everyone around the table was formally attired to an extreme. Edwin was still wearing his work clothes—in this case, a woven suit which Julia particularly hated because she insisted it made him look like Sherlock Holmes.

"I am so sorry, everyone," he said with all the sincerity he could muster. "I beg your forgiveness, especially yours, President and Mrs. Wilson. Do go on with your conversation."

Mortimer's father, who had been interrupted midsentence by Edwin's arrival, continued. "As I was saying," he said, "my theory is that the Germans are toying with us. They're very cunning people, you know. I suspect they captured a man-eating shark and brought it here just to antagonize us."

"Why would they do such a thing?" asked Mr. McAdoo, the secretary of the treasury.

"To rattle us, of course," he replied. "To distract and divide us. That way, we'll be focused on other things when they attack us."

"Well, I heard that it was the propeller from the German U-boat that hurt those poor young men, and not a shark at all," said Mrs. McAdoo.

"I don't see how that's possible," Mr. McAdoo said to his wife.

"Oh my," the president said, furrowing his brow. "The war! The shark! Could we talk of something else? Dr. Halsey, I believe this is the first time you've met Mr. and Mrs. Mortimer Weeks Jr., young Morty's parents. How nice that you've finally been introduced."

"Yes, indeed," said Edwin. Addressing Mortimer's parents, he added, "Again, please accept my heartfelt apology for being late. I meant no disrespect."

"Oh, that's quite all right," Mrs. Weeks said warmly. "I'm sure it goes with the territory—being a physician, I mean."

"I do hope that your patient—whoever it is—is recovering," said Julia. It was the first time she'd spoken. Then, to the others around the table, she added, "Father is very dedicated to his patients and has been working tirelessly, especially now, with the infantile paralysis problem."

"Well, that was not the reason I'm late," said Edwin, frowning. He felt the eyes of everyone around the table looking at him as if to say, *Well, then why* were *you late?* Seeking to fill the awkward silence and perhaps to defend himself, he added, "After the close call in Asbury Park this morning, which I'm sure you're all aware of, there was another frightful encounter with the shark this afternoon."

There were several gasps around the table.

"Where?" the president asked in dismay. "Where did it happen?"

Julia glared at Edwin so ferociously that he made a quick survey to be sure that no large forks or knives were within her reach. He looked at her helplessly. The president, unaccustomed to being ignored, repeated his question.

This time, Edwin answered. "In Bayonne," he said quietly.

"All the way up there?" asked Mortimer's father.

"Wait!" cried Mortimer. "If the shark was in Asbury Park this morning, how could it be in Bayonne later on the same day? Why, that must be fifty miles. It's not possible!"

"How do you know that?" Edwin asked him. "There is a scientist in Australia who believes that some types of sharks can travel easily that far in a few hours' time."

"I don't believe it!" replied Mortimer.

"And your opinion is based on what, exactly?" asked Edwin. "The man in Australia is knowledgeable about these creatures. Surely, we should at least listen to him."

"You're talking about *Australia*," said Secretary McAdoo. "We certainly don't have sharks like that here."

Edwin bit his tongue. *What will it take to convince people?* he thought. *The deaths of Vansant and Bruder aren't enough?* He cleared his throat and attempted to speak calmly. "Well, sir, a police lieutenant in Bayonne would beg to differ."

"A police lieutenant?" asked the president.

"Yes, he was the primary witness."

"But he wasn't hurt?" asked the president's wife.

"That is correct. I drove up there as soon as I learned of it."

"Well, do go on," Mortimer's mother said. "You *have* to tell us now."

Edwin glanced at Julia, who rolled her eyes and took an unladylike gulp of wine. "The police lieutenant was with three other men onshore when they heard children screaming," Edwin said slowly. "The children were swimming at a yacht club. All four men looked out at the water and saw an enormous black fin heading toward the children. At one point, the shark lifted its head from the water. The police lieutenant ran to the end of a floating dock. The shark was still heading toward shore, following the children. They scrambled out of the water just in time."

"Oh, thank God!" cried the president's wife.

"Yes, but there is more," said Edwin. "The shark seemed unaware that the children had escaped and continued toward shore. In doing so, it came straight by the dock where the police lieutenant was standing. He waited until it was close enough and then emptied his revolver into the creature's head. He succeeded only in stunning the shark, which lashed its tail fins and made a sharp turn. It headed toward the Robbins Reef Lighthouse and disappeared. The police lieutenant was still standing there, along with a crowd that had gathered with shotguns, when I arrived later. They were hoping the creature would return, but there was no sign of it."

"Too bad they didn't kill the shark," said Mortimer.

"Indeed," Edwin responded, "but it wasn't for lack of trying."

"The fellow in Asbury Park might have killed it had he followed instructions and had a gun with him," said Mortimer. Then, to Julia, he added, "Wasn't that what they said? That he was supposed to have a rifle in the boat?"

Edwin's heart lurched. "Wait a minute," he said. "Young man, are you saying that you and Julia were *there*?"

Mortimer didn't answer. Julia appeared to be studying the massive crystal chandelier which hung over their heads.

"Julia," demanded Edwin, his tone scathing, "what is the meaning of this? I asked you not to go to any ocean beaches. Last week, you went to Spring Lake. Today, you were in Asbury Park. Please tell me you were not in the sea this morning!"

"It's all right," said Mortimer. "I was with her, and we didn't swim out very far. Anyway, sir, with no disrespect, Dr. Halsey, I have to disagree with you. I'm not going to live my life in fear."

Edwin coughed. "You went into *the water*?" he asked, spluttering with rage. He could hardly get the words out. Then he remembered where they were and glanced around the table. Not a single soul would meet his eyes. They were embarrassed to witness this family fracas, at a formal dinner, no less.

"People will always be drawn to the sea," declared Mortimer. "It's in our nature. We cannot stay away."

Edwin closed his eyes. *Control your temper!* he told himself. When he opened his eyes again, everyone was staring at him.

"Are you all right, Dr. Halsey?" Mrs. McAdoo asked timidly.

"Yes, thank you," he lied.

He had not intended any of it to happen. He was not going to talk about the shark at all, but somehow he had. And he was not planning to humiliate his daughter, but that had happened too. *The shark is now even costing me what's left of my relationship with my daughter*, he thought.

Still, he had every right to be angry at her. *Julia has let me down in a very serious way*, he thought. *And Mortimer Weeks is turning out to be an even bigger fool than I could have imagined.*

The elder Mr. Weeks managed to make things worse. "Dear sir," he cried, addressing Edwin in a blustery, dramatic tone. "I beg you, allow me to apologize on behalf of my son's outrageous behavior! That he would disrespect your wishes and instructions for the safety of your daughter is unconscionable. I assure you, sir, that my wife and I are ashamed!"

The younger Mortimer, his face reddening, stared at his father with incredulity.

"Now, now," the president said hurriedly. "Let us move on, shall we?"

Julia remained silent, but she wore an expression that Edwin hadn't seen since she was a child. Her chin jutted out, and her bottom lip trembled.

Servants carried out platters of striped bass, cauliflower in cream, sauté of squabs on toast with mushrooms, duchess potatoes, sweetbread patties, and cherry sherbet, the latter being a palate cleanser after the main dish. Dessert was custard pie or Charlotte russe followed by Edam and Roquefort cheeses and coffee. Edwin scarcely ate any of the sumptuous dinner.

When the meal finally ended, the women went on a tour of the colonial mansion with the First Lady as their guide while the men retreated to a tapestry-draped room for Cuban cigars and an Italian liqueur, both of which Edwin declined. The president mentioned that he and the First Lady had decided, just prior to dinner, that Shadow Lawn would be their retreat.

"It has fifty-two rooms, not including outbuildings," noted Wilson. "Plenty of space to entertain heads of state."

"What year was it built?" asked McAdoo.

"1903."

"Ah," said McAdoo.

The evening lingered like a persistent cough. When at last it was time to leave and the hosts had been properly thanked, Julia turned her back on Edwin very obviously and walked down the front steps with Mortimer toward his automobile.

Edwin drove home alone and waited for her. Two hours later, Julia announced her return by clumsily closing the front door and dropping something—perhaps her purse—which was followed by a curse word Edwin hadn't realized she knew. She wasted no time in confronting him.

"I will never forgive you!" she screamed. "How could you humiliate me like that? You couldn't possibly have made me look worse!"

"How could *you* be so foolish and irresponsible?" Edwin shouted back. "I asked you not to go anywhere near the water, but you *did*! It is *you* who humiliated *me*! A daughter should listen to her father and obey his wishes!"

"Obey his wishes?" she mocked. She lost her footing and grabbed the piano for support, and he realized with dismay that she was drunk.

"Go upstairs to bed this instant!" he yelled.

"Gladly!" she screamed back.

But instead she plopped down heavily on the sofa and immediately passed out. Edwin checked her pulse but otherwise let her be. He went upstairs and went directly to bed. As he fell asleep, he wondered where the shark might be. He didn't dare hope that it had finally gone out to sea. Instead, he felt a strong premonition that it wasn't done with them yet.

JULY 9-11, 1916

CHAPTER 19

Julia did not get up until half past noon. Her hair was uncombed, her complexion blotchy. Edwin had been waiting for her in the kitchen for an hour. He had already gone on a morning walk, attended the early service at church, and visited the cemetery. It was Julia's mother's birthday, and Edwin always brought flowers to lay on her grave.

Hannah was in the midst of cooking a lavish Sunday dinner of pork roast and mashed potatoes. She took one look at Julia, however, and prepared coffee and cinnamon toast.

Edwin was so uncertain what to say that he had planned to keep his mouth shut and let Julia speak first, but he didn't like the way she looked and flew into doctor mode.

"You look dehydrated," he said. He got her a glass of water from the tap. She glared at him but drank it anyway.

It began to rain, accelerating from a drizzle to a wind-driven deluge in seconds. Edwin, with Hannah's assistance, raced through the house, closing windows. Now the house would quickly grow stuffy, but there wasn't anything they could do.

By the time they were done, Julia had finished her toast, and the look in her eyes indicated that she was ready to revive their argument.

When she started to talk, however, Edwin cut her off. "I'm sure Hannah doesn't want us arguing in her kitchen while she's cooking," he said. "Let us go into the parlor and try to have a civilized discussion, shall we?"

Julia followed reluctantly. She sat down heavily in a leather chair that had been the favorite perch of Edwin's father and folded her arms across her chest. Edwin began by apologizing for embarrassing her the night before. "That was never my intention," he said softly.

"Do you have any understanding of what you've done?" she asked through gritted teeth. "You were meeting Mortimer's parents for the first time! I needed you to make a good impression!"

"Julia, I'm very sorry I was late," said Edwin.

"You always ruin everything! Why must you do that?"

"What about *you*?" Edwin asked in reply. "You disappointed me as well! To think that you and Mortimer went sea-bathing in Asbury Park! And you weren't going to tell me either—that was clear!"

"Oh, Father, you and your precious rules," she said dismissively.

"Yes, I have rules, and I won't apologize for that. As long as you're living in this house, you are expected to follow them," Edwin said firmly.

"Father, you have never liked Mortimer. That's what this is all about, isn't it?"

Edwin hesitated. "You are correct. I do not like Mortimer. But he could still earn my trust if he tried. Same with you. For the time being, he is not welcome here. I will never forgive him for taking you swimming while the shark is a threat to life and limb!"

"The shark!" Julia screeched, which drew Hannah to the doorway of the parlor to check on them. "Father, what is it with you and that shark? Why do you care so much about that shark?"

"BECAUSE I SAW IT!" Edwin shouted back.

Julia leaned back and tilted her head quizzically. "You saw what? What do you mean?"

Edwin didn't answer.

"Father, I'm asking you, what do you mean?" Julia said. "How could you have *seen* it? You arrived *after* both of those men were killed. The shark was long gone, wasn't it?"

Edwin still did not reply. He looked at Julia and then at Hannah still in the doorway. And then he blurted out words he thought he'd never say. "I saw one just like it—thirty-six years ago. On the seventeenth of June, 1880."

Julia and Hannah stared at him.

Finally, Hannah spoke. "Where?"

"Sea Bright."

"Father, what are you talking about?" asked Julia. Her voice trembled. "Father, are you *ill*?"

Edwin laughed. "No, I am not ill."

"What, then? You aren't making sense. Please explain yourself!"

"All right, I will," he said. He spoke slowly and deliberately. "The summer that I was thirteen, your grandfather decided I needed to 'toughen up,' so he arranged for me to be a deck-hand on a small fishing boat. And I almost lost my life to that horrible shark."

"How can it be the same one?" cried Hannah.

"I don't know if it is," replied Edwin. "Probably not. But I did some research—remember, Julia, I mentioned that last night?—and there is a man in Australia who is knowledgeable about sharks, probably more than anyone in the world, and he believes that some types of shark can live fifty or even sixty years."

"Well, in a way I hope it *is* the same shark," Julia exclaimed. "Otherwise, that means there's more than one. Much better to think there's one rogue shark out there that's sick or lost!"

"I talked to some fishermen at the docks in Point Pleasant the other day," said Edwin. "They believe it's one shark. In fact, they have some kind of mystical relationship with it. They feel they know it. They think it lives here and has been tormenting the population for a very long time. I have no idea if they're right, but I do know that *something* is out there. I will not rest until it is dead or gone for so long we can assume it has disappeared back into the depths of the sea from whence it came!"

"Oh, Dr. Halsey, no wonder you've been so determined to warn people," Hannah murmured, still standing in the doorway, her hands now in her apron pockets.

"Unfortunately, the reaction has been inconsistent," said Edwin. "I don't know which is worse—the denial, conspiracy theories, defiance, or willful ignorance!"

"Father, now I understand why you've been so cross with me. But why have you never mentioned anything about this before?" asked Julia.

"Because I was thirteen years old when it happened, and there were people who didn't believe it—or didn't *want* to believe it. And maybe I'm still afraid people won't believe me."

Julia looked Edwin directly in the eye. "I believe you, Father," she said softly.

"I do too," added Hannah.

Edwin took a deep breath. Then he exhaled what felt like part of his soul.

He realized they were waiting for him to say more, so he continued. "At first, people were very sympathetic and concerned. It was the talk of the town. It was even in the newspaper. Since I was only thirteen, my name was withheld, and I was referred to as 'the deckhand' in the news story, but everyone knew it was me. It would have been okay if not for one boy who was a bully. I didn't know him well—maybe he didn't like the attention I was getting—but he started saying it couldn't be true, and he wouldn't stop repeating the lie. After a while, other children believed him, and then the adults did too. Everyone started to ridicule me. And this happened even though there were witnesses, including the captain and the crew of another fishing boat. I was devastated. It is a terrible thing to survive a horrific event only to have people doubt you afterward. My father and mother finally told me not to speak of it to anyone ever again. Over time, people forgot about it. On the rare occasion that someone brought it up, I said nothing. Not one word. I didn't add fuel, so to speak, so eventually the fire went out."

"Please tell us what happened, Father," Julia insisted in a voice barely above a whisper.

Edwin took a deep breath, steadied himself, and began. "We had caught a lot of fish and were going to head back in," he said, almost choking on the words. "Then this huge shark appeared from nowhere. It started circling us and then dove underneath the boat. For a second, I thought it was gone, but then it rammed the bottom of our boat. It struck the bottom of the boat so hard that it broke through. But its head was stuck."

Edwin paused and shuddered. They waited silently while he composed himself. "The captain was thrown overboard, but somehow I hung on."

He paused again, this time dropping his face into his hands. When he looked up again, he had tears in his eyes.

"Father, if you can't say anything more, that is all right," Julia said gently.

"No, no, I think I need to say the rest of it," he said. "The shark became frantic. It was so powerful that it shook the boat to get loose. It even lifted the boat and pounded it on the surface of the water. I didn't know such a thing was possible. And I don't know how I hung on, but I did. I even helped the captain get back in the boat. I'm still surprised I had the strength to do that.

"Just as I pulled the captain back in, the shark freed itself. Water gushed in, and we probably would have sunk in no time. We did our best to plug the hole, but what saved us was a fishing boat much bigger than ours. The crew had seen what was happening. They couldn't believe their eyes. But they came to our rescue. They boarded our boat and plugged the hole completely. Then we bailed all the water that had poured in. We all waited awhile, and no one saw any sign of the shark.

The boat was seaworthy, at least enough to get us back to port in Oceanic. So we thanked our rescuers and headed in."

"Oh, Father, how horrible," Julia murmured.

Hannah, wide-eyed, simply stared.

"Well, that's not the end of the story," Edwin added quickly. "The damned thing reappeared, and followed us all the way to the docks! We crashed the boat and ran for the hills. And the shark—well, a witness reported later that it turned around and went back out to sea."

"Mercy, who ever heard such a thing?" Hannah cried.

"What a terrible ordeal," mumbled Julia and hugged him. "And to think you were just a boy."

"Let me show you the newspaper story," said Edwin. "Wait here, I'll go get it."

He knew exactly where the old clipping was, even though he hadn't looked at it in more than three decades. He went to his office, his feet strangely light under the weight of his body, and retrieved an old box he kept high on a shelf in the closet. The clipping was at the bottom of the box, beneath old letters, school notes, and a yearbook.

The clipping, with the headline "The Monster off Sea Bright," was yellowed but legible. He brought it to Julia and Hannah waiting in the parlor, then left them alone to read it.

Edwin went into the kitchen where he drank a large glass of water, then another, surprised at how thirsty he was. Exhausted and restless at the same time, he paced the floor. *I have kept this secret all these years*, he thought in wonder, *and now here it is, out in the open.*

Finally, he could stand it no longer. As he left the kitchen to rejoin them, however, he no longer experienced a sense of freedom and release. Instead, he felt terribly vulnerable.

They were waiting for him, sitting side by side on the sofa. The clipping was set on the low table in front of them like an artifact. *They are staring at me as if I am the Ghost of Christmas Past*, Edwin thought. Julia had become so pale that he noticed a blue vein on her forehead.

"Father," she said, her voice strangely low. Then she simply shook her head.

"Lord be praised that you survived!" cried Hannah, making the sign of the cross.

"It is a miracle," said Edwin. "And you know that's a word I don't use lightly. Needless to say, I never went back to that job. I went straight home! My legs shook the whole time, and I stopped and rested for a while near the firehouse in Fair Haven. I could hardly walk."

"Have you ever told anyone about this—I mean, since you were a boy?" asked Julia.

"Just once," replied Edwin. "When I had my final interview

at Monmouth Memorial, the dean asked me if there was anything from my past that he should know about. I wasn't sure what he meant, so he elaborated. He said anything that could potentially embarrass me or the hospital if it became known. The only thing I could think of was the shark. The dean listened and then advised me to stay quiet about it. I'll never forget what he said: 'You don't want to be the doctor who claims he was nearly killed by a sea monster, do you? Being a doctor is about trust, and people will think you are not in your right mind. It is better not to talk of these things. This way you can forget it ever happened.' Of course, that's not true. I've never forgotten."

"Did you tell Mother?" asked Julia.

"No, I never told your mother. I thought it would just upset her, and there was no point."

"Father, do you think you should bring it up again now?" Julia asked. "Maybe people will take you more seriously since you actually saw the monster, even though it was years ago."

"I have been tempted to bring it up," Edwin admitted. "But Captain Longstreet died years ago, and I can't find any other witnesses to support my claims the shark has been here before. Some people already think I'm off my rocker. If I were to say that I saw the shark, or one like it, when I was a boy, they would dismiss my warnings altogether. I can't afford the risk that no one will listen to me at all."

"One would think it would give you more credibility, not less!" cried Julia.

"I agree," said Edwin, "but I'm reminded lately that human beings are fickle. As a doctor, I knew this already. I learned it as a lad because of the shark, and I'm learning it again, with the way people are reacting now. Human beings are complicated. And unfortunately, a large part of the population is easily confused or misled."

"I see," said Julia. "In other words, the problem is not so much with the shark, but the people."

Edwin nodded and felt a surge of pride in his daughter. *Julia*, he thought, *is smart*. More importantly, for the first time in a long while, she didn't sound angry.

CHAPTER 20

For the next two days, Hannah and Julia were subdued, the household quiet. Julia, uncharacteristically, stayed close to home in the evenings. Edwin was aloof and mostly stayed in his library when he was at home.

Their quiet preoccupation with the shark, past and present, was pushed aside abruptly, however, when a telegram was delivered late in the afternoon for Hannah from her kinfolk in Ireland. Her grandnephew from County Mayo had been wounded in the European war.

"I knew this would happen!" cried Hannah. She'd been on guard for bad news since a vicious battle began in a place called the Somme on July 1. Another horrible conflict at Verdun had started in February and was still going on. Her grandnephew could have been injured in either battle or somewhere else entirely. The telegram from her family provided no detail, and it was impossible to glean information from the newspapers.

Hannah, still wearing an apron, hurried off to her sister's home to share the news.

Edwin and Julia sat at the kitchen table and studied the latest newspaper, examining a map of the major battles. The place names meant little to a pair of Americans thousands of miles from the scene, but the extent of the carnage was clear.

"Enough of this!" cried Edwin. "I don't care what the president says. We must join the war effort! Our friends are being slaughtered!"

"Why should our boys be slaughtered too?" asked Julia. "It has nothing to do with us! This is an Old World war. Let them fight it out themselves."

"They need us!" Edwin said, his brow furrowed in concern.

"But, Father, it's a bloodbath—an absolute bloodbath!"

"I'm aware of that," Edwin said crossly just as Hannah returned.

"She got a telegram too," said Hannah, referring to her sister. "And it said the same thing."

"Do you have any idea where he was?" Edwin asked gently. "Because there are major battles going on—"

"No," Hannah interrupted tersely. "We don't know."

"Well, I'm sorry that the US isn't there helping," said Edwin. "It's the right thing to do, and besides, it's in our own best interests to go. If our friends lose, we'll be next in line and we'll end up fighting anyway."

"I'm sorry about your grandnephew, Hannah, but I wouldn't want Mortimer to go," said Julia.

Edwin hit the table with his fist. "We've had two whole days without hearing his name," he snapped. "Why, imagine that! I was beginning to hope you'd never bring him up again."

"Well, Father, I was wondering how long we could go without you ridiculing him! Or being sarcastic! Mortimer is a much nicer person than you give him credit for. And he doesn't have a mean streak like you do."

Hannah had turned her back to them both, rinsing dishes in the sink. She was handling the porcelain roughly, which was not her usual way. Suddenly, she pivoted toward Julia.

"That's enough from you, young lady!" she snapped.

Then, to Edwin, Hannah said, "Dr. Halsey, I would like to speak to Julia alone for a moment, if you don't mind."

In all the years she'd been part of the household, Hannah had never made such a request, nor had she reprimanded Julia.

Edwin exited the kitchen without saying a word. For a second, he feared that Hannah might quit. From the adjoining room, he was tempted to eavesdrop, but he didn't have to. Hannah was loud enough to hear.

"Let me tell you something about your father!" shouted Hannah. "Do you know how I know him? Did he tell you about the 1887 epidemic in the Limerick? That's what they used to call the Irish tenement in Long Branch. We all got sick from malignant diphtheria, and do you know what everyone said about us? They said, 'Let them die.' No one cared about us except *one* person—your father. He wasn't even a doctor yet. He was still studying. He was a young fool, they said, for caring about Irish immigrants. 'There are too damned many of them anyway.' That's what they were saying. *Except for your father.* He came into the Limerick and did what he could when no one else would. I lost all my children, missy. All seven of them. Lost my husband and my brothers too. But your father saved me and my sister. He didn't leave until everyone was either dead or recovered. So don't you be disrespectful of your father again, or I'll be washing your mouth out with soap."

Edwin heard Julia say something but couldn't decipher it.

Then Hannah spoke again, her voice shrill. "That's *right*," she said. "That's why, even though years had passed, when I heard about your mother and your brothers and sisters being sick, I came to help—dropped what I was doing and came! When it was all over and they were all dead except you and your father, I stayed, and after a while he hired me as a housekeeper and your nanny. Guess what else, missy? When he realized I didn't know how to read and write, he hired a tutor for me. Don't you remember me learning my ABCs the same time as you? So I'll stand no more of your disrespectful back talk. I won't have you treating him with no respect like that. Maybe I'm talking out of turn now, but I need to speak my mind."

Julia responded, but again Edwin couldn't understand. Her tone was subdued, however. Then there was silence. Edwin waited what he hoped was a reasonable amount of time and returned to the kitchen.

They looked worn out, like two prizefighters who had gone the distance in the ring. Julia was crying, curled up like a cat in her chair. Hannah was leaning against the icebox. Letting loose at Julia—and no doubt the bad news from the telegram—had taken a toll on her too.

Neither of them would even glance at Edwin, so he assumed they had more to say or sort through.

He grabbed his jacket and doctor bag and left quietly. Once again, the automobile gave him respite. He drove around for a while, thinking things through.

His mistakes had never seemed so glaringly obvious. Regret badgered him. He had shielded Julia from the past—his past, her mother's, even Hannah's. He hadn't shared the challenges and setbacks of his work, even when she'd asked and was old enough to understand. He had tried too hard to protect her from pain, and in the process all he had done was transform his grief into a different type of sorrow, one defined by distance and isolation. He had been surviving, not living, and both he and his daughter had paid the price.

He could only hope that the secrets of the past, now revealed, would loosen their grip. The veneer of normalcy had been wiped away, leaving a clean slate. With God's grace, perhaps there was still time for him to become a better father to Julia.

But first, he had to deal with the shark. As long as it was a threat, he could have no peace.

CHAPTER 21

"Meet me at the old dock" was shorthand among the boys of Matawan for swimming and roughhousing.

There was, in fact, no dock any longer, but everyone knew what was meant. Even the adults in town still called it the dock, although the structure was long gone, having collapsed into the creek during a February nor'easter, the year of which no one could remember. All that remained was a series of ragged pilings which once supported the dock but now simply jutted out of the water.

The youngest boys were about eleven; the eldest, fourteen. This was their last chance to be children before adult responsibilities took over their lives completely. Already, they rose before dawn all summer long to work in factories or on a family farm. A few also attended summer school. By three o'clock, most had put in a nine-hour day.

A hundred games had been invented at the pilings. Here, their imaginations soared. They pushed the limits, testing their athletic abilities and judgment. Sometimes, they would leap from one piling to the next, daring each other to reach the pilings that were higher, farther, or tilted. Often, they fell with a scream and a splash into the water.

They were pirates, brave naval officers, and sea captains. They "walked the plank," fired imaginary cannons at faux targets, and pretended to be lost in fog on a schooner while drifting precariously toward shoals that would rip their ship to pieces.

The boys had known one another all their lives and had always been friends. They made special allowances for Lester Stilwell, who suffered from spells and was small for his age, and Albert Novitis, who was born with a clubfoot. Lenny Yelverton was always included, even though he tended to exaggerate. While the other boys pretended to be swashbucklers from long ago, Lenny claimed he'd been a stowaway on a pirate ship or that he'd seen a strange sailing vessel flying a skull-and-crossbones flag on Raritan Bay. The other boys would simply roll their eyes.

At the moment they were all annoyed with Lenny because he was obsessed with the news about the man-eating shark. He had even invented a new game called "Something's in the Water."

It was preposterous to think that an ocean-swimming creature like a shark would ever come to their little creek, but the game was unnerving. The creature had killed two swimmers in the previous ten days.

"Stop it, Lenny," scolded James Finnigan when Lenny tried to launch the game again, just five days after the Spring Lake attack. "You're going to scare Albert and Lester." A farmer's son, James was strong, tan, and, at fourteen and a half, the eldest of the group.

"Do we need to worry about the man-eating shark?" asked Albert.

"Of course not," replied James. "Lenny is just being stupid." Lenny promised to stop. But an hour or so later, he jumped off one of the pilings, popped up for air, and screeched, "Something just brushed against me!"

James was livid. "Lenny, we've had enough of your stupid pranks!"

"Listen to me!" shouted Lenny, frantically treading water and putting on quite a show. "It's alive! There's something in here! Get out of the water!" Lenny swam for shore. From the banks of the creek, he called, "Please, please get out of the water! I think it's a shark!"

The other boys laughed. They didn't even bother to look around. A shark in Matawan Creek? Just to prove to the younger boys that Lenny was making it up, James, who had been standing on one of the pilings, jumped in.

Lenny continued to beg and scream, finally leaving only after James shouted, "Go home or I'm going to whip you!"

James and the other boys continued swimming, relieved that the obnoxious Lenny had left them in peace.

"There is an old log floating under the surface," one of the boys said after a while. "I just saw it. I'll bet that's what Lenny bumped into."

"Yeah," one of the other boys agreed. "Either that or he made the whole thing up."

The water was murky, made more so by the boys splashing and jumping, but they were used to it. They stayed for another hour until it was time to go home.

CHAPTER 22

"I'm going to have that telephone removed from this house," Margaret's father complained.

"Should I answer it or let it ring?" asked Margaret. If she thought it was Stanley, she would have rushed to the telephone, but she knew he was playing baseball with his friends at the empty lot next to Petersen's downtown.

"Let it ring," said her father.

"But what if it's important?" asked her mother.

"Oh, pshaw!" cried Margaret. "I can't stand it! I shall answer it."

It was Mrs. Yelverton, the mother of one of Margaret's summer-school students, Lenny. A widow with three other children, Mrs. Yelverton worked at one of the local factories where they manufactured tiles made specifically for New York City subway stations.

Margaret asked if Mrs. Yelverton could call back later, but Mrs. Yelverton replied that she couldn't. She was calling from a neighbor's house where she had borrowed the phone.

"I really need to speak to you," Mrs. Yelverton pleaded. "I'm taking Lenny out of school."

"You mean summer school?"

"No," Mrs. Yelverton said. "I'm taking him out of school altogether. He has gotten on my last good nerve, and I'm sending him to live with my brother in Texas. He has a ranch. Lenny will work on the ranch."

"Mrs. Yelverton!" cried Margaret. "Lenny is only twelve!"

"I am certainly aware of that," she said, "but you don't have to live with him. I do. And I'm at my wit's end." She sniffled and cleared her throat.

"Oh, Mrs. Yelverton, please don't cry. You must be exhausted. He is a very . . . spirited boy," Margaret said, struggling for the right word to describe Lenny.

She thought about her most recent interaction with the child, which occurred in front of the butcher shop. He was holding court with a handful of younger children, telling them the temperature in Matawan was 141 degrees, the highest temperature in the USA, and that it was likely they would get heat sick in their sleep and die in their beds. "You won't wake up in the morning," he told them.

Margaret had overheard and reprimanded him. She tried to reassure the younger children, but she could see from their wide eyes that the idea was planted in their minds.

"Mrs. Yelverton," Margaret said slowly, "I know he must be a very challenging child for you to handle at home. But what has he done this time that has gotten you so upset?"

"Well, he went too far with a prank," she replied. "He was swimming with the other boys this afternoon down at the creek. And he leaped out of the water, claiming that something alive had brushed up against him. He started screaming to the other boys to get out. He said the thing that brushed up against him might be a shark!"

"Oh dear," Margaret groaned. "He's heard about the stories in the newspapers."

"Yes, and that has put ideas in his head," Mrs. Yelverton complained. "The others laughed at him, of course. A shark in Matawan Creek? The other boys said there was something in the water with them, but it was just an old log. It's very muddy at the spot where the boys like to swim. But Lenny claiming it was a shark—that is just irresponsible. He knew perfectly well it was only an old log but pretended it was a shark just to create an uproar."

Margaret sighed. "I wish there was something else we could do rather than send him so far from home."

"Well, I'm hoping my brother can straighten him out."

"Maybe I could talk to him tomorrow morning," Margaret said hopefully.

"No, he won't be going anywhere tomorrow," Mrs. Yelverton replied. "He's not feeling well. You know how the boys always swim at the wood pilings where that old dock used to be? Lenny jumped off one of the pilings and got scraped up on the way down. Either that or he jumped right on top of the old log."

"Is he seriously hurt?"

"No, I don't believe so," replied Mrs. Yelverton. "He's got scrapes across his chest and belly. He said the shark caused that! Says it bumped up against him! I told him to shut his mouth, no more foolishness, and made him soak in a hot bath for an hour. Oh, he was mad as a wet hen. He missed his supper too. I made a plaster of honey for the scrapes to help them heal."

"Are you sure you shouldn't call Dr. Brewster?"

"I'll watch Lenny tonight and bring him over there in the morning," replied Mrs. Yelverton. "I expect there are splinters in those wounds. I didn't see any obvious ones, but they could be in deep."

"Oh, I would definitely have Dr. Brewster take care of that," said Margaret.

"I'll tell you something else," added Mrs. Yelverton. "I think it's about time some of the menfolk got together and cleared out the debris in that part of the creek."

"That's an excellent thought."

"Or maybe the boys could swim in another part of the creek, away from the pilings," said Mrs. Yelverton.

"That sounds like a good suggestion too," said Margaret.

When she got off the phone and rejoined her parents at the dining room table, Margaret relayed Mrs. Yelverton's ideas. To her surprise, her father reacted strongly.

"Perhaps the creek is in need of clearing out," he said. "But I used to swim in that exact location as a boy, as did your grand-father before me. The boys in this town should never be told to swim elsewhere."

JULY 12, 1916

CHAPTER 23

Margaret went to the little Matawan schoolhouse early and tried to open the windows but they were swollen shut. *This heat is ridiculous*, she thought, wiping sweat from her brow.

Anticipating that the building might be intolerably hot, she had brought with her several old quilts, with her mother's approval, of course. She spread them out on the ground in the shadow of a cherry tree. When the children arrived for summer school, she directed them to the quilts, where they plopped down happily.

For the first hour, this was fine. By the second hour, as the temperature rose, even being outdoors, motionless, was uncomfortable.

"Children, I never thought I'd say this, but it is too hot to learn," she said, dismissing them early.

As she gathered the quilts and walked slowly home, Margaret wondered how the principal would react and hoped she wouldn't get in trouble.

She couldn't wait to change her clothes and wash her face,

but first, she checked on her mother, who was asleep in a cotton nightdress, her arms and legs askew and mostly exposed. Margaret had never seen so much of her mother's body. *The heat has even overcome Mother's modesty,* she thought.

Margaret prepared a fresh pitcher of water and ice and carried it upstairs. Her mother was awake now, her feet dangling over the side of the bed. She was glassy-eyed, perhaps slightly delirious. She hadn't noticed that she was close to naked, nor did she realize that Margaret was home from school almost two hours early.

"Mother, shall I call the doctor?" asked Margaret.

"No," replied her mother.

"What shall we do, Mother? You look rather peaked."

"Sally said the same thing. She went to get me a root beer."

"Root beer?"

"Well, not root beer. Something else. Birch beer, I think she called it. She thinks it will cool me down from the inside out. And then I will get dressed and sit on the back porch."

"That's fine, Mother, but in the meantime, I brought you some cool, fresh water, just as you like it—not too cold." She supported the bottom of the glass while her mother drank.

By the time Sally returned with birch beer, Margaret's mother was looking better, anyway, covering herself with a sheet and ordering both Sally and Margaret to leave the room so she could get dressed in privacy.

Recognizing an opportunity, Margaret devoted the next three hours to persuading her mother to eat anything that appealed to her. Sally joined in the effort, agreeing to stay all afternoon. By half past two, Margaret's mother had consumed more food and liquid than she had in the four previous days collectively. Margaret felt relieved but also fidgety. Although the heat was soaring and going for a walk was not ideal, she announced a sudden need to take care of some errands.

"Oh, I see. You are hoping to run into Stanley," her mother said with a coy smile, noticing that Margaret had changed into a new outfit and braided her hair.

"Why, Mother, what would make you say such a thing?" Margaret asked in faux surprise. The mood had become so light that even Sally joined in their laughter.

"I'll be back soon," Margaret added more seriously. "And, Sally, thank you for staying late today."

Feeling carefree, Margaret strolled to Main Street, grateful for her broad-brimmed straw hat, which helped keep the sun at bay. She decided to stop by Stanley's shop first while she still looked somewhat fresh. As she headed there, five or six boys raced past her in the direction of the creek.

She knew them all by name, and they, of course, recognized her from school. As they dashed past her, they called, "Good day, Miss Margaret!" She smiled and shook her head. *How on earth can they run like that on a day like this?* she thought. It was remarkable, the strength and resilience of youth.

When she arrived at Stanley's shop, she saw through the plate-glass window that he was busy with a customer. Not wanting to interrupt their transaction, she waved and left. *Perhaps,* she thought, *if I come back in a few minutes, he will be alone.*

She walked two blocks to Mrs. Stoddard's Ice Cream and Confectionary Parlor to buy a frozen custard. She considered sitting down at one of the little wrought-iron tables, but all the seats were taken. Not enough time had passed to go back to Stanley's, so she ate her sugary treat while ambling over to Cartan's Department Store. A friend from high school, Deborah Irons, worked there and could always be counted on to help choose new hair ribbons—not that Margaret really needed any.

Margaret and Deborah were discussing shades of blue ribbon—what, exactly, was indigo?—when three women came into the store complaining loudly about Captain Cottrell, the retired sea captain, who, according to them, was shouting and making a spectacle of himself in the street.

"Something needs to be done about these old men with time on their hands!" said one in an irritated tone.

Another added, "Well, he's a retired sea captain. You know how they like to carry on."

The gist of the conversation about Captain Cottrell was not unusual, and Margaret secretly agreed the man's behavior was odd. *What is he carrying on about?* she wondered.

Margaret chose two shades of blue ribbon—mostly because she couldn't decide, and besides, Stanley's favorite color was blue, so how could she go wrong? She paid for her purchases and said goodbye to her friend. Perhaps by now Stanley would be alone at the shop.

As she left Cartan's, however, she realized what the three ladies had meant about Captain Cottrell's behavior. He was shouting and waving his arms and right in her path to Stanley's shop.

"Why doesn't anyone believe me?" he bellowed. "Please believe me!"

Margaret paused. "Pardon me, what is this all about?" she asked a woman standing in a doorway.

The woman laughed. "He's claiming he was standing on the trestle bridge and saw the dorsal fin of a huge shark coming straight up the creek toward the town." She rolled her eyes and laughed again. "Supposedly, it went right beneath him while he was standing on the bridge and just kept a-going. He said if no one believes him, two other men working on the tracks saw it too."

Before she could continue, another woman called out, "Old Captain Cottrell has been seeing things! He's been out in the sun too long!"

"Maybe he had a nip of Laird's applejack," a man in business attire said loudly.

Everyone laughed. Well, everyone but Margaret. She thought it was mean to make fun of someone. She slowly walked away but stopped short at the sound of a man's commanding voice.

Mr. Shuler, who owned the barbershop and doubled as the town constable, had come out of his shop to yell at Captain Cottrell. "I thought I told you to stop this nonsense!" Constable Shuler hollered. "Now get on home!" Then he turned to the bystanders and told them gruffly but politely that they should move along.

But Captain Cottrell would not stop. "Constable, I saw it! I saw a shark! A man-eater!"

"That's not funny!" Constable Shuler shouted. Then he told Captain Cottrell to come into the barber shop and calm down.

Instead, Captain Cottrell ran back toward the creek.

"Cottrell, we need to talk later!" shouted Constable Shuler.

The old sea captain paused and yelled back, "I'm going down to the creek to warn people," but the constable had gone inside already.

"How ridiculous!" cried a woman, the mother of one of Margaret's students. "Don't you think so, Miss Atkins?"

Margaret was put on the spot. "I'm actually a little worried about him," she replied. "Poor Captain Cottrell."

"But the very idea!" the woman continued. "How could there be a shark in our little creek? Sharks need salt water, and that creek is probably just as much fresh water as salt."

A man whom Margaret recognized as an employee of the post office agreed. "Sharks are ocean creatures, and we're eleven miles from the open sea!" he said. "It's just not possible."

"You know what I think?" asked Garrett Irons, Deborah's father. "I bet old Captain Cottrell's been hearing about those shark attacks south of here, and his imagination has gotten away from him."

Margaret thought of her student, Lenny Yelverton, who'd been scraped up badly from a log while swimming in the creek the previous day. He claimed it was done by a shark, but he was known to tell tall tales, just like Captain Cottrell occasionally did. Could there possibly be any truth to it?

The clusters of people on the sidewalk began to disperse. Margaret, by now a wilted mess, decided to go home directly and not try to see Stanley again. As she turned to go on her way, from the corner of her eye, she saw Captain Cottrell again. She couldn't tell what he was doing, exactly, but he tore off down a path toward the creek. *He's sure moving fast for an old man with a bad leg*, she thought.

A moment later, she saw the group of boys who had raced past her earlier coming up a different path from the creek. Something was amiss. *What is this?* she thought. They were running with their hands stretched before them, as if they wanted to grab on to something solid to keep from falling. Margaret stopped in her tracks. As they came closer, she saw that they were buck naked. *Something must be very wrong for them to run up to Main Street from the creek without putting on their clothes*, she thought.

She dropped the little paper bag containing her new ribbons and ran straight toward them. So did three or four other adults. Margaret got to the boys first, and they threw their arms around her, sobbing.

Mr. and Mrs. Hamilton's boy shrieked, "A shark got him! A shark got him!"

Another boy cried, "It took Lester! The sea monster took Lester!"

People started coming outside of shops and houses to see what the ruckus was about.

Someone yelled, "Something is wrong at the creek!"

And then Margaret heard others shouting, "The creek! The creek!"

Men of all ages started running toward the creek. Out in front was Stanley.

Margaret cupped her hands together and hollered, "Stanley, wait! The boys said there's a shark! Captain Cottrell said so too!"

Stanley slowed down long enough to call out, "Margaret, I have to help Lester!"

Most people in town knew Lester. He was eleven and small for his age, and he suffered from spells that sometimes incapacitated him. *The poor child has probably had a spell while he was swimming*, thought Margaret. *Perhaps he hit his head. He could be drowning.*

Margaret followed the crowd down to the creek.

Alfred Christie, one of the boys who had been swimming, was shouting and trying to get the men's attention. He yelled, "Listen to me; it grabbed Lester! We thought it was a log, but then it grabbed him! We saw its face! We saw its teeth! It had Lester in its jaws, and it pulled him under! It's a shark! A shark, I tell you!"

The men seemed to barely hear him, however. They were focused on finding Lester.

"Be careful! Listen to Alfred," Margaret pleaded with the men.

But Stanley and three of his friends had made up their minds. Everyone knew that when someone is drowning, there is no time to waste.

Lester's parents arrived on the far bank of the creek, and his mother began wailing and shrieking.

Stanley's friend Rusty Conover cried out, "We can't just stand here!" They took off their shoes and stripped down to their underclothes and dove into the water. Stanley went in first, followed by Rusty and the others.

The tide was high. *Higher than normal*, Margaret realized, *on account of the full moon.*

Again and again, they came up to the surface, took a deep breath, and dove back down again.

There was no sign of Lester.

Suddenly, Rusty panicked. "We have to get out of here!" he shouted. He swam and waded quickly toward solid ground, and when he stood up, his chest was covered with horizontal, bloody scrapes.

Margaret thought again of her student, Lenny Yelverton. His mother had described similar injuries to Lenny's torso. Lenny had even insisted he'd seen a shark and that the shark had brushed up against him. His mother didn't believe him, and Margaret hadn't been convinced either.

Perhaps Rusty got scraped up by an old tree branch or board, just as Lenny did, thought Margaret.

Rusty stood on the creek bank, begging the other men to leave the water. They all did, except for Stanley, who dove down one more time and then surfaced, shouting, "I've got him! I've got Lester!"

But at the moment of his triumph, the water behind Stanley rippled curiously, as if a small earthquake had occurred beneath the creek bed. The surface of the water parted, and the crowd gaped as a creature emerged like a dragon from deep inside the earth's crust.

It was a shark. *The* shark. The one that could not possibly bother them here. They had never seen a shark of any kind in their creek, and the enormous size and shape of this one was like a biblical vision. Its head loomed over Stanley, dwarfing him, yet Stanley, clutching Lester and facing the creek bank, was unaware.

The creature appeared far too large to be traversing and hiding in the shallow depths of their creek, and yet here it was, poking its head above the surface as if to take a good look around, its small eyes seemingly unfocused and lifeless, just like the glass eyes of a little girl's china doll. Its mouth was shaped like a bear trap, its teeth triangular and jagged. In a matter of seconds, and without ever making a single sound, the creature slipped back under the surface.

Before Margaret and the other stunned bystanders could react, Stanley let out a scream so loud and shrill that it almost wasn't recognizable as human.

"No, no, no!" Margaret shrieked.

Without thinking, she rushed toward Stanley, half sliding down the bank toward the creek, her hands outstretched, but someone yanked her back before she plunged into the water.

She watched helplessly as Stanley fought hard, pounding on the creature with his fists. The water all around him was turning a sickeningly bright red. Women screamed and dragged children away from the sight. Men shouted Stanley's name. Margaret wailed.

He broke free somehow. Now the men called to Stanley as he swam toward the water's edge.

"Keep going, Stanley! Come on, Stanley!"

Someone extended a boat paddle, but Stanley was unable to grasp it. His friends reached as far as they could with their hands. "You can do it, Stanley! You're almost there, Stanley!"

There was movement beneath the water. Margaret could see that the shark was about to attack again.

Stanley was almost within reach of safety. As he frantically pushed his way through the water, his friends sought to grab ahold of him. Finally, he was close enough. They grasped his hands and arms and hoisted him up on the bank.

And then everyone gasped as they saw what the creature had done. Margaret nearly fainted. A huge piece of flesh was missing from Stanley's thigh, from just above his knee to near his hip, so deep that it left bone exposed.

Stanley looked down, touched his leg, and said, "Oh my God."

Margaret tried to get near him, but his friends surrounded

him. They tried to make Stanley lie down on the ground, but he struggled against them. Finally, he collapsed. Rusty made a tourniquet with his belt and applied it to the top of Stanley's thigh. This, at least, stopped the blood from spraying in the air.

Rusty rushed off to get the doctor while Stanley's other friends knelt beside him.

Margaret saw it all through glazed eyes. Her feet felt as if they were cemented into the ground. Now someone reached for her hand and said to Stanley, "Margaret is here," but as she was led toward him, she slipped in the mud. She lay there, perhaps six feet from Stanley, unable to move or even turn her head, dead weight when people tried to help her up.

For a few peculiar moments, she imagined she was a red-winged blackbird flying high above the sea oats. Looking down, she saw scores of people rushing about as if they were ants moving in a swarm. All of these people, strangers and friends alike, were trying to help Stanley. He was surrounded by them. She saw herself lying on the ground, ignored, which was fine. She didn't care.

All that mattered was Stanley.

CHAPTER 24

Margaret could not remember how she got home. She was lying on her bed, upstairs in the house where she'd been born and lived her whole life. Of that much, she was certain. Her confirmation was an oil painting that had hung on the wall in precisely the same spot as far back as she could remember. She now stared at it, comforted. There were children in the painting—four of them, two blonds and two brunettes, each so familiar they might have been her friends or siblings. When she was little and had been lonely, she'd confided in them. In her imagination, they had spoken back.

When she closed her eyes, she could see her house from the outside, "the third Victorian on the left," as they always described it, white with light-blue shutters. The one with the prettiest turret in Matawan. In her mind, she saw Mother's ancient but much-loved cat, Essie, perched inside the bay window, staring wide-eyed at something in the branches of the holly tree. There were the overgrown evergreen shrubs and the old stone walkway that had sunk with time, leaving an uneven surface which Father kept promising to fix.

But if she were indoors, lying on her bed, why was she looking at the house from the outside? Then the bed began to spin.

Oh, I see! she thought. *I'm on the carousel in Asbury Park!
And maybe I have fallen! And they brought me home. But where
is Stanley? Why didn't he catch me when I fell?*

The scent of rose water and vanilla floated through the air.
She was overwhelmed with the need for sleep. But someone
was fighting to keep her awake. *No,* she thought, *two people.*
One gripped her right hand and rubbed it urgently while the
other blotted her forehead with a cool, damp cloth. She heard
her mother's voice say, "Margaret! Margaret!"

She struggled to focus. Mother and their housemaid, Sally,
loomed over her, both peering into her face. *Am I dying?* Margaret wondered.

"We need to get her out of these clothes," her mother said.

Margaret realized that her clothes were soaking wet. *Oh,*
she thought, *I must have a fever.* She lay helpless as Mother and
Sally tried to unbutton and remove her clothes, as if she were
a baby. Then she remembered being at the creek. *I'm soaking
wet because I was at the creek,* she thought. *It's not from a fever.*

That was a tiny bit comforting. She would rather have fallen
into the water than have a high fever. A fever was more worri-
some. But she couldn't recall anything about being at the creek.

"Look at her, she's like a rag doll," said Sally.

"We must get these filthy clothes off her!" her mother cried.

They began ripping her dress at the seams.

"Don't move, Margaret!" her mother admonished. "I'm
going to use scissors."

They literally cut Margaret's clothes off her body. *Why are
they doing that?* she thought helplessly. *I'm wearing my best petticoat. Why are they ruining it?*

But then Margaret noticed the clothing in their hands. She

saw the color red. *Perhaps*, she thought, *that's just mud.* Then she became aware of her nakedness. She wanted to cover herself with a blanket or sheet but didn't have the strength. Then they began examining her, and she realized they were looking for injuries.

"Will you look at that, there's not a scratch on her!" her mother cried.

"Thank you, Lord!" Sally shouted joyfully.

"Sally, go run the bath!" said her mother. "I'll use a washcloth in the meantime. I want to get this blood off her."

So it is blood, Margaret thought, alarmed again. *But if I don't have any wounds or cuts, whose blood is it?* She didn't think about it for long, however, because suddenly she was transported—half walking, half carried—and eased into a hot bath.

The bath did nothing to revive her. In fact, it did the opposite. She felt herself slipping into an unconscious state. *I think I should just close my eyes*, she thought.

Mother and Sally scrubbed her with a soft brush and emptied and refilled the tub three times. They hauled her from the tub and tried to make her stand while they dried her and pulled a nightdress over her head.

"Margaret, lift your arms," her mother said a little crossly. But Margaret was unable to obey.

Somehow, she found herself back in bed. One of them had changed the sheets. *They smell like they are fresh off the clothesline*, Margaret thought. *How lovely. Perhaps now they will just leave me alone so I can sleep.*

"She should have water," her mother announced. There was more bustling around, and this time her father's voice joined the chorus from somewhere near the door to the hallway.

"How is she?" he asked.

Sally and her mother propped her up in bed just enough to drink water. At first, Margaret could handle only a birdlike sip, but they all cheered her on, as if she were a year old and had taken her first steps. She got a few gulps down but then coughed and had to stop.

I'm coughing, she thought. *I guess I must be alive.* From listening to their conversation, all she could glean was that a man had carried her to the house.

"Perhaps she was hit by a train," she heard her mother whisper.

"Or trampled by horses," added Sally.

"Tell me again what he said when he brought her into the house," said her mother.

"He said he couldn't stay, that he had to go back right away and help, but I don't know what he was talking about."

"Where is that doctor?" asked her mother, irritated.

"I haven't been able to get through," her father said. "I'll go out and look for him. But what should I tell him? You said she's not hurt."

"Well, she has no injuries that I can see, but she's barely conscious!" cried her mother.

"It does seem like she's in some kind of shock," said her father.

Oh, Margaret thought. *So that's what it is.*

Her father wasn't gone long. Margaret heard him say, "Dr. Brewster can't come now, but he's sending his nurse, Tillie."

"I don't understand," her mother said. "I thought Tillie was retired. Where is Dr. Brewster?"

Margaret's father hesitated. In a hushed voice, he said, "Dr. Brewster is with Stanley."

Stanley. Margaret felt a sudden stab of pain. *Stanley is hurt. Something has happened to him.*

Her father added something in a low voice that Margaret couldn't hear, causing her mother and Sally to gasp.

"No, no, no! That can't be!" her mother cried.

Sally then spoke in a soothing voice. Margaret's father announced he was going back out again. Her mother climbed into bed next to Margaret—something she had not done since Margaret was five or six. Together, they waited for the nurse.

"Let me sit with Margaret for a while," she heard her father say. "Go get yourself some rest. Try to eat something."

It was long after dark when Tillie, Dr. Brewster's former nurse, finally arrived. Margaret had known Tillie all of her life; in fact, Tillie had assisted Dr. Brewster with Margaret's arrival in the world. But tonight, Tillie was different. *She is not herself,* Margaret thought uneasily. *She's usually so talkative and warm, but she seems upset, withdrawn.*

Tillie checked Margaret's pulse in a perfunctory fashion and asked questions about how she was feeling. Still unable to speak, Margaret nodded or shook her head in response.

Before she left, Tillie patted Margaret's shoulder. "There, there, Margaret," she murmured with a small, sad smile. "The best thing you can do right now is rest and regain your strength."

Regain my strength from what? Margaret thought helplessly. *Why won't anyone tell me what's wrong?*

CHAPTER 25

Edwin had seen patients all day in his home office. The weather was still irritatingly hot, but he finally had time to wash his automobile, still dirty from his excursion home from Beach Haven in the storm. Although it had rained since then, claylike mud still clung to the undercarriage of the car.

He was just completing the chore, having doused himself with a bucket of clean water, when Hannah came to the back door.

"Telephone call from the hospital!" she called, waving frantically. "You need to drive over there right away!"

Edwin rushed inside, toweled off, and grabbed his spare blazer. "Do I have time to change?" he asked Hannah. "What kind of accident did they say it was?"

She paused and looked him in the eye. "A shark attack."

"No! Not again . . ." He sagged against the wall to steady his nerves while she quickly reviewed her notes.

"The patient will be arriving in Long Branch by express train and will be met by hospital staff who will take the patient by gurney to the hospital and into an operating theater without delay," she said.

"By train?" asked Edwin. "He's arriving by train?" The Long Branch rail station was literally across the street from Monmouth Memorial, but the plan described by Hannah suggested desperation.

Edwin drove as fast as he dared, hopeful that he would actually be able to help this victim. When he reached the hospital, he hurried to the operating theater and prepped for surgery. Three nurses were already present and ready to assist.

At five thirty, the patient arrived. He appeared to be unconscious, or barely conscious. Edwin removed the blanket which covered most of the young man's body and observed a catastrophic injury nearly identical to the one suffered by Charles Vansant in Beach Haven eleven days earlier. The outer side of the right thigh was denuded from three inches below the great trochanter to two inches above the knee, all of the muscles and tissues were completely removed, and only a third of the muscular tissue on the inside of the thigh remained. Bones were intact.

Edwin began preparing to do an amputation. His patient did not respond to stimulants and saline transfusions, however, although he rallied slightly for reasons unknown—perhaps sheer willpower. One of the nurses noticed first.

"Doctor," she said, drawing Edwin's attention. She gestured to the patient's face. His eyes had opened, and he reached out his hand to Edwin, who took it, remembering Julia's admonition that he was not consoling enough with his patients.

"Is he trying to say something?" asked the nurse. She was surprised, as was Edwin. The patient was doing so poorly. How did he have the strength to lift an arm, let alone speak?

But he did. He mumbled something. Edwin heard the words, "I found him, I had ahold of him, I've done my duty."

He motioned for Edwin to come closer. He was fading. The best he could do was whisper.

Edwin leaned down, putting his ear close to the patient's lips, still gripping the young man's hand.

Barely audible, the man said, "Tell Margaret I'm sorry. Have a good life without me."

CHAPTER 26

Edwin had covered the young man's body with a sheet. Often, the nurses took care of that responsibility, but now Edwin chose to do it himself. He did so with a tenderness that he hadn't allowed himself to feel or express for a patient in a long time. *Poor young fellow,* he thought. *What a terrible ending, and so young. Just like the others.*

The nurses stared at him.

"Dr. Halsey, are you all right, sir?" one of them asked hesitantly.

He had tears in his eyes, but for once he didn't bother to hide them from the medical staff. "This is the third young man killed by the shark," he said forlornly. "A young man in his prime with a bright future, no doubt. I'm sorry, I've become sentimental. You must forgive me."

"No, no, that's quite all right, Dr. Halsey," another of the nurses said gently, dabbing at her own eyes.

The first nurse wiped tears off her cheeks as well, then resumed her usual professional yet kind demeanor. "Why don't

you go to the lounge and change, Dr. Halsey? The doctor who
came with the patient on the train is waiting to speak to you. I
think his name is Dr. Brewster."

Edwin pulled himself together. "I will clean up and speak
to him at once," he said with a grateful nod.

A few minutes later, he found Dr. Brewster seated on a
bench in the hallway outside the operating theater. He glanced
up as Edwin approached and said, "You don't need to tell me
what has happened to my patient. One of your nurses already
did. To be frank, I did not really think he would make it."

"I am so sorry," said Edwin. He sat down heavily on the
bench next to Dr. Brewster. Both men were exhausted, and their
shared calamity allowed them to forgo the usual formalities of
shaking hands and offering proper introductions.

They sat wearily side by side in silence for several moments,
as if they'd known each other for years rather than minutes.
Edwin leaned back with his head resting against the wall; Dr.
Brewster slumped forward with his hands on his knees and his
head tipped downward. With his chin nearly resting on his chest,
Dr. Brewster's most prominent feature was a jawline that had
blurred over time into a cascade of jowls.

Edwin guessed that Dr. Brewster was at least sixty years old.
He wondered if he would still be practicing medicine at that
age. Certainly, he would no longer be doing surgery. Even so,
he wondered how the older doctor was able to keep up with
what was very likely a demanding, small-town practice. And
certainly, the events of this day must have been extraordinarily
demanding—indeed, perhaps the worst day of the older doctor's
entire career.

"Dr. Brewster," Edwin began finally, "how did this happen?
I don't have any details—not even the young man's name."

Dr. Brewster looked up, his eyes exuding warmth and deep

sorrow. "His name is—was . . . His name was Stanley Fisher. He's twenty-four years old, and I got to him only a few minutes after . . . after they pulled him out of the water."

He explained that he had tried to save young Mr. Fisher but did not have the tools or experience to perform the amputation that might have saved him. Desperate, Dr. Brewster decided to bring Mr. Fisher on the train to Monmouth Memorial Hospital.

"I knew it was not likely to work," said Dr. Brewster. "But I had to try something." Then he added, "You know, I brought that young man into the world twenty-four years ago. His friends and his sweetheart, Margaret, too."

Margaret. The young man had said, "Tell Margaret I'm sorry. Have a good life without me." *Those were his last words,* Edwin thought. *Should I ask Dr. Brewster to pass on the message? No, it was a private communication between my dying patient and me. I will have to figure out a way to inform this young lady, Margaret, whoever she is.*

Edwin turned his attention to consoling Dr. Brewster. "What a terrible day you have had," he said. "Allow me to get you some water." He stood up to retrieve it before Dr. Brewster could reply.

The older doctor drank the water in one long gulp. "I did not realize I was so thirsty," he said with surprise.

"You have done a great thing, bringing him here," said Edwin. "I suggest you go directly home, and I will take care of things from here, and we can talk later."

"No thank you, I prefer to wait and bring him home with me on the train tonight, assuming there is another train," Dr. Brewster replied.

"There are several more trains tonight, but it could be a while before you can leave with him," said Edwin. "I'd like to examine the body more fully. I need to prepare a death certificate, and I have several officials I need to notify. That will include the superintendent of the Coast Guard in Asbury Park."

"Why do you need to contact the Coast Guard?" asked Dr. Brewster. "It happened inland, in the town of Matawan."

"What are you talking about?" Edwin asked sharply. "This is a shark bite."

"Yes, but it happened in Matawan Creek, close to our main street. It didn't happen at a beach along the ocean or even Raritan Bay."

"This took place in a creek?"

"Yes, a small tidal creek."

"Are you saying that a shark went from the ocean into a bay and—what? From the bay into a tidal creek? And then a mile or two *up* the creek?" Edwin could not hide his surprise and dismay.

"Yes, that's exactly what I'm saying. A group of boys were swimming in the creek, where they always do. One of the boys disappeared and was believed to be drowning. Stanley Fisher went into the water to search for the boy, and that's when the shark attacked him."

"Well, what happened to the boy?" asked Edwin. "Was he saved?"

"I don't know," Dr. Brewster replied. "We haven't found him yet. But I fear he might be another victim of the shark."

Edwin dropped his face into his hands. When he was finally able to find his voice, he asked aloud, "Dear God, what kind of monster are we dealing with here?"

Now it was Dr. Brewster's turn to comfort Edwin. "It is beyond comprehension," he said soothingly, patting Edwin's shoulder. "I, too, am flabbergasted. Who would believe such a thing?"

Edwin studied the pattern in the wood in a door opposite them. It looped and swirled, and he thought of the majesty of trees—how they were reduced from living things into desks, doors, and, worst of all, firewood. He had never noticed that the sign on the door, which read Supplies, had been painted over an earlier word, Apothecary. He could not remember it ever being anything other than a supply room, and he had been there a long time. He wondered how many times doctors like himself and Brewster had sat dejectedly in this very hallway outside the surgery, and it made him feel small. And then he thought of all the times a colleague had tried to cheer him up when a procedure had failed. A kind gesture and a few compassionate words went a long way.

"I have an idea," said Edwin. "You could take the next train back to Matawan, and I will accompany the body by train tomorrow. You could meet me at the station there, along with an undertaker."

Dr. Brewster sighed. "I must say, that would be a relief," he said. "It would give me the chance to make arrangements for the body since Stanley's parents are away. He deserves a proper homecoming."

After Dr. Brewster left for the train station, Edwin sat alone with the body, still covered with a sheet. He bowed his head and prayed. Then he got to work. There was paperwork to fill out and telephone calls to authorities to make. He took a deep breath and began carefully measuring the wound on Stanley Fisher's leg.

As Edwin returned home to Red Bank, the sun was close to rising.

What a life, especially lately, he thought. *Measuring the days in sunrises and sunsets.*

Hannah had not yet arrived to prepare breakfast, but to Edwin's shock, Julia was waiting for him in the kitchen. "Father, I made soup!" she declared. "I can also make you a sandwich. Here, let me get you some coffee."

Edwin was too tired and surprised to respond. He plunked

down onto one of the kitchen chairs. He'd never found them particularly comfortable, but at least he was off his feet.

Julia scurried around the kitchen. "When Hannah told me what happened, I canceled my outing last evening," she said. "I've been waiting all night for you to come home. Did your patient survive?"

He shook his head.

"Oh, Father," she said, brushing a lock of her cropped hair from her eyes. "How awful."

Edwin sipped the coffee.

"Father," added Julia, "you were right all along. About the shark, I mean."

"My dear, it's even worse than I thought. This time, the shark attacked in a creek, in an inland town!"

"What? Where?"

"In Matawan," he replied. "That nice little town we see from the train when we go to New York."

Julia started to ask another question but stopped herself. "Just eat, Father, and you can tell me the rest later."

"Thank you, Julia," he said. "I'm going to bed for a while. When Hannah arrives, could you ask her to check with Dr. Parker? I hope he will be able to see my patients today. Just the most urgent ones. He is aware of the unusual circumstances. If he can't do it, someone at the hospital will. They'll all know I was up until the wee hours."

"Are you going to stay in bed all day, Father? You surely need to."

"No, actually, there's something I must do. Late this morning or early in the afternoon, I'm accompanying the body of the patient on the train back to Matawan."

"Really, Father?" asked Julia. "But you're exhausted. Why must you do it?"

"Because I said I would."

"I don't work until tonight, Father," she said. "I could go with you to Matawan."

"You don't need to," replied Edwin. She bit her lower lip and looked away. Quickly, he added, "But if you're willing, that would be very helpful. I could use your support."

She beamed. "Go get some rest, Father. I'll take care of everything. I'll wake you up later when we're all set."

He wanted to thank her, but could only nod and stumble upstairs, clinging to the banister. Right now he had but one thought: *sleep, blessed sleep.*

JULY 13, 1916

CHAPTER 27

The smell of something burning awakened Margaret a few hours before dawn.

Is the house on fire? she wondered. She felt a little stronger and, with great effort, sat up partway in bed, leaning on her elbows. *Something has happened to me, and I am sick in bed*, she thought. *And now the house is burning down.*

She climbed out of bed, propelled by an instinctual fear of fire and prepared to wake up her parents and flee. The scent of smoke, however, was not coming from within the house. She followed the acrid smell to the open window on the far side of her bedroom and peered out.

To her surprise, her mother was standing in the backyard, her face illuminated by a fire in the metal bin used for the purpose. *What is she doing?* Margaret thought. She had never seen her mother burn anything. That task was usually left to Mr. McElroy, who did odd jobs.

Margaret leaned heavily on the windowsill, watching in silence as her mother methodically placed one item after another into the fire. *How strange*, Margaret thought. Then something glinted in the firelight, and with a jolt Margaret recognized the mother-of-pearl buttons that secured the front of the dress she had worn the previous day. *Mother is burning my clothes*, she realized with astonishment. *The ones I wore yesterday.*

The buttons . . . The fire . . . The oddity of her mother outdoors in the dark, burning the clothes in secret. *Mother does not want me to see this. She wants to protect me.*

Puzzled, Margaret remained at the window, fixated by the scene. *My clothes were covered in blood*, she thought. *Not my blood. Stanley's blood.*

In that instant, Margaret knew that Stanley was gone.

She stumbled back across the room and flopped facedown onto the bed and wept into her pillow until she could cry no more. Finally, she had the urge to sleep and escape this new reality. That she had slept earlier was puzzling until she remembered that Tillie had prescribed whiskey. At first, her parents objected.

Margaret vaguely recalled intervening. "I'm twenty-four years old, and if Tillie thinks it will help, then I shall drink it!"

Father's bottle of whiskey was still sitting on the nightstand. She took a slug of it. *Well, it worked a few hours ago*, she thought. *Maybe it will work again now.*

She awoke hours later, startled to see Mother staring anxiously at her from a chair pulled up close to her bed.

"Oh, I am so glad you are awake!" her mother cried. "I have hot tea, and I will ask Sally to make some toast."

How odd, Margaret thought. *Mother is taking care of me, rather than the other way around.*

Margaret's head was pounding, especially at her temples. She rubbed her face. "Mother," she whispered, "I know he's dead."

Her mother would not look her in the eye. "Margaret, you must eat."

"Mother, don't be ridiculous! I don't want to eat anything! Did you hear what I said? Stanley is dead! I don't know how I know, but I do."

"Margaret, you must eat," her mother said firmly. "Tillie said you must try. She telephoned a half hour ago to check on you. We told her you were sound asleep, and she said that was good, that you were resting your mind. She said ideally you should get full bed rest for the next three days. The police were here and someone from the state, but your father told them you were in no condition to talk."

"Why do they want to talk to me?" asked Margaret.

"It's a formality," replied her mother. "They're interviewing all of those who were . . . present . . . at the . . ." Her voice trailed off. "Anyway, it's the law," she added.

"Why shouldn't I talk to them?" asked Margaret. "It's all coming back to me now. I'm not afraid to talk to them. If everyone is supposed to be interviewed, then I should participate. It's the least I can do for Stanley." Tears flooded down her cheeks as she said his name.

"This is what I mean, you are in no condition!" said her mother, dabbing Margaret's face with a handkerchief.

"Oh, Mother!" Margaret wailed. "You are treating me as if I am a child."

Now it was her mother's turn to cry. "I'm sorry, Margaret," she said. "I'm not sure what to do."

Her mother's tone softened Margaret's heart. "Oh, Mother, this is bad enough without us quarreling. We will get through this together. Now you and Father must trust me. I do want to talk to the police, the Coast Guard—whoever it was that came by earlier. Please ask Father to call them and see if they can come back this afternoon."

Her father wasn't pleased with Margaret's decision. "I think it is a mistake," he said after her mother summoned him to Margaret's room. "You are too fragile."

"Father, I would prefer to get it over with," Margaret said firmly. "I think it's my responsibility."

There was more disagreement, but in the end, Margaret prevailed. Her father contacted the authorities, and an hour later, they returned. Margaret, wearing a pale-gray linen dress, her hair pinned loosely to her head, joined them in the parlor.

"I have one request," she announced after they were all seated. "I will tell you what I remember—but only once. Whatever I say here, I hope it will suffice for the inquest, which I will not attend. After today, I will never speak of this again."

CHAPTER 28

A small crowd jostled for position at the Long Branch Rail Station as Edwin and Julia, wearing black, boarded the noon train heading north. Somehow, word about the death of Stanley Fisher was out already. The coffin was loaded last, under the supervision of the conductor. A few people pointed, and someone took a photograph.

Julia had done a remarkable job with the arrangements. She had even convinced the owner of a Long Branch funeral parlor to donate a modest but respectable coffin. Thus, the body of Stanley Fisher would travel the dozen or so miles back to his hometown of Matawan with dignity.

Edwin and Julia settled into bench seats facing each other, with a shared view to the east through a window which, in the bright sunlight, revealed streaks, fingerprints, and dust. Edwin suppressed the urge to clean it with a handkerchief.

The engineer came back to speak to Edwin, saying that this was the same train that had brought Stanley Fisher to Long Branch the previous day and he'd been on duty when the gravely injured young man was transported. "'Tis a pity," he said, shaking his head sadly.

A few minutes later, the train lurched forward. There were many other passengers on the train, most of them probably heading to New York, but the car in which Edwin and Julia sat was empty, except for the coffin, which was secured by an exit. Allowing them the entire car, Julia explained, was a courtesy granted by the railroad.

They were both very aware of the presence of the coffin, although it was twenty feet or more away. Julia turned and looked at it occasionally. Mostly, she and Edwin stared out the window, welcoming the distraction provided by the constantly changing view.

Then Edwin had a jarring memory of the funeral procession for his wife and other children many years before. *Julia and I—we were the survivors*, he thought. *We sat just like this, directly across from one another in the first carriage.* He struggled to remember more details. Julia, not yet two, had been held in the sturdy arms of a distant relative, but it was the same scenario. *I could have spoken to her, my one remaining child*, he mused sadly. *I could have held her. But instead, I looked away.*

He looked at her now and asked, "Have I told you lately how very much you look like your mother?"

She smiled. "No, Father, as a matter of fact, you haven't."

"I also meant to thank you. You did an excellent job organizing our journey today, and I appreciate that you have accompanied me."

"You're welcome, Father," she said.

Returning the topic to the reason for their mission caused them both to become subdued, however. Still, he was glad to have brought it up. *One cannot always wait for perfect timing to say what needs to be said*, he thought.

The train passed through small towns and farmland, past small factories and tidal marshes. In two locations, the tracks were laid across narrow, freestanding bridges, with nothing but open water on either side, giving the impression of being not on a train but a boat. Usually, Edwin deliberately looked away. This time, he scanned the horizon for a large dorsal fin. *Where is the shark?* he wondered. *Is it out there just beyond this window?*

Julia broke the silence this time, startling him. "Father, I confirmed that Dr. Brewster will meet us at the station," she said. "Other than that, I have no idea what will happen when we arrive. Do you?"

"I don't believe anything is expected of us," he replied. "Most likely, we'll take the next southbound train for Red Bank. If you want, we could go for a walk and get some air before we return home."

Julia looked a little ashen, and he realized she was nervous. He reminded himself that she was, after all, just nineteen years old. He reached over to give her hand a reassuring pat just as the conductor entered their car.

"Next stop, Matawan." In a voice that seemed a little sadder than usual, the conductor sang out, "*Mat*-uh-wahn. *Mat*-uh-wahn. *Mat*-uh-wahn Station." He walked through briskly, moving on to the next car.

The train slowed, then stopped. Edwin stood up, ready to disembark.

"Father!" cried Julia. "Who are all these people?"

Edwin stooped down to peer out the window. He, too, was taken aback. He scanned the crowd and estimated that five or six hundred souls stood silent and unmoving on the platform and beyond. Several younger men were perched on the gabled roof of the station. All of the men had removed their hats and held them against their chests. Most of the women were crying.

"What are they doing?" whispered Julia.

"I believe they are waiting for us," Edwin replied softly.

As they departed the train, the conductor tapped Edwin on the arm. "No need to rush, sir," he said. "We've allotted extra time."

Dr. Brewster stepped forward from the crowd. Edwin shook his hand and introduced Julia. Then Dr. Brewster motioned for a clergyman in full vestments to join them.

"I am Reverend David Rutledge, pastor of First Methodist Episcopal Church here in Matawan," he announced to the crowd. "I am here at the request of the family. As many of you know, the Fishers are members of the church. However, the parents of Stanley Fisher are on a trip to Minnesota to visit their daughter. They have been notified and are on their way back. Stanley was much loved in our town, as was the little boy he tried to rescue, Lester Stilwell. We are hoping and praying that Lester's body will be found, but we take comfort in knowing that Stanley and Lester are together with our Heavenly Father. Those of you who are members of our church will recall with fondness that Stanley was an esteemed member of our choir in the tenor section. Lester often attended our Sunday school. As of this morning, there are no funeral plans yet for Stanley. When arrangements have been made, we will announce them at the church."

As the reverend stepped aside, the crowd made a collective gasp or groan. Behind him, six men were unloading the coffin from the train. The throng parted without waiting to be asked, and the pine box was carried to a horse-drawn funeral wagon waiting nearby.

A few people started to follow the wagon as it moved away, then it seemed almost everyone did, including a group of newspapermen and photographers who had been held across the street behind a barrier.

Dr. Brewster followed Edwin's gaze. "Yes, the newsmen are here," he said with a grimace, "and I fear we shall never be rid of them. Our constable made them agree not to take photos of the unloading of the casket from the train. We've been trying to work with them and communicate our priorities and sensitivities."

"I haven't seen a newspaper yet today," Edwin commented, "but perhaps it would not be a bad thing if people were warned of the danger."

"Oh, I agree, but unfortunately the newspapers have gone berserk," said Dr. Brewster. "I dread to see the late-afternoon editions. If you think the attacks in Beach Haven and Spring Lake received a lot of attention, what happened here has reached another level."

"I'm sure it is quite obnoxious," said Edwin. "But perhaps people will finally listen."

The train pulled out of the station. The conductor, in a poignant gesture, saluted Edwin, Julia, and Dr. Brewster, the only ones left on the platform.

"Dr. Brewster," asked Julia, "what time do you suppose the next train will be—southbound, I mean?"

"Oh, where are my manners!" he exclaimed. "Please come to my house for coffee and something to eat before you leave. It's not far, and we could walk."

Edwin let Julia decide, and she welcomed the idea. As they strolled along Main Street toward Dr. Brewster's home, Edwin remarked upon the quaintness of the town.

"I admit I have been here only two or three times in my life," said Edwin. "Of course, I have passed through here many times on the train. But I must say, what a charming place."

"Why, thank you," said Dr. Brewster. "We still consider ourselves an old-fashioned farming town. Although nowadays produce is moved by trains. Farmers used to load their crops onto flat-bottomed boats that would go down the creek and out to the bay. Then they'd transfer the produce to larger boats that would go to New York. It was a great system. But I guess everything changes. I'm sure something will come along that makes trains obsolete one day."

"I thought Matawan was also known for making tiles," said Edwin.

"That's true," said Dr. Brewster. "The mud along the creek is perfect for making tiles and bricks. Have you ever traveled by subway in New York City? Matawan tiles are used extensively there."

"How many people live here?" asked Julia.

"Well, let's see, the last federal census was in 1910, and I believe at that time there were about sixteen hundred souls," said Dr. Brewster. "A nice size," he added. "Not too big, not too small. The town itself covers about two and a half miles."

One of the newsmen had noticed them. He broke with the group that had followed the horse-drawn funeral wagon.

"Oh, no, here comes one of those reporters," Dr. Brewster groaned.

"Aren't you Edwin Halsey, the shark doctor?" the reporter called out.

The shark doctor? Edwin wasn't sure how to respond, or if he wanted to, but the newspaperman persisted, clarifying his request. "I read all the stories from Beach Haven and Spring Lake, and I remember your photograph," he said. "You're the doctor who examined the shark victims."

"And you are . . . ?" asked Edwin.

"Oh, I'm sorry," the reporter replied. "I'm Jake McGuire from the *New York Herald Tribune*."

"I can't talk to you at the moment," Edwin said abruptly.

"My daughter and I are on the way to Dr. Brewster's home for a private conference."

"Well, just a quick question or two," he pleaded. "Do you believe this is the same shark that killed Mr. Vansant in Beach Haven on July first and Mr. Bruder in Spring Lake on July sixth? And then there was that close call in Asbury Park two days after that. Matawan must be at least thirty miles north of Asbury Park if you're traveling by water. That seems kind of far for a shark to swim, don't you think?"

Edwin thought, *I might as well answer the man.* He took a deep breath, then replied: "I have not had a chance to look into it yet. I have only just arrived."

"Are you surprised this could happen here?"

Edwin paused. "I am indeed very surprised that it happened here, so far inland," he replied. "But I am not surprised that it happened again somewhere. I have been saying since July first that any person who goes in the water anywhere along the shore is in danger, but unfortunately, the public has been distracted by conspiracy theorists, as well as those who think a man-eating shark in these waters is impossible or entertain the preposterous idea that it might be a hoax.

"Once the message is muddled, people stop paying attention. There has not been one clear and repeated official communication, which should have been quite simply, 'There is a man-eating creature, evidently some type of shark, attacking and killing people. Stay out of the water until we understand what it is and what we might do about it.' And now, tragically, we know that this includes even very minor tidal estuaries, of which there are hundreds along the shore."

"Isn't that an overreaction?" asked the reporter. "I mean, the chances of any one person being attacked must be very small, am I right?"

"Well, you don't want to be that one person, do you?" Edwin asked wryly. "The chances are not high, but the outcome is so terrible for the individual that it hardly seems worth tempting fate. One must think also of the family and friends—and the rescuers and witnesses—who must live with the tragedy for the rest of their lives. Waiting a bit until the creature is killed or has evidently left the area doesn't seem like much to ask."

The reporter, writing in his notebook as fast as he could, said he had one last question. He was looking for someone named Margaret Atkins, a local schoolteacher and Stanley Fisher's sweetheart. He'd heard she was at the scene when the fatal attack occurred.

"I know nothing about that," said Edwin.

The question rattled Dr. Brewster, however. "I will not tell you where Margaret Atkins lives," he snapped. "And even if you find your way there, I can guarantee that her father will not let you near her. Now leave that poor girl in peace."

"So you are confirming that she *was* there?" the reporter asked.

"I am not confirming anything!" Dr. Brewster roared. "Now get away from me or I shall report you."

The reporter tipped his hat and sprinted in the direction of the crowd that had disappeared down the street.

A dozen questions gathered in Edwin's mind, competing for attention. Still, he kept silent until they reached Dr. Brewster's house and settled outside on the verandah in Adirondack chairs, relaxing contraptions that were, nevertheless, awkward for Julia in her narrow skirt. A servant offered lemonade and crackers.

"Would you like lunch?" asked Dr. Brewster. "I can arrange that immediately, if you wish."

Edwin glanced at Julia. She had never been able to eat when under duress, so he was not surprised when she shook her head.

"We are fine, but thank you anyway," said Edwin.

"How about something stronger in your lemonade?" asked Dr. Brewster, taking a flask from his vest pocket.

"Oh, no thank you, not at this hour," replied Edwin.

"I understand," he said. "But I hope you don't mind my partaking."

"Why, of course not," said Edwin, and Julia smiled slightly and shrugged.

"It's just that, well, I have never . . ." Dr. Brewster began. "I have never . . . I should say *we* have never, meaning the town . . . *we* have never experienced a tragedy like this."

Edwin nodded sympathetically. "It is not impossible, scientifically speaking, but it certainly seems bizarre that the shark made its way here."

"*Bizarre* is a good word," Dr. Brewster agreed. "Are you familiar with what happened? I'm not certain how much I told you yesterday."

"Not really very much at all," replied Edwin. "There wasn't time."

"Well, I shall give you a brief overview. It is a sad story indeed. Oh, wait! Perhaps you would prefer that your daughter not hear this."

Julia glowered and started to speak, but Edwin interrupted her. "Julia is a nursing student," he said. "She's not squeamish. However, it's up to her, not me, if she wants to hear the story. As she often reminds me, she is able to make her own decisions."

"Oh my, oh my," Dr. Brewster said, looking back and forth between Edwin and Julia. "All right, then I shall rephrase my question. Julia, would you like to hear the story? We can go in another room and leave you here for a few minutes, if that's your preference."

"I would like to hear it," she said simply.

"Then I shall commence," said Dr. Brewster. "Don't say I didn't warn you. I will try to be succinct, but I know a lot more than I did last evening. As I mentioned to you then, Dr. Halsey, there is a place in Matawan Creek where local boys go swimming in the summer. Always have, went there myself as a lad. But yesterday, one of the boys, an eleven-year-old named Lester Stilwell, disappeared in the water. At first, it seemed he might have drowned. There were multiple witnesses, but all were young boys, confused and scared. However, it seems that— just as I feared, Dr. Halsey—Lester was, in fact, attacked and dragged under by a shark. Unfortunately, so far, his body has not been found.

"At the time there was a great deal of confusion; the other boys ran into town naked and screaming hysterically about Lester. Several young men rushed to the creek. They went into the water in an attempt to rescue the child, unsure exactly what had happened but realizing that time was of the essence. One of these young men was Stanley Fisher. As you know, he was attacked by the sea monster and later died after I brought him by train to your hospital.

"Everyone in this town knew and loved Stanley. He will always be a hero. He died trying to save a child. That is why so many came to meet the train carrying his body home."

Edwin was about to say something when, from an indeterminable distance away, came the sound of gunshots.

"Hunting, here?" Julia asked, alarmed. "So close to homes and shops?"

"Oh, that's coming from the creek," replied Dr. Brewster. "They're shooting into the water."

"Who is shooting into the water?" asked Edwin.

"Those are local residents trying to kill the monster," replied

Dr. Brewster. "If they think they see something, they shoot at it—men and women out there with rifles and shotguns. They've also put wire fencing across the creek in several places, hoping to capture it."

The sound of shots, twice as many as before, ricocheted against buildings. Julia recoiled.

"If you think this is bad, you can't imagine what it was like late last night when they were throwing dynamite into the creek," said Dr. Brewster. "They are determined to kill that shark! But they're also hoping to get the child's body to rise to the surface. Oh, and did I mention there's a third victim?"

"Third victim?" cried Edwin.

"A nine-year-old boy named Joseph Dunn from the Bronx. He is at a hospital in New Brunswick. As of this morning, he was alive."

"Tell me more about him," said Edwin.

"Well, he was attacked downstream from Lester and Stanley, maybe an hour or so later. It happened close to where the creek meets the bay. Joseph Dunn was playing on a dock with his older brother and a friend of his brother's. The tide was going out, so my guess is that the shark was passing by them on its way into the bay. His leg was mangled, but the arteries and veins, miraculously, were intact. I only got a quick look at him, but I thought he might make it to the hospital in New Brunswick by automobile, and a Good Samaritan took him."

"Why didn't he take Stanley too?" asked Julia.

"Oh, as I told your father last night, I was quite certain that Stanley would not survive the road trip," replied Dr. Brewster. "That's when I came up with the idea of taking him on the train to your hospital, Dr. Halsey. I had to try something. At least the train would be a smooth ride."

"And it was indeed a good idea and worth a try," Edwin said warmly. "But tell me, how did the boy, Joseph, get away from the shark?"

"He was pulled out of the mouth of the shark by his older brother and their friend."

"How extraordinary! Such raw courage!" exclaimed Edwin.

"And then an old sea captain named Cottrell, who had been warning everyone on the creek about the shark, took Joseph in his boat and brought him straight to me, where I was working on Stanley."

"Can you draw this on a map for me?" asked Edwin. "Or better yet, take me to the creek?"

"Father!" cried Julia. "Are you sure?"

"I wouldn't go near the water," said Edwin. "But if Dr. Brewster can figure out a way to ask the, uh, vigilantes to stop their shooting, it should not be particularly hazardous."

"What about your clothes, Father?" asked Julia.

"I don't care, except for my shoes," he said. "If I could borrow a pair of work shoes or boots . . ."

"Why, of course," Dr. Brewster quickly replied. "But are you certain you would like to go?"

"Yes, if it's not too much trouble."

Dr. Brewster excused himself to make a telephone call. When he returned, he reported that the constable would halt the shooting at the creek and escort Edwin there. Julia and Dr. Brewster did not wish to go.

"I shall stay here and make telephone calls," Dr. Brewster announced. "There is a young man named Rusty Conover whom I would like you to meet before you leave. I will see if I can track him down."

A few minutes later, a Model T almost identical to Edwin's pulled up at the curb.

"That will be him," Dr. Brewster said. "The constable, I mean. Shall I introduce you?"

"Thank you, but it's not necessary," replied Edwin. "You look so comfortable here on the verandah."

Dr. Brewster breathed a sigh of relief and his jowls drooped toward his chest. "Well, we shall be awaiting your return," he said. Julia took a book from her purse and began reading. She paused and gave Edwin a worried look.

The constable's name was Tom Shuler. He greeted Edwin by saying, "I've seen you in the papers" in a flat tone. A middle-aged man with the tense posture and developed muscles of a boxer, Constable Shuler was not the talkative type, at least under these circumstances, for Edwin could not get another word out of him and promptly gave up. After driving a planked road for a brief time, Shuler pulled the automobile to the side of the road.

"This is the shortest way to the creek—well, to the place on the creek where . . ." He paused and reconsidered. "The place on the creek that you want to see," he said finally. With no further explanation, Shuler exited the automobile and stepped down from the road onto an embankment disappearing into a thick patch of sea oats and eelgrass. Edwin hurried after him.

The constable pulled aside a curtain of low branches partially knit together by a clinging vine, and the muddy creek loomed just below and in front of them. A gurgling, gentle stream zigzagged into the distance, a picturesque waterway surrounded by a broad vista of salt marsh.

"This is it?" asked Edwin. Jolted by the weight of what had transpired here, his voice shook slightly.

"Yes," Shuler said simply.

"Such a beautiful place!" cried Edwin. "It's hard to accept that something so terrible happened here just twenty-four hours ago."

Shuler folded his arms across his chest. A tall man who, as

constable, wore a gun in a holster slung across his hip, he was an intimidating figure.

"I know what you mean," said Shuler, opening up for the first time. "The fact that it's such a beautiful place—well, somehow that makes it even worse. Like it's some kind of cruel joke."

A snowy egret soared across the expanse. Where the tide was receding, a blue heron stood patiently waiting for the precise moment to spear a fish. A pair of red-winged blackbirds scolded and fussed, then flew away, annoyed by the presence of humans. A gentle breeze swept through the marsh. Sea oats swayed and danced in errant patterns, creating a hushed song of innocence and times gone by.

"My grandmother used to say that the sea oats whisper," said Edwin.

"You mean that whooshing sound when the wind blows through them?" asked Shuler.

"Yes," said Edwin. "My grandmother lived on a creek just like this one, down in Red Bank. I used to play there."

Shuler nodded. "Kids have been swimming and playing here for generations," he said. "There's all kinds of stuff to find here," he added. "Indian arrowheads. Bullets from the Revolutionary War. And of course, the kids are always searching for pirate treasure since Blackbeard, Captain Morgan, and Captain Kidd used to hide out here."

Without saying anything more, Shuler walked farther along the path. He disappeared but then popped back into view, standing on a bluff of ten or twelve feet that seemed to stick out slightly over the creek. Beyond Shuler, Edwin saw a series of wood pilings—all that was left of an old dock.

Edwin caught up with the constable, who pointed to an area below them where the sea oats and eelgrass had been trampled. "See that, over there? That's where they pulled Stanley out," he said. He paused and then asked, "What do you think, Dr. Halsey? Do you suppose we'll ever find Lester's body?"

"I don't know," replied Edwin. "Probably not. And very likely, you've seen the last of the shark too."

"Some of the men put up steel netting farther down the creek, hoping to catch it," the constable said. "But I would think a creature like that could just tear right through it."

Edwin shrugged, then asked, "Several trails lead to the creek?"

"Yes," he replied. "This one is the closest to the road."

"The entire creek is closed to swimming since this all happened?" asked Edwin.

Shuler was irritated by the question. "Of course it is!"

"Well, there are people still swimming at Beach Haven and Spring Lake," said Edwin. "And Asbury Park, where they had a close call. Some people are just defiant. They say it's their choice."

"It's their choice to go over Niagara Falls in a barrel, but that doesn't make it smart," said Shuler.

"Well, you know how we Americans are," Edwin said dryly. "Independent to a fault. I've always thought it had something to do with the type of people who came here from Europe. They must have been a feisty bunch. They weren't the ones who stayed home. They were the risk-takers."

"That's one way to put it," said Shuler.

"What's another way?" asked Edwin.

"That we are stubborn as hell."

The two men stood shoulder to shoulder, lost in their own thoughts. Edwin could feel the sun on his face. "Constable," Edwin asked finally, "how big was the shark? What did witnesses say?"

"Oh, some said ten feet, others said fifteen," he replied. "The estimates are all over the map."

Edwin nodded. "Yes, the witnesses said different things in

Beach Haven and Spring Lake too. It must have looked especially enormous, proportionately, here in the creek as compared
to the ocean."

"Yes, and people only got a quick look at it," said Shuler. He
thought for a moment. "One thing I didn't realize," he added,
"is that sharks can hide under the water like that. I thought you
could always see the fin."

"There's a lot we don't know about sharks," said Edwin. "I've
been looking into it. There are many different kinds, and information is scarce. But this doesn't seem like normal behavior. It's
astonishing that it came all the way up here in the first place."

"No one ever thought a shark—any kind of shark, let alone
a man-eater—would come up the creek," Shuler agreed.

"But the ocean, the bay, and the creek are interconnected,"
said Edwin. "I only mean that it could happen. And in fact, it
did happen."

"We just never thought of it that way," Shuler said sadly.
"We had no reason to think this could happen."

Edwin took out his notebook. "How deep is it here?" he
asked.

"At high tide, maybe eight feet," replied Shuler. "We had a
full moon yesterday with an extreme high tide, so it was a little
higher than that. But, heck, that's still not very deep."

"Oh, yes, the full moon," Edwin said. "I wondered if it
played a role. That extra foot or two of water in the creek could
have made all the difference. The shark might never have entered
the creek if not for that! Strange to think about, isn't it?"

Shuler nodded. "Makes you wonder if there's some truth
to those old stories about a full moon—I mean about strange
things happening."

"It's science, that's all," Edwin said. But within himself,
he felt uneasy. *A full moon in Matawan*, he thought. *The belief*

among the fishermen in Point Pleasant of the strange creature they called the beast. Even the most unflappable believer in science would be a little shaken.

"What is the depth at low tide?" Edwin asked, determined to get back to the facts.

"In isolated spots, as low as one foot," replied Shuler.

"What!" cried Edwin, looking up with a start. "How is that possible? I wonder if it swam upstream in high tide and found itself trapped here at low tide. Then maybe it left, assuming it has, when there was another high tide? Something is very strange about this!"

"Maybe there's something wrong with it," said Shuler. "It could be sick. Maybe it was hit by that U-boat that was out there and its brain was damaged."

"Oh, no, not the U-boat!" Edwin groaned. "All these theories about the U-boat and the shark! They are so far-fetched!"

"I'm just trying to make sense of it," said Shuler, a little defensively.

"Yes, yes, I understand," Edwin said, nodding. "I'm sorry. It's just that I have been dealing with this situation for twelve days—oh, now thirteen days!—and it shows no sign of ending. Now tell me this, how wide is the creek?"

"Well, the mouth of the creek—where the creek meets the bay—is about two hundred feet," Shuler noted, "but then it narrows quickly, all the way down to just twenty feet wide, as you can see here."

"And how far are we from the bay?"

"Well, as the crow flies, probably a mile and a half, but since the creek zigs and zags, I would say it had to swim close to three miles," replied Shuler.

"Three miles!" Edwin exclaimed.

"Yes, and we must be eleven miles from the open ocean."

Edwin shivered despite the heat. "All the way up here in the creek, why, the water must be brackish."

"Yes," said Shuler. "Part salt, part fresh. But with an extreme high tide pushing water up from the bay, it would become much saltier."

"Ah, that's true," Edwin agreed.

"There's at least one type of shark, a bull shark, that likes brackish water," Shuler continued. "At least, that's what Captain Cottrell says. He's one of our main witnesses. He saw it from up on a trestle bridge. Says it could have been a bull shark, but if he had to bet money on it, he would say it was a great white shark."

"I wonder if we'll ever find out," said Edwin.

"I wish I had listened to him," Shuler muttered softly, almost to himself.

"To whom?"

"To Captain Cottrell. Before any of this happened," he said slowly, "Captain Cottrell ran into town, shouting that he'd seen a shark in the creek, but I didn't believe him. You know how these old sea captains are. They can tell a good story. And it's been so hot. I thought maybe he'd been out in the sun too long. If only I had believed him."

"Are you saying the attacks here might have been prevented?"

"Possibly," replied Shuler. He looked at the ground and, with the toe of his shoe, started kicking a root that protruded from the soil.

"Constable, you mustn't judge yourself so harshly. Were you the only one who didn't believe him?"

"No, there was a crowd of people, and no one believed him," Shuler said. "But still, it was my decision. I'm the constable."

"You couldn't possibly have known," Edwin protested. "You know, in my line of work, as in yours, we see tragedies all the time. It never does any good to second-guess. You sound like everyone I've ever encountered who has suffered a tragedy. And that includes me."

"You?" asked Shuler. He finally looked up.

"Eighteen years ago, my wife and five of our children died of typhoid fever," said Edwin. "I survived, as did our youngest child. All these years, I have blamed myself. I had been treating patients with it, and I probably brought it home. I couldn't save them—except for the littlest one, Julia, who is now a grown woman. Until recently, I felt crushed by guilt every day."

"I'm so sorry for your losses," Shuler said solemnly. "What a terrible burden you have carried. You said, 'until recently'— so what has changed, if I may ask?"

Hmmm, what has changed? Edwin thought. *So* much *has changed.* He struggled for the right way to put it. "I finally saw myself through my daughter's eyes," he replied. "And I didn't like the person I had become."

CHAPTER 29

Julia was waiting impatiently for Edwin's return from the creek. He'd been gone longer than she had expected, and she was worried about his safety but also that she might be late for her shift at the hospital. When the constable finally dropped Edwin off, she rushed to greet him.

"Father, I'm so glad you're back." She looked at him with curiosity. "Did everything go all right at the creek?"

"I had a very good tour from the constable," replied Edwin. "Now I have a better understanding of what occurred."

"Well, I'm glad you're all right, but I must rush off to catch the next train—I'm due at the hospital in a few hours." Julia kissed Edwin on the cheek, thanked Dr. Brewster for his hospitality, and hurried off on foot to the station.

"What a lovely, mature, responsible girl!" said Dr. Brewster after she left.

Edwin smiled. "Thank you," he said. "I'm quite proud of her."

Dr. Brewster nodded agreeably. "Well, let us get back to the matter at hand. I will telephone Rusty, and he'll come straight over."

"Excellent," said Edwin, "but who is Rusty and why am I to see him?"

"Well, it is the most peculiar thing," replied Dr. Brewster. "I am entirely flummoxed, and I would like you to examine him. He was with Stanley yesterday at the creek—one of several young men who dove into the water to try to rescue Lester. Just before Stanley was attacked by the shark, Rusty says something brushed against him. He climbed onto the bank of the creek to see if he'd been injured, and he had these large scrapes horizontally across his chest and abdomen. And he is the second person this week to have this happen! A boy named Lenny Yelverton had the same experience." Lowering his voice to a near whisper, he added, "Could these scrapes be from the shark? It sounds preposterous, but so does an attack in Matawan Creek."

"I would be most interested in examining both of them," Edwin said.

"I was only able to reach Rusty," Dr. Brewster said apologetically.

"Then that will have to suffice," Edwin said, adding, "and I thank you for your effort."

Dr. Brewster made the telephone call, and Rusty arrived within a half hour, apologizing that he couldn't come more quickly. True to his name, Rusty had a mop of burnished hair and a constellation of freckles, which made him look boyish, although, as he mentioned to Edwin, he was twenty-five years of age. He shook Edwin's hand firmly and thanked him for seeing him. With Dr. Brewster leading the way, they walked to the wing of the house that contained an office and examining room.

Edwin offered his condolences to Rusty. "I'm very sorry about your friend Stanley."

Rusty had seemed so composed, but Edwin's words, perhaps the mention of Stanley's name, stopped the young man in his tracks. With no warning, he fell to his knees in grief. "He was my best friend!"

The enormity of what had happened cut through the earlier polite banter.

"There, there," said Dr. Brewster, patting Rusty on the shoulder. Edwin and Dr. Brewster exchanged glances and waited while Rusty sobbed, his face cupped in his hands.

"I'm sorry," Rusty mumbled finally, getting to his feet.

"Nothing to be sorry about," said Dr. Brewster.

Edwin nodded his agreement. "Would you prefer to skip the examination?"

"No, no," replied Rusty. He walked ahead of them into the examining room and unbuttoned his shirt.

Edwin resisted the urge to gasp.

There were indeed scrapes, nearly two inches wide, across Rusty's torso. Edwin, like Dr. Brewster, was stymied, but did not wish to add to the young man's worries unnecessarily by speculating.

"I do not know what these are," said Edwin, peering at the wounds through a magnifying glass, "but my guess is that they are harmless. I will try my best to find out. In the meantime, keep the wounds clean and let them get air. Don't let them get sun, or they may become scars. And don't put any kind of lotion on them."

This is very likely the work of the shark, but how? He remembered reading a theory that sharks might be capable of emitting a toxin or poison. *If that were the case, the young man would probably be dead already,* he reflected glumly. *Anyway, I must find out, for his sake—and the other boy who sustained these same injuries.*

As Edwin made notes, he said, "I wish there was a way for me to have photographs of these abrasions. Is that possible?"

"Oh, I think that could be arranged," replied Dr. Brewster.

"I meant immediately," said Edwin, "so that I may take them home with me."

Dr. Brewster made several telephone calls and found a professional photographer willing to help. Edwin, who by now was eager to return home, feared this could take several hours, but the photographer came and did the job right away, and prints were developed without delay in the darkroom at the photographer's own studio just a few blocks away. The whole process took about an hour, and Edwin was relieved to catch the next southbound train with photographs of Rusty's injuries in his vest pocket.

The train ride home promised to be his first chance for a respite in many hours. Edwin found a seat, sat down, and closed his eyes. The physically and emotionally demanding aspects of a very trying day were soothed almost instantly by the rhythmic sounds and rocking motion of the passenger car.

He was awakened, however, by two men talking. *Why do some people's voices carry so far?* he wondered crankily. Wide awake and livid, he sat up and rubbed his eyes. To Edwin's great dismay, the man sitting directly across from him was reading the *Evening Mail*, a New York newspaper which carried a front-page headline in over-sized type that declared:

HUNDREDS SEEK TO SLAY SHARK; THINK MONSTER TRAPPED IN CREEK

Looking more carefully around the passenger car, Edwin was appalled by the realization that everyone with a newspaper in hand was reading about the shark. It wasn't hard for him to see, since the size of the headlines were huge.

My God, I can't get away from it, he thought.

When he departed the train in Red Bank, a woman was reading a copy of the *Asbury Park Evening Press*. The front-page story displayed a photograph of women firing shotguns into Matawan Creek.

He longed to think about something else for a while but as soon as he got home, he began his inquiries into the strange scrapes on Rusty Conover's abdomen. Somewhere, someone had to have some answers—if only he could discover who that person might be.

JULY 14, 1916

CHAPTER 30

Margaret's mind would not rest. Awake and in her dreams, she was tormented by visions of water and blood. The continuous loop of memories did not, however, include Stanley's attack. She could not picture the wound at all. This, at least, was a blessing.

Reporters came by and asked to interview her, but her father promptly chased them off. Part of her wanted to talk to them, to be sure that Stanley was remembered as a hero. That's what she would tell them if she could, but she didn't have the strength. Her mother weighed in unhelpfully, reminding Margaret that "a woman should be in the newspaper only twice—when she is married and when she dies." Margaret rolled her eyes, not bothering to disguise her reaction.

No one was allowed in the house except her school friend Clementine, who cried so much that Margaret was relieved when she left; Dr. Brewster, who popped in twice; the Reverend Rutledge, whose visits were calming, especially because they helped settle her mother; and Stanley's friend Rusty.

Margaret didn't talk to Rusty, but her mother and father

did. They depended on him for the latest information. Margaret eavesdropped from the top of the stairs. This was how she found out that it was Rusty who carried her home from the creek.

"How is she doing?" she heard him ask.

"Well, we're very worried," replied her father. "Rusty, when you brought her home from the creek, did she say anything?"

"No," he replied. "Not really. Just sort of mumbling about Stanley. You know, I feel bad that I rushed out of here so quickly and didn't stop to explain everything, but there wasn't any time to lose. I had to get back to the creek to help Dr. Brewster with Stanley. I'm very sorry."

"Oh, don't be," Margaret's mother said quickly. "We're awfully glad it occurred to you to get her away from there! You did the right thing."

"Indeed, you did," her father said heartily. "And we thank you."

Rusty cleared his throat nervously. "Well, I have some news. That's the reason I stopped by." He paused. In a sad, low voice, he said, "They found Lester's body this morning."

Margaret's mother gasped.

Rusty provided the details. Mr. Hopkins was on his morning walk beside the creek. It was just after dawn. Out of the corner of his eye, the retired farmer saw something partly submerged. He couldn't tell what it was, but something about its size and shape concerned him. He left and returned in a rowboat.

It was Lester. Parts of the body were missing, and what was left was very badly mangled except for the face, which was untouched. Mr. Hopkins removed the remains from the water.

"He didn't dare leave the body and go get the constable, which would have been the correct thing to do, because he feared the body would sink again or go out with the tide," said Rusty.

"Have they told Lester's parents?" asked Margaret's father.

"Oh, yes, they were the first to know," said Rusty. "Mr.

Hopkins wrapped the body in his overshirt and took it straight to their house. When Lester's mother saw Mr. Hopkins walking down the road at that hour with a bundle in his arms, she started screaming."

"She did?" cried Margaret's mother.

"Yes," replied Rusty. "My aunt lives across the street, and she said Lester's mother started screaming and collapsed right in the road. My aunt is the only one on that street with a telephone, and she called the constable. They also called Dr. Brewster. They showed the face to Lester's father, and he confirmed it was Lester. I don't know what happened after that, except that Lester's mother had to be carried inside her house and Lester's body was taken to the funeral parlor."

Margaret was ready to creep back into bed when she heard her father say the word *funeral.*

Rusty replied, "The choir is planning something special, and the reverend is working on the eulogy. Stanley's parents are supposed to be back home today, and if they are, I think the funeral will probably be tomorrow."

Riveted, Margaret continued to eavesdrop, even though her legs began to shake.

"Poor Mr. and Mrs. Fisher," Rusty added.

"Oh, we have been worried about them!" said Margaret's father. "Do they know the whole story?"

"Yes, they know," said Rusty. "Someone sent them telegrams. I think it was either Dr. Brewster or Reverend Rutledge."

Then Margaret's mother said something that Margaret couldn't hear.

"Well, first, his parents were told that something had happened to Stanley and they should return home," Rusty said. "Then I believe they got another telegram saying that Stanley's condition was very serious and they should return home on the next train. Finally, just before they left Minnesota, they got a telegram that said Stanley had not survived."

"Oh, how horrible!" said Margaret's father. "But do they know *how* he died?"

Rusty sighed. "They saw a newspaper story when they switched trains in Chicago," he said. "They called the constable, and he confirmed it."

"What do you mean, saw a newspaper story?" asked Margaret's mother, her voice rising.

"Stanley's father bought a newspaper at the station in Chicago," said Rusty. "There happened to be a story about the New Jersey sea monster. The story said the monster had killed again, this time in a place called Matawan. They included the names of the victims—Stanley Fisher and Lester Stilwell. So they telephoned Constable Shuler right then and there, to ask if it was true. And Constable Shuler had to tell them that it was."

There was a pause, and then Rusty added, "I don't know which train they'll be on. Their daughter is with them. She told the constable she'd call from Pennsylvania Station in New York to let us know exactly when they'll arrive here. Constable Shuler thinks that if he meets them at our station, it will tip off the reporters, so I offered to get them home."

The front door creaked as it did whenever it was opened, a few more words were said, and the door closed shut with a *thunk*. Rusty had left.

Margaret tiptoed back to bed. She expected her mother or father to come upstairs to relay Rusty's news, but they did not. Two hours passed before Margaret heard her father's footsteps on the stairs.

"Rusty was here and inquired about you," he said from the doorway. But that was all.

A half hour after that, her mother appeared with a tray of

food, none of it appealing, although it included some of Margaret's favorites: a grilled cheese sandwich, an orange, a sliced peach, a small bowl of butter pecan ice cream, a glass of milk, an oatmeal cookie.

"Thank you, Mother, but I have no appetite," she said.

"Margaret, I will not stand by whilst you wither away!" her mother cried.

"It might help if you and Father didn't treat me like a baby!" Margaret snapped. She had never used such a harsh tone with her mother before.

"Margaret, what on earth are you talking about? I'm just trying to get you to eat. Dr. Brewster says you have acute melancholia brought on by a terrible shock and that you simply must eat, drink plenty of water, and rest."

"When were you and Father going to tell me what Rusty said?" Margaret asked, her voice growing louder with rage. "NEVER?"

"How do you know what Rusty said? Margaret, were you eavesdropping? Shame on you!"

"I have a right to know what's happening!"

"What is the matter?" asked her father, appearing in the doorway. He was out of breath, and Margaret realized he must have dashed up the stairs.

"I do not wish to seem ungrateful," Margaret said, drawing out the words emphatically as she struggled not to scream. "I am a grown woman, and I insist that you treat me that way."

"Now, Margaret," said her mother. "Your father and I are only trying to do what's best for you."

Margaret responded by shrieking and pounding her fists into her pillow. Only when she was worn out did she stop. She rolled over to see her parents standing stock-still, their mouths agape.

They look so frightened, so old and fragile, she thought.

The mirage that she had control over her life was unraveling. She had thought of her parents' lives as never ending, that they would always be there for her, a blind assumption that was easy to indulge when life was normal. Now the pretense was stripped bare, and she understood that one day her parents would die and leave her behind, just as Stanley had done. If Stanley could die, so could they.

"I'm sorry," said Margaret, her voice raspy. "Please forgive me. I know you're trying hard to help me. You are such lovely parents, and I'm grateful for you. But you can't protect me from life anymore."

CHAPTER 31

Edwin had gotten nowhere in his attempt to learn if the scrapes on Rusty Conover and Lenny Yelverton were from the shark, and if so, whether their wounds might have been exposed to a toxin or poison. *Suppose there is some special treatment we know nothing of?* he thought. *Suppose we are running out of time?*

He had sent telegrams and made telephone calls to scientists and doctors around the US and beyond. To his frustration, he was now in the position of waiting helplessly for replies.

The only call he received was unrelated to his medical inquiry. It came from the news vendor at the Red Bank train station, alerting him to the fact that newspaper coverage of the "Jersey shark" story was expanding to new cities. While newspapers in New York and Philadelphia had already been fixated on the topic, the press in Washington, Baltimore, Boston, Chicago, San Francisco—and even London—had now published stories too. He thanked the news vendor and hung up.

While Edwin felt queasy about the sensational coverage, he understood the story's appeal, especially how events had unfolded in Matawan. The fact that a small town far from the open ocean had been invaded by a sea monster was a reminder of the precariousness of life itself. If a group of American boys without a care in the world couldn't swim safely in a creek on a hot summer's day, there was no such thing as innocence. No one anywhere could be assured of getting through a day unscathed.

There was also the heroic aspect of the story. A well-liked young man with a bright future was killed while bravely attempting to save a doomed boy. This was a story as old as time. This was humanity at its best.

No wonder everyone wants to read about it, Edwin mused.

It was one thing to read about it from a distance, and quite another experience to be involved, however. He knew he would worry about Dr. Brewster's patients, Rusty and Lenny, until he found answers. In the meantime, the best he could do was stay busy, and Edwin was relieved that he had a full schedule of patients to see for the next few hours.

Unfortunately, even his patients couldn't refrain from talking about the shark attacks—in most cases even broaching the topic ahead of their own health concerns.

One of his patients insisted the shark attacks were a message to mankind sent by the Almighty. "If God had meant for us to swim with the ocean fishes, we'd have been given gills and fins," he told Edwin in all seriousness. "And the last time I checked, I have neither."

Some blamed the shark attacks on women's bathing costumes. The styles that summer bared more flesh than critics considered acceptable. This same group also objected to the practice of fanny-dunking, a pastime in which women locked arms and, screaming with laughter, dunked their rear ends into breaking waves.

Others concluded that the shark attacked only men and

boys, sparing females. Thus, this theory went, it was safe for girls and women to go sea-bathing.

"It's not that it only attacks men and boys," protested Edwin. "It's that close to a hundred percent of ocean swimmers are male. Vansant and Bruder had both been swimming in water deeper than most women ever go near."

But what, he was asked, about Matawan?

"In Matawan, girls didn't swim in the creek," replied Edwin. "Boys always went skinny-dipping, and so the girls stayed away."

Edwin rarely changed anyone's mind, and in fact, he noticed that the more ridiculous the theory, the more fervent the believer. He was both fascinated and frustrated by this phenomenon, and wondered if the ability to think logically was innate or could be taught. *The extent to which the human mind will contort itself to search for explanations of the unknown or unfathomable is a wonder*, he thought. *Perhaps I will study this one day.*

And yet he couldn't blame his patients for their imaginative attempts to address the events which had altered what they thought they knew and understood about where they lived. The Matawan shark attacks, in particular, had hit too close to home, as there wasn't a single one of his patients who hadn't frolicked in a similar tidal creek as a child. For some of his poorer patients, tidal creeks were the source of fish and crabs for their daily meal.

As the day wore on, the discussions exhausted him, however. When his last three patients of the day posited their theories, he offered no opinion and simply changed the subject to the reason for the patient's visit.

When it was time, at last, to turn out the lights, he was eager to return to the main part of the house and find out if there were any responses to his inquiries, which Hannah had monitored. There had been two telegrams and four telephone calls, none of which shed any light on the injuries of Rusty Conover and Lenny Yelverton in Matawan.

Edwin changed his clothes and tried to relax in the parlor while Hannah prepared dinner. He kept getting up and peering out the front window, however, as he awaited the arrival of the evening newspaper. He was anxious to read it and, at the same time, dreaded seeing it, wondering what news it might contain. Finally, he resolved to stay seated and read a medical journal.

When the paper's arrival was announced by a distinctive thud as it landed by the front door, tossed with astonishing accuracy by the neighborhood newsboy from his bicycle, Edwin leaped from his chair, very nearly knocking over the glass lamp.

And yet he did not rush to retrieve the paper. He froze for a moment, visualizing the newspaper carefully rolled up and neatly tied with twine. He considered ignoring its presence and pictured himself stepping over it the next time he left the house. In his mind, he then went even further. *I could leave it there forever in the sun and rain, and it will disappear. The ink will run, the newsprint will rot, and the twine will blow away.*

"Father, did I hear the newspaper arrive?" asked Julia, suddenly standing in the doorway to the parlor.

"I believe so," he replied.

"Do you want me to get it?" she asked, puzzled.

"Not really."

"What does that mean?"

"I am allowing myself the pretense that I can keep bad news at bay if I don't know about it," replied Edwin. "I think I have finally gained some insight into the human desire for denial."

"You think there will be bad news?"

"Well, yes," he said, "because that's all there is of late."

"Father, you need a vacation from all this," she said, sitting on the piano bench. "It is too much, really, the way you are taking the lead on this."

Edwin sighed. "I didn't set out for that to happen."

"I think it's time for you to step back."

"I have one more responsibility—something I'm looking into for two of Dr. Brewster's patients—and then I will stop," he said.

"Well, after that, I think we should go on a little trip," said Julia. "Maybe bring Hannah too, if she wants to go."

"Where?"

"Some place far from the sea," she replied. "Perhaps the mountains."

"There are bears in the mountains," he said, half teasing. "And wolves."

"That's fine," she said. "As long as there aren't any sharks."

"We could go to the Adirondacks or the Berkshires," he said, warming to the idea.

"Adirondacks? Berkshires? What are you talking about?" asked Hannah, standing in the doorway. She wiped her hands on her apron. "Where's the paper? I want to see if there's any news from the war."

"We haven't brought it in yet," said Julia.

"All right, I'll get it," Hannah announced before bustling off.

"Well, Father, I guess your respite from the news is over," whispered Julia.

Hannah returned, unfolding the paper as she walked, and said, "Oh, Lord!"

"What is it?" asked Edwin. "Is it the war?"

"No, it's not the war," replied Hannah. She handed the paper to him. A huge headline was splashed across the front page.

BODY OF BOY VICTIM OF SEA WOLF FOUND AT MATAWAN

Julia peered over Edwin's shoulder. "How sad," she said softly. "But isn't it sort of good news?"

Edwin took a deep breath. "Yes," he replied. "At least now his parents will be able to bury his body. I didn't think they would ever find it."

"Father, did you notice they called it a sea wolf?" asked Julia. "Is there such a thing?"

"I don't believe so," replied Edwin.

"Maybe the newspaper editors are just getting tired of using the word *shark* in a headline," said Julia.

Edwin half smiled. "That could be it," he said. "The simplest explanation, as they say, is usually the right one." But then he grew serious again as he read the article. "It says the boy's body was badly mangled and— Oh, never mind the details. How horrible."

"His poor mother!" cried Hannah.

"Indeed," said Edwin sadly.

"Now what happens?" asked Julia.

Edwin thought for a moment. "This confirms he was a victim of the shark and that he didn't simply run away or drown—not that anyone has seriously suggested that. The descriptions by witnesses of the attack on the boy match completely with the injuries on the body. Somehow, we must hope and pray that we can capture this creature, kill it, and then hopefully study it."

"I suppose it's too much to wish that it will simply disappear," said Julia. "Perhaps it will go back to the deep sea and leave us alone."

Edwin was struck by Julia's choice of the word *us*.

Julia, he thought, *now shares the sense that the shark attacks have become personal. The creature has killed a vacationer in Beach Haven, a hotel bellhop in Spring Lake, and now it has gone to great lengths to stalk and take the lives of a young man and a child in Matawan. How dare it? How dare it turn a pleasant pastime into a scene of horror? It is a betrayal! The shore, whether on the beaches or in the myriad rivers and streams, is a refuge from the world. It is not meant to be a place where such things happen.*

That evening, Edwin reluctantly telephoned Dr. Brewster, telling him that so far, he had received no new information from his inquiries into the source of the peculiar injuries suffered by Rusty Conover and Lenny Yelverton. "I will keep trying," he promised Dr. Brewster.

Edwin was running out of options, however. He reached a surgeon in Port Arthur, Texas, who had been recommended as a possible source of information, but the man was as stymied as Edwin.

Out of desperation, Edwin tracked down the home telephone number of Dr. Mervot, the director of the American Museum of Natural History in New York City. Edwin had been upset with Dr. Mervot and two of Mervot's colleagues, who, after the first shark attack on July 1, had publicly refuted any suggestion that the culprit was a shark. Now, reached on the telephone, Edwin found Dr. Mervot had made a 180-degree turn. At the same time, Dr. Mervot had seen Edwin's name in the paper and realized that Edwin was knowledgeable.

Both men comprehended the truth, though, and freely admitted it to each other. Neither of them was, in fact, an expert.

They were simply scientists, albeit with different training, who were doing the best they could with very limited information.

Dr. Mervot urged Edwin to talk to a man named Michael Schleisser. "I should warn you, Schleisser is a bit odd," added Dr. Mervot. "He lives in Harlem, but I strongly advise that you not go to his house."

"Why?" asked Edwin.

"Because it's bizarre, not to mention dangerous," replied Dr. Mervot. "Schleisser is a strange fellow, like a showman at a circus. He's able to train wild animals. He's also a big-game hunter. He's traveled the world and captured or killed all kinds of creatures, like polar bears and tigers. Apparently, he keeps some of them as pets at his house, where they are tied up in the backyard or wander about the yard—or even in the house. Some are trained, but not all. Oh, and he's also an outstanding taxidermist, and he does the work in his basement. I'm told the house has an odd smell."

"How is it that you know this man Schleisser?"

"One of our curators has purchased items from him for our collections," replied Dr. Mervot.

"And you think he may be able to answer some of my questions?" asked Edwin.

"If anyone can, it would be Schleisser," said Dr. Mervot. "Including your questions about the scrapes on those two swimmers in Matawan Creek. Schleisser is likely to give you an explanation and, more importantly, know whether there's any reason to be concerned about a toxin or poison released by the shark."

Edwin thanked Dr. Mervot for the information.

"That's quite all right," Dr. Mervot replied. "Perhaps someday, someone will figure out how to study sharks, perhaps with a way to track them. Until then, I'm afraid we are mostly guessing."

JULY 15, 1916

CHAPTER 32

Margaret shouted in her sleep, awakening herself and her mother, who had taken to dozing in Margaret's room on a daybed, which, in better days, had been Margaret's favorite place to curl up and read a good book.

"What is it?" her mother cried, leaping to her feet.

Margaret sat bolt upright. "Today is the funeral," she said.

"Margaret," Mother said. "Go back to sleep. It's half past four in the morning."

"But I must get ready! Today is the day!"

Her mother put on a robe and slippers and shuffled to Margaret's bedside. She sat down heavily at the foot of the bed and began to rub Margaret's feet. The room was partly lit by a light in the hallway, and all Margaret could see of her mother was a silhouette.

"Please, Margaret, go back to sleep," she begged.

"But the funeral is in a few hours!" cried Margaret.

"How do you even know that?" Mother asked and sighed.

"I don't know! I must have overheard."

"Well, my dear one, you are correct." Her mother paused. "It's in the late morning. A double service for Stanley and Lester."

"Then, Mother, I must get dressed! I need to get ready!"

"Don't you think the funeral will be another enormous shock to you? You are nowhere near recovered!"

"Oh, Mother," she shrieked, "I doubt I will *ever* recover! Please, I must go!"

"I don't think you should!"

"I need to see Stanley's parents."

"You can see them later."

"Mother," Margaret said, "I insist on going. Remember what I said yesterday? I don't want you and Father making decisions for me."

"Well, we are trying to respect your wishes. Your father and I talked about it. We will step back. But please remember, this hasn't been easy for us either! We are all terribly upset. I admit I did interfere just a wee bit yesterday, but that was before you . . . before you said what you did about us interfering. But you may as well know. I telephoned Reverend Rutledge to ask if the service could be held off another day or two in the hope that you might feel a little stronger and perhaps attend. But he said they'd already had to wait for Stanley's parents to get back from Minnesota, and everyone decided they had to go ahead because of the condition of the bodies . . ."

She stopped, horrified at what she had just said. "I'm so sorry, Margaret! I can't imagine why I said such a thing!" she cried out. "I'm just so tired and on edge."

"I know you didn't mean it, Mother," Margaret said. "Please don't distress yourself. Now help me up, please. We have work to do."

"Work?"

"You know I don't own a black dress," said Margaret. "We have to figure out something for me to wear. Because, Mother,

I am going to the funeral. It's my choice. You and Father can come with me if you like. But mark my words, I'm going."

Just before eleven o'clock, Margaret walked to First Methodist Episcopal Church with her parents on either side of her, their arms entwined.

They navigated their way through clusters of mourners who lined sidewalks, hovered in doorways, and even spilled onto Main Street, essentially closing it to traffic. Solemn faces peered from second-story windows of homes and stores, and a few boys had climbed onto gabled roofs to watch.

Why, the entire town has turned out for Stanley and Lester, Margaret thought.

"Mr. and Mrs. Atkins and Miss Margaret Atkins," the constable called out and beckoned them forward.

The crowd parted and let them through.

Someone took her picture.

The constable scolded the photographer. "Hey, you!" he shouted. "Get back across the street!"

Margaret glanced over her shoulder. Reporters and photographers were jammed together behind a rope suspended between two hitching rails. The newsmen were being supervised by a man in uniform.

As Margaret and her parents crossed the threshold and into the back of the sanctuary, she was disoriented.

This is my home church, she told herself, but she had the sensation of remoteness, as if she were looking at photographs of her surroundings rather than being there in person. *This is the church I helped decorate for Christmas and Easter. Up there, in the loft, is where Stanley sang with the choir.*

"Do you see any empty seats?" Mother whispered. They were still standing with arms locked, Margaret between them.

"I see a few near the front," replied her father. He started to pull them forward, down the center aisle.

I do not want to go to the front, Margaret thought helplessly. *I do not want to walk down this aisle.* Out of habit, she glanced at the choir, expecting Stanley to be in his usual place. *But he is not there and never will be again,* she thought forlornly. *He never missed singing in the choir. Now they will be singing for him.*

They were halfway down the aisle. Still, there were no seats. Several men spotted them and stood, indicating they would forfeit their seats, but her father did not see them. He plunged forward, hurtling them, or so it seemed to Margaret, toward the front.

Then Margaret stopped short, jerking her parents to an awkward stop. A wrenching thought consumed her. *I ought to be walking down this aisle as a bride. Stanley should be waiting for me at the altar, smiling and maybe a little nervous.*

Instead, at the front of the church were two coffins, one for Stanley and a smaller one for Lester. Rather than a white bridal ensemble, Margaret wore her mother's Victorian mourning gown, a black silk confection that they had quickly altered that morning, and which now seemed presumptuous if not grotesque.

A thought went through her mind: *I wouldn't want Stanley to see me in this awful, out-of-date dress.* And she gasped, realizing that Stanley would never see her again, not in this lifetime.

Her cry was more like a desperate gulp of air, and her parents gripped her arms tighter, digging their fingers into the flesh of her upper arms, apparently fearing she was about to faint. Her father spied a few empty spaces on the right and moved toward them with astonishing speed, dragging her behind him and causing her mother to trip.

The service soon began. Lester's and Stanley's mothers moaned and sobbed, and it was hard to hear the Reverend Rutledge. Margaret couldn't focus anyway, although she perked up when the minister read from John 15:13, "Greater love hath no man than this, that a man lay down his life for his friends," and said that Stanley was "a hero who had immortalized himself."

The choir sang "Blessed Assurance," Stanley's favorite hymn, and it was all Margaret could do to keep from running out of the sanctuary. Even the menfolk were weeping. It was the first time Margaret had ever seen her father cry.

At the closing, the Reverend Rutledge spoke of the community's loss. "In a sense, this has happened to all of us," he said. "We have lost two sons of Matawan. We will support one another and get through this by leaning on one another and on the Lord."

Margaret averted her eyes as two sets of pallbearers gathered around the coffins, lifting them from the matched pair of funeral biers on which they rested. When the pallbearers passed by the row where she and her parents sat, she looked up. Lester's small casket was carried first, his immediate family walking behind it; then Stanley's, his parents and sister trailing behind.

"Margaret," her father whispered, "do you want to go to the cemetery?"

An image of Stanley's coffin being lowered six feet into the ground flashed through her mind. "No, Father," she replied. "I don't think so."

They exited the church with the stragglers.

"Should we wait until the procession has left?" asked her mother.

"Yes," said Margaret.

In the shadow of the church spire, they watched from a distance as the caskets were settled onto funeral wagons, each pulled by a magnificent black horse loaned for the occasion by a gentleman farmer in Freehold. The pallbearers stepped back, their duty done for the time being.

Mourners who planned to walk to the cemetery gathered behind the funeral wagons, followed by those going on horseback, then horse-drawn carriages and humble farm wagons—one of which, pulled by a mule, was carrying a half dozen children. Bringing up the rear was a line of automobiles, nearly all Ford Model Ts indistinguishable from one another. All awaited the tolling of the church bell indicating that the procession should begin.

"This must be the largest funeral ever held in Matawan," Margaret remarked. She moved into the shade of a sycamore with wilted leaves, a location which offered a slightly better vantage point. Her parents followed.

"Margaret!" her mother said suddenly, drawing her attention to a woman headed in their direction.

It was Mrs. Fisher, Stanley's mother. Margaret had always been a bit intimidated by Mrs. Fisher's demeanor, so decisive and confident. Now she was barely able to walk—as though treading on grass, with its uneven surface, was more than she could handle.

Margaret rushed to her, and they embraced.

"Oh, Margaret," whispered Mrs. Fisher. "How are we going to live without him?"

Of all the things she could say, this comment struck Margaret as the simplest, most profound, and accurate. There it was, all wrapped up in one basic question: What was life without Stanley?

CHAPTER 33

Edwin waited for the grandfather clock in the hallway to chime eight times, indicating the earliest hour in the morning that a civilized person could telephone someone they didn't know. He hoped to have a conversation with Michael Schleisser.

On the first try, there was no answer. The telephone operator asked if Edwin wanted to try again, and he said, yes, in five minutes. That call went through, and a woman answered, identifying herself as Mr. Schleisser's housekeeper. She reported that he was not available, but when Edwin expressed great disappointment, she told him that her employer had gone, as he frequently did, to Perth Amboy, New Jersey, where he kept his boats, and that if Edwin hurried, he might be able to locate him before he left to go fishing.

Edwin changed quickly into more suitable clothing, which included his one and only straw boater. The docks, he knew, would be scorching with the sun fully ablaze, even if there was a breeze.

It was great luck that Schleisser was in Perth Amboy, not

Harlem. Still, it would take an hour to drive there. Edwin knew that Schleisser might be out on his boat already by the time he arrived, but it was worth a try. If he arrived too late to speak to him, well, he'd simply wait at the dockside. Edwin was quite desperate to talk to anyone with knowledge of sharks. He kept checking to be sure that the photographs of Rusty Conover were squared away in his inner jacket pocket.

Other than getting stuck for a mile behind a sluggish delivery truck, it was a smooth trip, and Edwin was pleased. He found a place to park his automobile and, hurrying onto the docks, asked the dockmaster on duty for the location of the boat slips belonging to Schleisser. He was told that Schleisser hadn't left yet and that he'd be the guy wearing a green-and-blue striped shirt.

Still here! Edwin thought gleefully. *My good luck continues!*

There was indeed an athletic-looking man in the correct attire who seemed to be refereeing an intense disagreement between two fishermen. Edwin waited politely to the side. No good could come from his interrupting this spirited argument, although he was tempted. He longed to ask Schleisser to look at the photographs.

Edwin studied Schleisser. He was not as big a man as one might expect, considering his occupation, but he moved with the power and grace of a jungle cat that has vanquished all challengers. Gauging Schleisser's age was difficult. Midthirties, perhaps. His hair was dark, but streaks of silver intruded here and there, mostly along the temples. He might have been handsome at one time, but his rugged lifestyle and too much time in the sun had mottled his complexion and created a web of lines around his mouth and eyes and across his forehead. Edwin had assumed the man was American born but detected a hint of an accent that might have been Dutch.

Schleisser suddenly grew tired of the two fishermen and

their rivalry. "Oh, sort it out yourselves," he said in disgust. He turned and, for the first time, spotted Edwin.

"Mr. Schleisser," Edwin said quickly, approaching him. "I am Dr. Halsey, a surgeon at Monmouth Memorial Hospital in Long Branch. I spoke on the telephone last night with Dr. Mervot of the American Museum of Natural History, and he suggested I speak to you."

Schleisser nodded. "I've seen your name in the papers," he said. "I was just about to head out." He gestured to a boat of perhaps twelve or fourteen feet in length.

"You're going out in that?" asked Edwin.

"I'm not going out very far," he replied. "Just to catch a few fish to pan fry." Then he pointed to a boat, the *Rose Marie*, perhaps forty feet long, in a nearby slip. "That's my baby right there. She's the one I take when I want to do some real fishing."

"She's a beautiful boat."

"Yeah, well, for now she stays at the dock. Had a little engine trouble with her midweek, and my mechanic is coming today to take a look. Now tell me, how can I help you?"

"It's about the shark," replied Edwin.

"I figured," said Schleisser. "But now's not really a good time. I've got to do my fishing this morning or I probably won't get to go out at all." As he spoke, he began to untie the small boat, loosening the rolling-hitch knot that secured it to a dock piling.

"I won't detain you for very long," pleaded Edwin.

"Why don't you come along? We can talk while I'm fishing."

Edwin flinched. "I'd rather not. Perhaps I'll wait here until you return."

Schleisser frowned. "But I don't know if I'll have time to talk to you when I get back."

Edwin eyed the boat. He had never been out on the water in a boat that small. In fact, except for the ship that took him to Cuba during the Spanish-American War, he hadn't been in any size or type of vessel since that terrible day thirty-six years earlier off Sea Bright.

"Are you sure we can't take the *Rose Marie*?" he asked. "I'd prefer the bigger boat."

Schleisser stared at Edwin. "As I said, I've had some engine trouble with the *Rose Marie*. And she's really not the appropriate boat for my little jaunt, anyway."

"I don't think I could go out in that," said Edwin, pointing to the smaller boat, which featured a newfangled motor attached to the stern.

Schleisser gave Edwin a contemptuous look. "Don't tell me you're worried about the shark!" he said. "For God's sake, man, it's long gone! Probably way past Coney Island by now. Heck, halfway to Nantucket! We'll never see it around here again."

Edwin realized they had acquired an audience of several nosy fishermen. He felt his face flush with shame.

"Now are you coming with me or not?" demanded Schleisser.

One of the fishermen on the dock snickered loudly. Edwin felt as if he were in grammar school, being dared to do something he'd rather not. But then he thought of his duty to Dr. Brewster's patients, Rusty Conover and the boy, Lenny Yelverton. What if the appalling scrapes on their torsos were infected with some kind of toxin? What if there was a way to treat their injuries—perhaps even something relatively simple, such as a cleansing agent or poultice—but time was running out? And what if this unusual man, Schleisser, knew the answers?

Edwin took a quick look around him. He spotted a broken oar in a pile of debris on the dock. Impulsively, he grabbed it and climbed into the boat. Once seated, he kept his eyes cast downward so that he wouldn't have to look at the water. He fought a wave of nausea.

Schleisser laughed. "What are you bringing that for?" he asked, pointing to the broken oar.

Edwin didn't bother to answer. He'd had enough humiliation for one morning, but he could tolerate it, he decided, along with his fears, as long as he remembered why he was there. *Dr. Brewster's patients are more important than my comfort or pride*, he told himself. *All will be fine. Nothing will happen.* Nonetheless, he kept a tight grip on the broken oar.

"Well, suit yourself," said Schleisser, starting the engine.

As Schleisser piloted the boat toward the broad expanse of the bay, there was a moment when Edwin forgot his feelings of dread and was overcome by a surprising emotion: pure joy. There was nothing comparable to being out on the open water on a beautiful summer day. *I have not felt this freedom since I was thirteen years old*, he mused. But as they left the docks farther behind them, the sensation faded and trepidation returned.

From the middle bench seat, he swung his legs so he was facing Schleisser, who sat in the back to pilot the boat. Their knees were about a foot apart. *This boat is way too small*, Edwin thought, panicking. He tried to comfort himself with rational thoughts. *We are on Raritan Bay, a little sister to the ocean, and the swells are gentle. There is nothing to fear. The shark is long gone.*

Not that Raritan Bay was insignificant in size or lacking in hazards. Growing up in the region, Edwin knew there were sunken boats and the occasional rock pile in the bay as well as other infrequent but hazardous obstacles left by long-ago sailors. On the far side of the bay, near Sandy Hook, sandbars were a particular hazard. A sandbar had even stranded the explorer Henry Hudson and the crew of *Half Moon*, who had to wait for the tide to rise before their ship floated free.

Edwin's mind turned to Matawan Creek, one of many tidal streams that emptied into the bay. *We must be a few miles from*

Matawan, he reasoned, *and anyway, the attacks were three days ago. The shark is far, far away.*

"This is one of my favorite things in the world," Schleisser announced. It was the first time he'd spoken since they left the docks. "I come out here at least twice a week," he said. "Unless I'm traveling, of course."

"Haven't we gone out far enough?" asked Edwin. There was only so long he could endure this.

"Yes, this'll do," replied Schleisser. He put the engine in neutral and attached a fishing net to the stern. Then he gently accelerated the motor and tossed the bulk of the net into the bay. It trailed behind them below the surface.

Edwin did not like the slower pace, for it made the boat ride lower in the water. Silently, he said the Fisherman's Prayer posted over the bar in Point Pleasant. *Oh, Lord, thy sea is so vast and my boat is so small . . .*

"So what is it you want to ask me?" asked Schleisser.

Edwin snapped to attention. "Well, it's a peculiar situation," he said, quickly gathering his thoughts. "I am very concerned about the well-being of a man and a boy from Matawan who were in the creek when the shark was present. They both have large, horizontal scrapes on their bodies, almost like welts." Edwin reached into his pocket, removed the photographs, and handed the first one to Schleisser. "Could these marks be caused by the shark?"

Schleisser said nothing until all of the photos had been passed back and forth, one at a time. "Yes," he replied. "These injuries would be from the shark's skin. The skin is extremely rough, worse than sandpaper."

"So it brushed up against them?" asked Edwin.

"Yes, probably to help it decide."

"Decide what?"

"If they were worth eating."

"Oh," Edwin said. "I see."

"They are extremely fortunate," added Schleisser, shaking his head.

"I have heard many times that a shark bite is toxic or poisonous," said Edwin. "Do you know if this is true? Could there be a toxin or poison in these scrapes?"

"No," Schleisser said. "That is not true. There is nothing to be concerned about. The bite is not poisonous, and neither is contact with the skin."

Edwin was so relieved he felt a few tears trickle into the corners of his eyes. "When we get back to shore, I will be sure to let their physician know immediately."

"Is there anything else?" asked Schleisser.

Edwin swallowed hard, working up his nerve. He hadn't expected to have this opportunity but plunged ahead. "I had an experience long ago that I would like to tell you about."

Schleisser listened intently as Edwin described the harrowing event off Sea Bright in his youth. It was a little easier to tell the tale this time, and Edwin felt encouraged that Schleisser did not laugh or minimize the experience. In fact, Schleisser seemed mesmerized.

"Punched a hole right through the bottom of the boat?" he asked. "What a magnificent creature."

"Magnificent!" cried Edwin. "I beg your pardon, Mr. Schleisser, but you're not supposed to root for the shark! Anyway, I survived, as did the captain. Although I must say I've spent the last thirty-six years trying to forget it."

Schleisser softened. "Yes, I can imagine," he said. "Sorry about earlier. Had I known, I wouldn't have teased you about coming out with me in the boat. What a terrible ordeal."

"Have you ever heard of anything like it?"

"Yes," said Schleisser. "It's a wild story, but white sharks have been known to attack boats. About fifty years ago, one attacked a fishing boat near Nantucket, but way out to sea. It destroyed the boat, then ate the fishermen."

This was the first time Edwin had ever heard, other than his own story, of a shark trying to sink a boat.

He told Schleisser about the Point Pleasant commercial fishermen who spoke of a beast that stalked the waters along the shore. "Surely, that's just a silly folktale," said Edwin.

Schleisser shrugged but cautioned Edwin. "We should never dismiss such stories. Around the world, you hear such things, and there is usually some truth to the story."

This gave Edwin pause. "Is it possible," he asked, "that the shark I encountered in 1880 is the same one that has been perpetrating these attacks, in 1916? It seems preposterous!"

"Do I think it's the same one? Yes, it could be," Schleisser said. "I believe a white shark can live as long as a human. Plus, there's a pattern to this one's behavior—the series of deliberate attacks and coming in so close to shore—that's very rare."

The boat moved forward, dragging the shallow net, the pace almost hypnotic. Edwin was relieved when he realized that Schleisser was making a wide turn and they were, in fact, heading back to the docks.

"I'm sure we've got some fish in the nets," said Schleisser. "I think you've had enough for one day."

"Thank you," said Edwin.

"Doc," said Schleisser, "I guess it's safe to say you aren't comfortable in boats."

"That is correct," replied Edwin.

"You are very brave," said Schleisser.

"I would hardly call myself brave," said Edwin. "I'm extremely nervous even though I know it's irrational. Sometimes

I suspect I have a problem similar to one they've been noticing in the European war. They call it shell shock. I read about it last year in a medical journal, *The Lancet*. Have you heard the term?"

"Yes," replied Schleisser, "but shell shock is not a new condition. It used to be called soldier's heart or nostalgia. It can happen when a person experiences a great trauma."

It occurred to Edwin that Schleisser, considering his occupation, had likely been exposed to a good deal of trauma himself. *I wonder why it doesn't seem to affect him*, he mused. *And yet my experience affected me.*

Edwin was lost in thought about ways that science could address the condition of shell shock, or whatever one might call it, when something caught his eye. In the distance, he saw a large, dark seabird—perhaps a cormorant—flying close to the water. He almost smiled.

Maybe it wasn't so bad being out on the water again after all.

CHAPTER 34

The seabird flew in arcs, sweeping back and forth, searching for prey. Edwin welcomed the distraction. It was almost as if it was keeping them company as they headed back in.

Then it disappeared.

Oh, drat, it's gone, he thought, scanning the open water.

But then he saw it in the distance on the starboard side of the boat. How odd. Had it flown past them without him noticing?

Schleisser was oblivious. He was fixated on what types of fish and how many he might have snared in the net. "There is a little drag, so I'm sure we've got a nice catch," he said confidently.

The seabird reappeared once more, to Edwin's delight. This time it was closer, and Edwin thought it might be following them in the hope of stealing some of their catch. "I wish I had binoculars," he commented.

A cloud in the distance passed over the area where the bird flew back and forth, changing the color of the water from sparkling silver to dull gray. But when the cloud scooted on its way, and the bright rays of the sun returned, Edwin realized that the object he believed to be a large bird was in the water, not above it.

His throat tightened.

"What is that?" he spluttered, barely getting the words out. Schleisser looked up. "Way over there." Edwin pointed.

"I don't see anything," replied Schleisser.

I must be imagining it, Edwin thought, forcing himself to stay calm. *My being out here on the water, after all these years, has triggered a hallucina—*

"Dear God," Schleisser cried.

Edwin followed his gaze. The shape was closer now, and there could be no doubt. The black thing on the surface of the water was a large dorsal fin.

"It's circling us!" Schleisser shouted. "Quick, we must lose the net! It wants our fish!"

Or maybe, thought Edwin, *it wants us.*

Schleisser was struggling to release the net when the boat jerked to a stop, stalling the engine and hurling both men backward to the bottom of the boat.

Schleisser managed to get to his feet first.

"Did we hit something?" Edwin called out.

"No!" shouted Schleisser. "It's the shark! It's caught in the net! It's trying to free itself!"

For a moment, Edwin felt a tiny quiver of hope. Perhaps if it broke loose, the shark would simply swim away.

Crouching, Schleisser peered over the stern. He turned to Edwin to say something when the boat began to move backward, slowly at first, then faster.

"Jesus, Mary, and Joseph! It's going to pull us under!" shouted Schleisser.

Indeed, the bow rose in the air as the stern was dragged downward.

Edwin threw himself into the bow, instinctively trying to counterbalance the force exerted by the shark. And it worked—for a moment. The shark paused, and the boat stilled.

There was silence, and no movement except for the gentle swells of the bay.

Then the shark took a different tack. Its head, partially entangled in the net, rose out of the water behind the stern. With jaws wide open exposing rows of serrated teeth, bloody from having devoured the fish in the net, the gaping mouth of the monster was an opening to hell. They looked at one another—the men and the monster. Was it sizing them up or just trying to figure out how to get free of the netting? For an instant, they were frozen in place.

Then with astonishing power, the creature tried to leap into the boat, snapping at Schleisser, who was closest. Both men moved back, and the boat tipped precariously from the shifting weight.

We are dead men, Edwin thought. *Poor Julia, she will never know what happened to me.*

The shark tried again, leaping toward them, but this time they saw that something was holding it back. The same netting that had entangled the shark was now preventing it from destroying the boat and killing them.

As understanding dawned, Schleisser leaped into action, seizing the broken oar Edwin had brought along at the last minute. Each time the shark lunged, Schleisser clubbed it on its nose and eyes and sometimes the gills when he was able to get at them.

Edwin wondered what, if anything, he might do to help Schleisser, but he could think of nothing. There was no way to release the netting from the boat without coming within inches of the shark's teeth, and if Edwin tried, he would only get in

Schleisser's way. The only weapon on the boat was the broken oar, which Schleisser was using.

The shark responded to the beating by pausing for a moment. Instead of backing off, however, it mustered its strength and took its biggest leap yet. It almost got Schleisser's arm but missed, though in the process, the creature's skin brushed against Schleisser's forearm, leaving deep, bright-red scrapes.

The scent of Schleisser's blood seemed to give the shark yet another burst of energy. It vaulted onto the stern of the boat, where, this time, its head and the front of its body stayed.

My God, it must be as long as the boat, thought Edwin. *It's going to flip us over.*

Schleisser staggered backward, away from the shark, and dropped the broken oar. Instantly, Edwin reached for the impromptu weapon, which meant moving toward the shark, but for a moment he was unafraid. He felt not fear nor the courage that comes with fighting to survive. What spurred him forward in that moment was something akin to revenge.

Edwin pushed past the wounded Schleisser and rushed at the shark with a fury he didn't know he possessed. He clubbed the creature just as he had seen Schleisser do—on its nose and around its eyes. When the creature turned its head away from him, he struck its gills. Each blow carried the weight of living for thirty-six long years in the shadow of the monster. He had no hope that he might vanquish it. He wanted only to fight back as long as he could.

The shark seemed dazed. It slid slightly backward toward the water. Now was not the time to stop hitting it, but strangely, Edwin no longer cared. *I should keep hitting it,* he thought. *Don't give up now.* Instead, he collapsed.

Schleisser crawled toward Edwin and pried the broken oar from his tight grasp. While Edwin now lay helpless, Schleisser approached the shark and clubbed it one more time. Slowly, still entangled in the net, it slipped into the sea. Schleisser watched for any sign of life, but the fierce shark was dead.

Neither man could speak, nor did they look at each other. Finally, Schleisser turned to Edwin. "You all right, Doc?"

"I think so. Is it really dead?"

"Yeah," replied Schleisser.

"Are you sure?"

"Uh-huh."

"Now what?" asked Edwin, after a pause in which neither of them could speak.

"Um, we need to get back," replied Schleisser. "I'll see if I can get the engine started. If not, we'll have to wait for someone to come looking for us."

"Boat seems okay, doesn't it?"

"Yeah," replied Schleisser. "Seems seaworthy." He tried the motor, and it started right up. He laughed giddily. "How about that, Doc? Did you ever hear such a beautiful sound in your life?"

"Where's the, uh, creature?" Edwin wasn't sure he could ever say the word *shark* again.

"Oh, it's right here, still tangled in the net. If I can keep the netting away from the propeller, we can tow it back to the docks with us."

"No! For God's sake, let it float away!" cried Edwin.

"Doc, you're not making sense," Schleisser said calmly. "We have to bring it in. It has to be examined—measured and all that."

"I don't care about that," Edwin snapped.

"Well, you should. Otherwise, no one's going to believe it."

"I don't care if no one believes it."

"Doc, think for a minute," said Schleisser. "For the sake of the families—you know, the families of the victims. And all the people who live at the shore. They're going to want evidence that the shark is dead. Otherwise, it's just a story."

Edwin buried his face in his hands. *I can't bear this another moment*, he thought.

"Please, Doc, we have to bring it back for proof. For the sake of science. And for the families."

"Are you absolutely sure it's dead?"

"Yeah, take a look for yourself."

Edwin craned his neck and looked at the lifeless creature, then leaned over the side of the boat and vomited.

"Everything's okay now, Doc," Schleisser said soothingly. "Look, here comes help now."

A fishing vessel was heading straight toward them. As it drew close, a crew member cupped his hands and shouted to them, "Everything shipshape over there?"

Schleisser chuckled ironically. "Hear that, Doc? He wants to know if everything is shipshape!"

They both burst out laughing so hard they gasped for breath.

"Do you need help?" the crew member shouted, puzzled by their behavior. At that moment, however, a wave shifted the crewman's perspective, and he caught sight of the dead creature in the net. "Good God!" he screamed. "You've caught the shark!"

The rest of the crew of the other boat rushed to see the creature.

"You caught it from that little boat?" one of them yelled.

"How did you do it?" shouted another.

"Come aboard, we'll take you to shore," the first one called. "We'll tow your boat. And the shark."

Edwin started to accept, but Schleisser told him not to. "Why?" Edwin asked.

"Because we caught it, not them," he replied. "We're going to take it back to the docks at Perth Amboy where we started."

"Do as you wish; I'm going back in the other vessel," Edwin said.

"I need you to stay with me, Doc," said Schleisser. "You're my witness. We need to return to Perth Amboy together. There's another reason: this needs to be done properly. You know as well as I do that there's a good possibility there are human remains in this thing's gut, and we'll need a medical doctor to make that determination."

The last thing Edwin wanted to do was examine the creature's stomach contents. But Schleisser was right. If there were human remains, especially bones, it might prove whether this was the same monster that killed four people and badly injured a fifth all in the space of twelve short days.

"So what do you say, Doc?" asked Schleisser. "We need to bring it back ourselves, agreed?"

Edwin groaned. "Yes, yes," he said. "Agreed."

Schleisser called to their would-be rescuers, thanking them but insisting they were fine. Edwin watched with mixed feelings as the bigger boat departed.

The return voyage with the shark towed behind them was agonizingly slow. Edwin moved to the bow of the boat, as far from the creature as he could get. He looked at the shark repeatedly, not totally convinced that it wasn't going to spring back to life. He could not maintain his vigilance indefinitely, however, and despite his best efforts, exhaustion took over, and he closed his eyes.

The sounds of other boats and people jolted him awake, and he realized with a sudden burst of euphoria that they were approaching the Perth Amboy docks.

Suddenly, Edwin remembered that Schleisser had been injured. "Your arm all right?" he asked.

Schleisser seemed to have forgotten about it too. "Oh," he

said, peering at the injury. "A new one to add to my collection of scars," he replied lightly.

Yet he didn't give the impression that he was feeling triumphant. He was excessively pale, and his eyes were deeply bloodshot.

On the docks, a curious crowd began to gather as they came near. Passengers lounging or sunning themselves on anchored boats spotted the dead shark tangled in netting. People shouted and pointed at the strange sight, drawing ever more onlookers. Edwin realized that he and Schleisser were a spectacle—or rather, the shark was.

"That shark is bigger than your boat!" a man called from a sailing vessel.

"Hey, Schleisser, whatcha got there?" an old man called out.

But Schleisser ignored them. He piloted the boat straight to an official weigh station used in tournaments. Murmurs of surprise and something close to admiration swept through the marina as the shark's body came into full view at the dock.

"Look at that!" shouted one fisherman. "Never saw the likes of it 'round here!"

"They caught it!" a young boy screamed. "They caught the monster!"

But the two men in the small boat had come too close to death to celebrate. They were fatigued mentally and physically, especially Edwin. The tide was going out, and he would need to climb up a ladder to reach the dock—a task that seemed impossible. Without waiting for him to ask for help, two burly dockhands pulled him to the dock. A woman brought him fresh water to drink and insisted that he do so.

Schleisser recovered more quickly. "I need a messenger!" he shouted. A lad of about six or seven years volunteered, and Schleisser sent him scampering to the nearest newspaper office in the hope that he might return with a photographer.

Under the supervision of Schleisser and the dockmaster, the

shark was hoisted from the water to be weighed officially as if it were the grand-prize winner in a fishing competition. As the shark dangled in the air, Edwin forced himself to look at it. It was at least twice as long as he was tall. *I could have ended up in that thing's belly*, he thought. He wondered how many other fishermen had disappeared that way. Suddenly, he felt sure the beast had been roaming these waters a long time.

The netting that entangled the shark was cut away, and the moment everyone was waiting for had arrived. The size of the creature would be determined, the frightful numbers written down for posterity.

The dockmaster's voice rang out. "Thirteen feet, three inches in length," he declared. Then he announced the weight. "One thousand four hundred pounds!" He shook his head in amazement. "A record for around here, that's for darn sure!"

A few onlookers moved forward, eager to get a closer look at the beast. But then a groaning sound was heard, and the shark began to move.

At first, it merely quivered, then it wobbled from side to side, and finally, bucked wildly. A sound came from Edwin's throat that even he didn't recognize—a yelp or gasp.

A child's anxious voice asked, "Mommy, what's it doing?"

"Get out of the way!" someone screamed.

Schleisser shoved the dockmaster out of the way, then leaped aside. The creature crashed to the dock, sending people scattering.

Edwin pushed his way shamelessly past several women.

It's alive. I have to get away . . .

But it was not alive. The apparatus had collapsed under the weight of the beast.

Schleisser was the first to figure out what had happened. "Nothing to worry about, folks," he yelled. "It broke the scale, that's all."

Assured that the shark was indeed dead, the crowd surged

forward, eager to peer closely at the lifeless form, remarking on its tremendous dorsal fin and especially its cavernous mouth. Grotesquely, it had died with its jaws wide open, its mighty teeth on full display.

"Don't touch it!" Schleisser snapped at several men who had gotten too close. "The skin is like very rough sandpaper," he explained, holding out his wounded arm. "Almost like broken glass."

The messenger boy returned with a news photographer, who looked grumpy until he spied the carcass on the dock. "It's the man-eater!" he bellowed. "This'll be the photograph of the year!"

He took pictures of the shark from different angles while Schleisser told the story. Edwin stood to the side, but Schleisser pointed him out. "This is the man who helped save the day," he declared, gesturing to Edwin.

Embarrassed, Edwin cringed and declined to be interviewed.

"Well, you must be in the photographs, at least," Schleisser declared. The photographer pleaded, and Schleisser pulled Edwin forward. "Come on, Doc," he said. "This is history."

The crowd lingered. They expected, as Edwin did, that Schleisser would cut open the shark's belly to examine the contents of its stomach right there on the dock, as was the custom. To everyone's disappointment, however, Schleisser announced that he'd had second thoughts. The dissection should be done using the proper tools and under professional circumstances because of the likelihood of human remains.

He asked volunteers to roll the creature onto a tarpaulin—with gloves so they didn't touch the skin—and bring it to his truck. It took twelve men to carry the beast, six on either side. It barely fit in the back of Schleisser's truck.

Edwin followed wearily. "Shouldn't you wait until the Coast Guard is notified?"

"The dockmaster will take care of that," Schleisser replied. "Now that it's been weighed and measured, and there are photographs of it, there's no reason not to move it."

"Where are you taking it?"

"To my house in Harlem," he said. "You're coming with me, right?"

Edwin groaned. He just wanted to go home. More than anything, he longed for this day to be over.

There was another factor that made him reluctant, however. Going to Manhattan meant taking a ferry. He did not want to be on any kind of boat ever again.

"Please, Doc," said Schleisser. "I have everything we need in my basement. You know as well as I do that there will be human remains in its stomach. You're a doctor and a witness. I need your help. We have to do this right."

"Then I shall follow you there," Edwin said quietly.

Ferries made the trip from Perth Amboy to Manhattan frequently, Edwin was relieved to learn. Waiting, he knew, would increase his anxiety.

The moment he dreaded was when he'd have to drive onto the ferry, but it was not as daunting as he feared. The ramp was wide, and he simply followed the vehicle in front of him. Once the vessel pulled away from the dock, however, Edwin felt queasy. The ferry, although enormous, was still subject to the sway of currents and tides that impacted New York Harbor. Edwin stayed in his car.

On the New York side of the Hudson River, as they were about to exit onto the solid ground of Manhattan Island, Edwin saw that Schleisser's truck, freighted with the weight of the shark, was unable to clear a bump where the ramp met cobblestone. Two policemen walked over to talk to Schleisser.

Now what? Edwin fretted. *What if he has to unload the truck?*

But Schleisser jovially waved to the police, gunned the engine, and the truck lurched ahead.

Edwin felt much better once they were on solid ground. Now all he had to do was trail behind Schleisser on the drive up to Harlem, a journey that went quickly due to Schleisser's apparent knowledge of side streets and shortcuts for circumventing slow-moving traffic.

Schleisser's brownstone, at least from the outside, was surprisingly ordinary in appearance for such a decidedly unusual man. Edwin pulled to the curb and parked while Schleisser did a three-point turn, lining up the rear of the truck to the entrance to the basement.

"How are we going to get it inside?" asked Edwin, joining Schleisser on the street.

"Oh, that won't be a problem," replied Schleisser. Edwin went back to his automobile, leaning against it with his arms folded, and watched as Schleisser approached a group of young men loitering at the corner. He handed them money. They followed him to the truck, and Edwin overheard Schleisser explain that they were to haul the tarp—and its contents, which he didn't name— through the cellar doors and lift it onto an examining table.

When the young men finished the chore and departed, Schleisser called to Edwin, who approached gingerly. The steps into the basement were dank and uneven, and at the bottom, Edwin was greeted by the stuffed head of a snarling lion affixed to the wall. As he entered the expansive cellar, he was repulsed at the sight of a stuffed lynx which loomed over a massive dissecting table. On an adjacent table lay the hulking shape of the shark inside the tarp.

"Can you shut the cellar doors?" asked Schleisser. "Oh, never mind, they're tricky." He seemed to have fully recovered his energy on the trip to Harlem. With little effort, he pushed past Edwin, jauntily bounced up the steps, and slammed the metal doors, securing them with a latch.

Trapped in this subterranean space, Edwin felt light-headed and suggested they take a short break.

Schleisser agreed with some reluctance.

"Say, you don't look too good, Doc," he said, finally taking a good look at Edwin.

The stairs to the main level were narrow and steep. As he followed Schleisser, Edwin recalled the warning from the director of the American Museum of Natural History that Schleisser kept wolves and tigers—or was it bears?—wandering the grounds and even indoors.

"Wait here while I make sure the critters are out back," Schleisser announced, as if reading Edwin's mind.

Critters, thought Edwin. *My God, this man is peculiar.*

Schleisser rapped on the door at the top of the stairs, and someone, perhaps the housekeeper Edwin had spoken to on the telephone that morning, opened the door almost instantly. "Are the animals loose?" Schleisser asked, as if he were referring to a pair of spaniels.

To Edwin's relief, she shook her head, and the two men entered the kitchen.

"My friend here needs something very plain to eat and some water," said Schleisser, and the housekeeper agreed to prepare a light meal.

When she began setting the table, Edwin excused himself and used the facilities to wash up. The mirror over the sink in the bathroom revealed a face much changed from the ordeal. There were deep, dark circles under his eyes. He was deeply sunburnt, especially on his nose and cheeks. His lips were badly parched or perhaps he had bitten them. His hands were red and raw, and he noticed that the muscles in his left shoulder twitched.

After a meal of tea and toast, Edwin felt markedly stronger. He asked to use the telephone to make a quick call home, just to share his whereabouts, but no one answered.

"Would you like a stiff drink before we get started?" asked Schleisser.

"Why, no, I wouldn't," replied Edwin, finishing his tea. "I mean it's an outstanding idea, but I would instantly go to sleep for about ten hours if I were to drink alcohol right now. I'll wait till I get home, at which point I might say a toast to the demise of the shark and wonder why I seem to be cursed."

"It is strange that it happened to you twice, but I wouldn't say you're cursed," said Schleisser.

"But what are the chances I would be attacked by a shark a second time—especially since I'm such a landlubber?"

"Doc, all kinds of weird things happen. I met a man who was struck by lightning twice. The first time on the day he became engaged. The second time, on his honeymoon."

"My," said Edwin. "Talk about a bad omen."

"Probably just bad luck," said Schleisser.

"As a man of science, I don't want to believe in bad luck—or omens, for that matter."

"Aw, c'mon, Doc. Something somewhere is always going wrong for somebody."

"Why are we even talking about this?" asked Edwin.

"Because I hope you won't dwell too much on what happened today. Remember, it didn't just happen to you. It happened to me too. And it's all my fault, frankly. I was wrong, thinking the shark was far away by now. I shouldn't have convinced you to come along. Heck, I shouldn't have been out fishing at all. It's no wonder the shark came after us, dragging a net full of fish!"

Schleisser's words were unexpectedly calming. "Thank you for the apology," said Edwin. "Also, thank you for the perspective."

"You're welcome," said Schleisser. "Now let's get to work. The sooner we finish the job, the sooner you'll be home."

They returned to the basement where Schleisser's first task was to cut through the tarp with a pair of tin snips. As the shark was unveiled bit by bit, Edwin felt nauseous. Schleisser suggested that he take notes, and Edwin was happy for the diversion.

"I want to start by reconfirming the weight and length measurements," said Schleisser. "Here, you hold the end of the—"

"No, no," cried Edwin. "I will not touch it."

"Okay," said Schleisser.

"And don't remind me how big it is," added Edwin. "I'd rather forget."

He stepped back, leaned against the wall, and closed his eyes. He could hear the sounds of measuring devices and gritted his teeth, wishing that Schleisser would hurry up.

"All set, Doc, you can open your eyes now," said Schleisser. "I hate to say it, but I think I should start with the mouth."

Edwin felt bile rise in his stomach and into his lower esophagus.

Schleisser peered into the creature's mouth and began to count out loud. "Write this down, please," he told Edwin. "Three thousand."

"Three thousand what?"

"Teeth," replied Schleisser. "Want to take a look?"

Edwin wanted to punch Schleisser. Then he realized that, for the sake of science, he had to do a visual examination of the shark's mouth. "Cover its damn face," he snapped at Schleisser, who complied, tossing a rag across the strange eyes that looked no different in death than they did in life.

He approached the creature cautiously. *Calm yourself,* he thought. A memory of the first time he examined a cadaver in medical school—the fear and the strange, medicinal smell— flashed through his mind. *If I could get through that, I can get through this,* he thought.

While it was repulsive that the creature had died with its jaws wide open, this now proved an advantage to Edwin, for all he had to do was stand close enough to peer into its mouth. *I will do this for science,* he told himself. *I will do this for the victims.*

He peered into the shark's mouth, half expecting the creature to lunge forward. He forced himself to concentrate, scanning the upper teeth and then the lower. Only when he was certain did he speak. "The spacing and size of the teeth and jaw are consistent with the wounds on Vansant, Bruder, and Fisher," he said, moving away from the creature.

"Catch your breath, Doc," said Schleisser. "Stand over there. I don't mind."

Next, Schleisser cut into the abdomen. "It's a female," he announced.

"Oh," Edwin said. He had never even considered its gender.

"I know you don't want to be reminded of its size," Schleisser said slowly, "but did you have the impression, when we were in the boat, that it was bigger than the one that went after you when you were younger?"

"As a matter of fact, yes," said Edwin.

"Well, that would make sense," said Schleisser. "It would have been a pup back then. Now it's a matriarch."

"It's hard to think of it as a mother," Edwin mumbled under his breath.

"When I was in Australia, I knew a man who said they're lousy mothers, at least, this type of shark is," said Schleisser.

"And the pups are born killers. As a matter of fact, I was told the pups cannibalize each other in the womb," he added.

"That's disgusting," said Edwin.

"Survival of the fittest," Schleisser responded with a shrug. "I have to say, this is a particularly mean one."

Edwin let that sink in. "So you think some are more aggressive than others?"

"Sure," replied Schleisser. "Same with any wild animal. Same with people." As he was talking, he folded a bandanna, covered his mouth with the brightly colored cloth, and tied it behind his head. Then he made one for Edwin. "You'll want to put this over your nose and mouth," he said.

Schleisser cut again, this time into the stomach. An indescribable stench burst into the air, so strong it passed right through the facial mask and stung Edwin's lungs like an acid. Using a pair of tongs, Schleisser began removing material from the creature's gut. Much of it was partially digested and unrecognizable. The identifiable items were set aside. These included

- a red-tailed hawk, still with feathers;
- five sand sharks, whole;
- part of a leather trunk, including the hinges, clasp, and lock;
- a piece of wood, approximately two by three feet;
- a man's trench coat;
- a sailor's cap, British;
- a woman's boot; and
- miscellaneous bones, some with flesh attached.

Edwin was most interested in the last grouping, of course, and stepped back while Schleisser transported the bones to a separate examining table. The question was: Were these *human* bones?

Now it was Edwin's turn to dissect while Schleisser took over the note-taking. Edwin's hands ached, but his long years of surgical practice helped him complete the task. The material that included bones with attached flesh weighed a total of fifteen pounds, three ounces. In Edwin's opinion, they were clearly human. They included an eleven-inch tibia of a child—possibly from Lester Stilwell—and a large section of rib belonging to a young adult—Charles Bruder, perhaps.

There was no definitive proof, however. The human remains could have belonged to unknown victims. Another possibility was that the remains belonged to a person or persons already dead, perhaps by drowning, before being consumed by the shark.

Still, the fact remained that there were human remains in this particular shark's stomach. The creature fit the unusual description by multiple witnesses of the type and behavior of the shark. And lastly, it was caught within a few miles of Matawan, the site of the most recent attacks. Schleisser pointed out that thousands of sharks had been killed in the previous two weeks by hunters up and down the Jersey coast, but none of those creatures matched the description or behavior of the one they encountered.

Edwin and Schleisser concluded that it was probably *the* shark, although they argued a bit over the wording. Schleisser wanted to say "almost certainly" while Edwin felt that was an exaggeration. They settled on "likely."

As Schleisser began the process of removing the rest of the organs and stuffing the thing for posterity, Edwin asked if he was still needed.

"I will take it from here," said Schleisser. "Leave everything to me."

Edwin could not depart fast enough. He had seen what he needed to see.

Now it was time, at last, to go home.

JULY 16-17, 1916

CHAPTER 35

Where am I? Edwin wondered. His eyes were blurry. He was aware that he was lying on his side, facing a blank wall. After a while, he discerned that he was looking at white tile and green paint. *This is a hospital,* he thought. But it didn't seem like Monmouth Memorial, although at first, he couldn't figure out why.

What was different, he finally realized, were the sounds. *I'm on a high floor of a very large hospital,* he thought in astonishment. The first clue was the constant rumbling from truck and automobile traffic. The second was the strange echo of big-city sirens combined with an extraordinary amount of horn-honking. This was not Long Branch, even at its busiest.

A nurse came into his room and explained that he'd been found unconscious behind the wheel of his automobile, which had crashed into a light post. He was at Presbyterian Hospital in Manhattan and had been there overnight.

"My name is Alice Munroe," she announced cheerfully. "I'll be looking after you. Your daughter should be here soon."

"My daughter?" asked Edwin.

"Yes, your daughter," she said. "You do remember that you have a daughter, don't you?"

"Yes, yes," he replied. "I'm just surprised that you knew to reach her, that's all."

"We looked in your wallet," she explained. "We telephoned your address in New Jersey. You live at the shore! Lucky you!"

"Uh-huh," said Edwin.

"I may move down there, to Ocean Grove," said Alice. "My sister lives there, and she wants me to move in with her."

"That's nice," Edwin mumbled.

"Anyway, we reached your daughter on the telephone and explained your condition. She sounded awfully worried."

Oh no, thought Edwin.

He wondered if he'd suffered damage to his heart. "What is my diagnosis?"

"The doctor isn't sure yet," said Alice. She looked at his chart. "You were dehydrated when you came in—severely dehydrated and suffering from exhaustion."

"Where is my automobile?" he asked.

"It was towed by the city. I'll find out where. Apparently, it needs some repairs."

She insisted on helping him sit up, and then she poured a glass of water from a pitcher. "I'm not leaving until you drink every drop of that," she said playfully but firmly. He did as he was told. The nurse then announced that he would be served a meal of soft-boiled eggs, dry toast, and applesauce within the next hour and that he would eat it "whether you like it or not."

The doctor came by and informed Edwin, whom he addressed as a colleague, that it was very likely an issue with his heart. "What had you been doing yesterday prior to blacking out while driving your car?"

Do I dare tell him? Edwin thought. *He might send me to the psychiatric ward.*

In the greatest understatement of his life, Edwin said, "I went fishing yesterday morning."

"Well, no more fishing or anything else for the next three weeks," the doctor said. "Complete bed rest. You must allow the heart muscle to recover. You know this as well as I do."

For the first time in Edwin's life, the concept of complete bed rest, which he often prescribed to his own patients, held a certain appeal. He slipped into a deep, healing sleep and was awakened by a stirring in the room and the nurse, Alice, saying to someone, "He'll be so glad you're here."

He opened his eyes to find Julia staring at him with wide eyes. "I'm with you now, Father!" she cried, squeezing his hand.

Ah, my child is here! he thought, and the relief in his heart and soul almost brought tears to his eyes.

He longed to stay awake now that she was present, but the need for more sleep was too strong. When he awoke again, he felt noticeably better. Julia was still there, in a chair pulled up next to his bed. Mortimer stood near the door, slouching against a wall, but Edwin was too tired even to be annoyed.

Julia followed her father's gaze and said that Mortimer had brought her straight here to New York City when she got the news.

"You look a little better than you did two hours ago," Julia said, and Edwin could hear the joy in her voice.

"I feel all right now," Edwin murmured. "I had a very difficult day yesterday."

Julia hesitated. "Father, we know all about it. It's in all the newspapers."

"Oh?" Then he remembered the scene at the dock and how he had reluctantly agreed to be in a photograph.

"Father, you were very nearly killed!" she cried. "What were you thinking, going out on Raritan Bay in such a small boat! How do you even know this man Schleisser? It said in the papers he's a big-game hunter and taxidermist! Were you deliberately hunting the shark?"

"Actually, no, not at all," replied Edwin. "I desperately needed to discuss something with him, and he was just going out to get a few fish to pan fry and said the only way I could talk to him was to come along. I had absolutely no idea that any of this was going to happen, and neither did he. Why, he thought the shark was off Long Island by then, or maybe even the coast of Massachusetts."

Mortimer took a step toward him. "Are you up to seeing the newspapers?" he asked. "You're quite a hero."

"Schleisser is the hero," replied Edwin. "He killed the shark."

"Yes, but you sure did your part. And you brought along the weapon—a broken oar, it says here in the *Post*."

"What else did he say?"

"He said the shark attacked more ferociously than any grizzly bear or African lion he'd ever encountered," replied Mortimer.

This was too much detail and brought the whole scene back into Edwin's mind. He told Julia and Mortimer that he needed to rest again. Julia said they'd return the next morning when he was expected to be discharged. As they prepared to leave, he noticed she'd been crying. She kissed his cheek, which she had not done since she was a little girl.

Suddenly, something popped into Edwin's mind. He had not yet told Dr. Brewster that he'd shown the photographs of the mysterious scrapes on Rusty Conover's abdomen to Schleisser and that the big-game hunter had said there was no cause for alarm. Both Rusty and the boy named Lenny, who had similar scrapes, needed to be informed.

"Julia," Edwin said, trying to collect his thoughts, "would you do something for me?"

"Anything, Father."

"I need to get a message to Dr. Brewster in Matawan. Please tell him that I believe Rusty and Lenny will be just fine."

She wrote the names down. "You can count on me, Father."

As they left, Edwin noticed a man in uniform stationed outside his door. When Alice, the nurse, came in, he asked her about it, and she said one policeman stood guard at the elevator and another at the door to his room to keep the newsmen away. Everyone, she explained, wanted to interview him and take his photograph.

"Oh," said Edwin. "I hadn't thought of that."

"We didn't recognize you when you were brought in," she added. "You're a hero, Dr. Halsey!"

Edwin groaned. "I really just want to go home."

"Can't say I blame you," she said soothingly.

Edwin slept well but woke up grumpy. He was very hungry and wanted a bath. He knew these were signs that meant he was close to being ready to go home.

Julia and Mortimer arrived and had tea in his room. Mortimer brought copies of three New York City newspapers. It seemed that Schleisser had taken the newly stuffed shark to the *Home News*, a newspaper owned by a friend in the Bronx, and the ghastly thing was displayed on a row of wooden supports behind a huge plate-glass window. Within hours, thirty thousand people had come to see it. Meanwhile, Schleisser got permission from the coroner's office to send the unidentifiable human remains to the American Museum of Natural History.

As Edwin was preparing to depart the hospital, a telegram arrived from President Wilson, stirring up even more excitement among the staff on Edwin's floor. *Congratulations on your extraordinary accomplishment*, it read. Edwin shook his head. He didn't feel like he'd accomplished anything except surviving.

Julia and Mortimer insisted that Edwin be pushed in a wheelchair, which he didn't like, but he was hardly in a position to argue. Newspapermen clogged the lobby and peppered Edwin with questions. He managed to say a few words, mainly condolences to the families of Charles Vansant, Charles Bruder, Stanley Fisher, and Lester Stilwell. He tried, also, to steer all of the credit for killing the shark to Schleisser.

He hoped, more than anything, that in time his role would be forgotten.

JULY 20, 1916

CHAPTER 36

How is a person supposed to convalesce when that detestable telephone is ringing all the time? wondered Edwin. He tried shutting the bedroom door, but the sound traveled up the stairs from the main hallway.

At least Hannah had succeeded in discouraging the reporters who showed up in person. She had covered the brass door knocker with a sign that stated No Visitors! Only one person, a news photographer from Philadelphia, had dared to knock on the door anyway, and he'd retreated quickly when faced with Hannah's wrath.

Both Julia and Hannah were handling the situation with great efficiency; nevertheless, it was disturbing, and they, too, were getting tired. "If this keeps up, we'll have to go somewhere else for you to recuperate," said Julia.

But in a surprising turn of events, there was no need for Edwin to recover elsewhere. Schleisser and Edwin's heroic deed became yesterday's news. Reporters were interested in finding new angles to keep the story going.

While many people were satisfied that the shark killed by Schleisser and Edwin was the man-eater, some refused to believe it. For tabloid newspaper owners, the story was pure gold, and attention-seeking hunters still held out hope that *they* would kill the monster.

Not to be outdone, the federal government belatedly responded to the shark problem, which made news. Two days after Edwin and Schleisser had dispatched the likely culprit, the *Washington Post* reported that Congress agreed to spend an additional five thousand dollars to aid in the campaign. The *Post* carried the following front-page headlines, which, to Edwin's dismay, were about two weeks too late:

U.S. WAR ON SHARKS
WILSON AND CABINET
TO MAKE PLANS
TO PREVENT MORE TRAGEDIES
COAST GUARDS TURN HUNTERS
FEDERAL CUTTERS ALSO ARE
ORDERED TO FISH FOR THE
MONSTERS

Realistically, Edwin recognized the possibility that he and Schleisser had not killed the "right" shark or that perhaps there were two or even three. True, their shark had human remains in its stomach, but there was no proof that those remains belonged to any of the recent Jersey Shore victims.

It was so comforting to indulge in the thought that *it* was dead, however. And that perhaps this was the very same shark that had nearly killed him back in 1880. That way, Edwin could put the whole thing to rest—provided he could get the image of the monster out of his mind. But there were no certainties to be found.

And it was impossible to avoid the subject. Although Julia advised against it, Edwin insisted on continuing his habit of reading newspapers, which continued to include breathless coverage of the shark attacks, even though very little new or pertinent information had been reported in days.

The impact of the fatal attacks at the Jersey Shore was enormous and far-reaching, which surprised Edwin. From newspaper coverage, it was clear that Americans had developed, almost overnight, a fascination with sharks, a species long ignored and largely considered harmless, now widely seen as a dire threat. Most unforgivable was the awareness that a man-eating sea creature could ruin a perfectly innocent pastime: a dip in the ocean or a tidal creek beneath a bright blue sky.

Most intriguing to Edwin was the sudden appearance of sharks in editorial cartoons as metaphors for evil. The first one Edwin saw was a drawing of a shark labeled *Deutschland.* In another, a shark shaped like a U-boat attacked Uncle Sam, sending him flying out of the water. But the editorial cartoons were not limited to commentary and fears about war with Germany. One drawing depicted a handful of sharks each labeled *lawyer.* Multiple sharks dubbed whiskey, late hours, gambling, and other vices fell under a headline, "Some Sharks Everyone Should Dodge." Another poked fun at women's bathing costumes, implying that they were so tacky they could scare off sharks.

Julia was right, he decided. So he tried to read medical journals instead of newspapers. Unfortunately, this increased his restlessness and led him to become obsessed with getting back to work.

Even with the beast dead, Edwin could not find peace.

Julia discussed her concerns about Edwin's mood with the Reverend Winterberry from St. Ann's Episcopal Church, where Edwin had been a member his entire life. The reverend agreed to stop by, though he warned Julia that Edwin might not let down his guard, even with him.

"My experience with your father is that he is a very private man," the reverend told her. "He may not confide in me at all, but I shall do my best to help him."

But Edwin was more than ready to talk. He welcomed the reverend and immediately shared his concerns.

"I want to go back to work," said Edwin, "but I'm told by everyone to wait until I'm stronger. Meanwhile, I can't help but wonder what is happening with my patients. Are they well? Are they responding to treatment? And then I think, what if they like Dr. Parker better and don't want to return to me? And what if I don't improve? What if I am never able to practice medicine again? Or perform surgery?"

The reverend nodded sympathetically. "This is understandable," he replied. "You are going through a very challenging time in your life."

"But what if . . ." Edwin's voice trailed off. Then he began again. "It's just that I don't want to be *replaced*."

"Replaced?"

"What if I can't go back because I've lost my position? What if some devious, opportunistic young surgeon—of which there are several!—uses this time to engineer my ouster?"

Reverend Winterberry listened patiently. "Worrying is a waste of the gifts God has given you," he said gently. He reminded Edwin of the scripture which, paraphrased, means there is a time for everything.

"Edwin," he added, "this is your time for healing. All these years, you have been the healer. Now it is your turn."

A time for healing. The words calmed him. Edwin repeated these words each time he felt a new wave of anxiety.

Little by little, he grew physically and mentally stronger. Sometimes he was able to get ahead of these concerns for himself, but in the evening hours, melancholia descended upon him if he couldn't sleep. That was when he would imagine the despair of the victims' families. And he had left one thing undone in Matawan, which began to nag at him. He hadn't told the woman named Margaret that Stanley had spoken his last words and asked Edwin to deliver those words to her.

Finally, he broached the topic with Julia.

"I'm not sure what to do," said Edwin. "I'm only guessing who Margaret is. Suppose Stanley Fisher had a sister named Margaret. I can't just write a letter or telephone Margaret Atkins unless I'm sure."

"We could ask Dr. Brewster," said Julia. "I could call him and ask."

"Oh, good idea!" Edwin said with relief. "You might also tell him why I need to reach her and ask how he would suggest I handle it. I suppose I should write a letter. I don't want to tell her on the telephone."

"I will call Dr. Brewster right away and ask his advice," she said.

"Thank you, Julia. You will be doing me a great favor," said Edwin. "You are becoming an excellent nurse. You are helping the patient enormously, in every possible way."

"What patient?" asked Julia, brows drawing together.

Edwin smiled. "Me."

AUGUST 1916

CHAPTER 37

Margaret was waiting in the parlor a full hour before her guests were to arrive. Weeks had passed since Stanley's death. Each long day was the same. She grieved. She struggled to accept it. She cried, pulled herself together, then cried again. When she awoke in the morning, she did not want to face the day. When night came, she was afraid to fall asleep, fearing her dreams.

She did not care what was going on in the world. Nothing fazed her. Even one night in late July, when a strange percussive sound rocked the town, followed by a series of shock waves, Margaret barely reacted. While her parents and what seemed like half the town fled into the street in their nightclothes in terror, Margaret stayed behind, hardly showing any concern or interest.

At breakfast the following morning, her father told her the news: a huge munitions depot in Jersey City, at Black Tom Island, had exploded. Rumors swirled that it was an act of sabotage by German spies.

Normally, Margaret would have been horrified by the deaths and destruction from an explosion that was heard and felt as far away as Philadelphia. She would have worried that it was an act of aggression against the US—one more reason that America would get dragged into the war in Europe and that Stanley would have to go.

But Stanley was no longer here, and the many hours she had spent fretting that the war would take him away from her now seemed sadly ironic in retrospect. He was gone, and it had nothing to do with him serving in any war. It had happened under freakish circumstances in their town's creek.

Sometimes she dreamed of the creek and, at other times, of Stanley when life was normal and they were happy and their future was bright and limitless. Both types of dreams were devastating.

She saw only a few visitors, always the same people, but she had received a request that she couldn't turn down. The doctor who had been with Stanley when he died was coming to visit, along with his daughter, a nursing student. Margaret had surprised her father by agreeing to take the call when the doctor's daughter telephoned.

"My father has been ill," Julia Halsey had explained. "He was recently hospitalized and I am working as his assistant. He was with Stanley when he died, and he wants to share Stanley's last words and assure you that his death was quite peaceful."

Margaret was stunned. "How did you know to reach me?"

"I called Dr. Brewster, and he suggested that Father and I come to see you—if you agree, of course. Dr. Brewster thinks these things should be done in person for the benefit of the bereaved."

"What about Stanley's parents?" asked Margaret. "Will you be seeing them too? It seems to me that you should see them first."

"They have declined our visit," said Julia. "They wish to be left alone. But we wanted to give you the option. Father feels strongly about it. He could write you a letter if you prefer."

"No, no," Margaret said quickly. "I would like to meet your father, since he was the last person to be with Stanley. And you too, of course. I'm sure, since his hospitalization, that he appreciates having you as his assistant. I'm aware of who your father is. I have seen his name in the papers. But I did not know he was the surgeon who tried to help Stanley at Monmouth Memorial. No one told me."

"He is the chief of surgery at the hospital."

"I have just one request," Margaret added. "I'm aware that your father was involved in killing the shark, and for that we are all grateful, I'm sure, but I don't want to hear about it. On your visit, I mean."

"Oh, of course," said Julia. "He doesn't want to talk about it either."

"When would you like to come?" asked Margaret.

"Father finished his three weeks of bed rest and is finally able to leave the house. We can come whenever you're ready."

They agreed on the following afternoon. Miss Halsey and her father would arrive at Matawan station and walk to the house. Margaret looked at the mantel clock; they would arrive shortly.

Now that the time had come, Margaret was so agitated that she chewed her nails—a habit she thought she had ended when she turned twelve. She hadn't even attempted to join her parents for lunch, which upset them greatly. She sat in the parlor, her foot tapping nervously.

Her father appeared in the doorway. "Margaret, are you sure this is a good idea?" he asked for the fifth or sixth time.

"How can I not hear what he has to say?" she replied. "I would always wonder. At the least, I should thank him for trying to save Stanley."

"Margaret, are you sure you want to be alone with Dr. Halsey and his daughter?" asked her mother, suddenly appearing at her father's side. "Or do you want us to stay with you? We could do that if you prefer."

Margaret almost smiled. *They are getting so good about asking my opinion.* "Thank you," she replied, "but I think I will be just fine on my own."

"We don't even know this man, Dr. Halsey," her father grumbled.

"Dr. Brewster knows him," said Margaret.

"I just hope he doesn't say anything that will upset you," said her father.

"I know it might be upsetting, but I have to do this."

"I understand," he said reluctantly. "We were going to wait in the kitchen, but perhaps your mother and I should go for a little drive."

Margaret was relieved when she closed the door behind them. She had prepared some refreshments—iced tea and a small plate of Mother's favorite gingersnaps—and kept relocating the tray until she decided on the perfect place.

She paced back and forth. This did nothing to steady her nerves, however, so she perused her mother's new copy of *Ladies' Home Journal*, a calming diversion until she flipped through the pages and came across a photo montage entitled, "Beautiful Bridal Trends for Fall 1916."

She tossed the magazine aside. She would never be a bride. She stared at the engagement ring Stanley had given her days before he died. Telling her parents and Stanley's that he had asked her to marry him was hard, but it had felt necessary. It was a part of his story. And she wanted to wear the ring as a memento and to feel close to him.

Someone tapped gently on the front door. Margaret jumped,

then told herself to take a deep breath. She smoothed her hair and checked the buttons on her shirtwaist.

Now or never, she thought.

She opened the door. A man in his late forties, well-dressed, with a mustache and beard, stood on the front step with a young woman with whom he shared the exact shade of chestnut hair. While he appeared a bit old-fashioned, the young woman gave the opposite impression with her stylish sailor-collar dress and a daring shoulder-length bob.

"Hello," said Margaret, attempting what she hoped was a reasonably friendly smile. "Please come in, Dr. Halsey and Miss Halsey."

Dr. Halsey took off his hat and made a small bow while Julia Halsey cried out, "Oh, Miss Atkins, thank you for seeing us!" She was as irrepressible, it seemed, as her father was solemn. The young woman's obvious empathy put Margaret at ease.

"Oh, it is I who should be thanking you for coming," said Margaret, swinging the door open wide. She ushered them into the parlor and indicated where they should sit, then perched across from them.

"This is Father's first time leaving the house since his hospitalization," said Julia while Edwin slowly made his way to a chair. "He's a little tired after the walk from the train station."

"Oh, I should have arranged for you to be picked up," cried Margaret. "I'm so sorry."

"No, no, it's quite all right," replied Edwin. "The walk was good for me. Nothing to concern yourself with, I assure you."

"It's hard for Father to be a patient," Julia said to Margaret with a conspiratorial smile. "He especially doesn't like to take orders from me."

Margaret poured the iced tea. "I'm so anxious to hear what you have to say, Dr. Halsey, but I'm also quite nervous," she admitted. She folded her hands tightly in her lap, her blue eyes wide with fear and expectation.

"Quite understandable. How would you like to proceed?" asked Dr. Halsey. His voice was kindly.

"Well, I suppose we should just get to the subject at hand," replied Margaret. "I know you want to share Stanley's last words. Before you called, it hadn't even occurred to me that he had any last words. It's going to be very difficult for me to hear them, but as I have learned in the last month, I'm stronger than I knew. So I prefer to face it, even if it hurts."

Edwin nodded. He began by explaining how he had been at home in Red Bank when he got the call to go directly to the hospital in Long Branch and that a patient was arriving by train.

"I did everything I could," said Edwin. "I was ready to perform surgery the instant they brought him in. I'm afraid it was already too late by the time Stanley arrived at the hospital. Still, I tried my best, as did the nurses assisting me. Stanley didn't respond to stimulants or saline transfusions."

"Am I correct to assume he was in terrible pain?" Margaret asked, wincing.

"On the contrary, he did not seem to be in pain at all," said Edwin. "This sometimes happens. If he had been in pain, I would have given him something, but he showed no sign. He said a few things about having done his duty. That is the word he used, *duty*. Now that I know the full story, I think he meant that he had tried to rescue the child. He said, 'I found him, I had ahold of him, I did my duty.' Frankly, I was surprised he was able to talk at all. He made one last effort to speak to me. He reached out his hand, and I took it. At this point, he was able only to whisper, so I leaned down to hear what he wanted to say. He spoke slowly and very clearly, 'Tell Margaret I'm sorry. Have a good life without me.' And then he simply passed away. There was no time to get a chaplain."

Margaret held back her sobs until Edwin finished. "He said my name!" she wailed.

"And he wished you a good life," added Julia, who hopped up from her place next to Edwin and moved next to Margaret, consoling her.

"Dr. Halsey," said Margaret, her voice now hushed and hoarse. "I am so glad you were with him. I'm so glad you held his hand. Thank you, with all my heart."

"I'm glad it's helpful," he said. "Here, let me pour you some more iced tea—for both of you."

"You should have some more too, Father," Julia urged.

Margaret mumbled, "I promised myself I wouldn't cry, please forgive me."

"Don't be silly!" protested Julia, tears in her own eyes. "Now here, drink this. Take your time."

"There's a lot conveyed in those few words," Edwin noted.

Margaret nodded slowly. "I think he knew he was going to die and he was sorry that he was leaving me behind."

"His last thoughts were of you," Julia said gently.

"I ought to let Stanley's parents know that he was at peace," said Edwin, "but they're too upset to talk to me."

"Oh, they aren't doing well at all," said Margaret. "Their daughter—Stanley's sister—went back to Minnesota to be with her husband. Mr. Fisher sits outside all day, smoking his pipe. And Stanley's mother hardly gets out of bed. I visit them almost every day. I'm about the only person they'll see. Well, except for their neighbors, who are still bringing meals." Margaret paused. "I suppose I could tell them that you came to see me and that we talked and that I feel much better. And if they ask for details, I could tell them. Would that be all right?"

"Yes, that will do nicely," said Edwin.

"The first time I went over there after Stanley died, it took all my courage," added Margaret.

"I can imagine," Edwin said, nodding.

"I've never had to be brave before. I didn't know I had it in me. Have you ever been through such a loss?" she asked. "Oh, forgive me, I shouldn't ask such an intrusive question!"

"It's quite all right, please don't concern yourself," said Edwin.

"We had a terrible tragedy in our family," Julia began, then stopped. She looked at her father.

"My wife died," Edwin explained, "along with all of my children, except for dear Julia here. Thank God I did not lose her too."

"I wasn't even two," added Julia. "This was eighteen years ago, in 1898. Typhoid fever."

Margaret sighed. "Oh, I'm so sorry," she said, barely audible. "I lost twin brothers to the measles when they were quite small, and it's been very difficult—for my mother, especially," she added. "May I ask you another question, Dr. Halsey?"

"Certainly," he said.

"How have you lived with it, year after year?"

He thought for a moment. "I didn't live with it year after year," he replied. "I lived with it one day at a time for many years. There's a difference."

"I see," said Margaret. "So I shouldn't think far ahead. Just day to day. Well, I'm trying to keep myself occupied. At first, I wasn't accepting any visitors except Dr. Brewster and our minister, Reverend Rutledge. This week, I've started pushing myself a little. I realized that Stanley and I were so completely focused on each other that I had neglected opportunities to make good friends. I'm having lunch with a friend next Tuesday. That will be my first time out in public except for church."

"I hope, for everyone's sake, that the reporters and photographers have moved on," said Edwin.

"Thankfully, yes, it seems so."

"This poor little town," said Edwin. "You all have been through a trauma. I imagine people will still be talking about this a hundred years from now."

"Everyone is shocked that anything so terrible could happen here," said Margaret. "There's this sense that we must have done something wrong, but we can't figure out what that is. Reverend Rutledge and I were talking about this. He said the townspeople are asking, 'What did we do to deserve this? Why us?'"

"I suppose it's human nature to try to make sense of things," said Julia.

"I have to say, I have some regrets," said Margaret. "We were all so busy worrying about the epidemic, fussing about the war—and complaining about the heat! We let our guard down! It seems so naive that we didn't think it could happen here. The creek is tidal! What were we thinking?"

"Oh, Miss Atkins," said Edwin, "the chances of it happening here were so very, very slim."

"But we had warnings! It was in all the newspapers that the shark was out there somewhere. Captain Cottrell tried to warn us. And Lenny did too! Do you know about them, Dr. Halsey?"

"Yes," said Edwin.

"Why didn't we believe them?" cried Margaret. "Why didn't we listen?"

"Because the boy had a history of pulling pranks or exaggerating, and the old man was a retired sea captain and everyone knows how they can spin a yarn," replied Edwin.

The conversation lagged for a moment, and Margaret worried that perhaps she had shared too much and was keeping them too long. This was, perhaps, more than they had bargained for. "You are so kind to have come today," she said, "but Dr. Halsey, you must be exhausted. I'm so honored that this was your first excursion since taking ill."

"We probably should be getting back," Julia agreed. "Father usually rests this time of day."

"Goodness, Julia, you make me sound like a complete invalid," muttered Edwin.

"Just for now, Father," Julia said soothingly. "While you're getting stronger."

"Well, let us end on a cheerful note," said Margaret. "I received a letter that I found absolutely charming and I think you would too. It's from the boy who was badly injured but survived. Joey Dunn is his name."

"I don't know a thing about him, but I am most curious!" said Edwin.

Margaret retrieved the letter from a small rolltop writing desk in the corner of the room. "Listen to this," she said, returning to her seat and reading the letter aloud.

Dear Miss Atkins,
    My name is Joseph Dunn.
My friends call me Joey. You
can call me that if you want.
I'm very sorry about Mr.
Fisher. You must miss him a
lot. I'm from the Bronx. I was
going to see my aunt when I

got bit. Now I'm stuck in the
hospital. The food is good.
Everyone is nice. I don't
know when I can go home. I
hope soon. If you would like
to visit me, that would be all
right. If you do come, just so
you know, I like Oreo Biscuits.

Margaret laughed. "Isn't that the most adorable thing?" she asked. "It's quite good overall for a nine-year-old."

"What a delightful little boy!" cried Julia. "Are you going to visit him?"

"Well, I hadn't really thought about it," said Margaret.

"Well, if you go, don't forget the Oreos!" Julia teased. "He sounds like quite a rascal. You know, it was in the newspapers that the first thing he said to the doctor was, 'Don't tell my mother! She'll be very upset!' And when someone asked his home address, he said, 'Oh, no. I'm not telling you that. You'll only go find my mother and tell her what has happened.' Isn't that funny?"

"I'm so glad you told me that, because it makes me like him even more," said Margaret. "I have avoided reading the newspapers. At first, when he wrote to me, I had no idea who he was until I showed the letter to Father, who recognized the name. And of course, the return address is Saint Peter's Children's Hospital in New Brunswick. Someone must have written that on there for him because it's in a nice, grown-up hand."

"I have wondered about that child," Edwin murmured thoughtfully. "And I have meant to find out how he's doing. Perhaps I should call the surgeon."

"Maybe you could do more than that, Father," said Julia. "We could go visit. We could meet the child, and maybe you could talk to his surgeon."

"Oh," said Edwin, sitting up straighter. "That does sound intriguing."

"Would you call me afterward and tell me what you find out?" Margaret asked Julia. "I would like to know how the little boy is."

"Why don't you meet us in New Brunswick?" asked Julia.

"Julia, you are getting ahead of yourself," warned Edwin. "We don't even know if we're going yet. There is protocol with these matters."

"All right, Father," said Julia, rolling her eyes. Then, to Margaret, "If I can arrange for Father and me to visit the boy, would you consider going with us or joining us there?"

"I'd like to think about it," said Margaret. "I haven't been out of town since all this happened."

"Of course," said Edwin. "We shall look into it and find out what is feasible. And then we will telephone you."

After they left, Margaret knew what she must do. She wrote in her diary, starting with Dr. Halsey's account of Stanley's final moments. Over and over, until she could stand it no longer, she read the passage in which she had preserved Stanley's last words. Then she lay down on Mother's divan, awaiting her parents' return, exhausted and expecting to sleep. Yet she could not. Her mind was too alert, and to her surprise, her thoughts soon made what seemed an extravagant leap, which in turn opened a tiny portal of hope. Instead of ruminating about the loss of Stanley, her attention shifted to the funny little boy who had survived.

CHAPTER 38

They met in the lobby of the hospital, in a waiting area designated for visitors, with long wooden benches that reminded Margaret of the seating at a railroad station.

She and her mother arrived first, positioning themselves so they could see everyone who entered through the revolving doors. They didn't have long to wait for Dr. Halsey and his daughter, Julia, who was sporting a silk blouse paired with a fashionable white skirt with big black dots.

Dr. Halsey followed, looking a bit peaked. Always the gentleman, he held out his arm for his daughter to take once he caught up with her.

Julia spotted Margaret and her mother and waved like they were long-lost friends who had found each other after a lifetime apart. Julia made Margaret smile. Perhaps this was what it would have been like to have a little sister.

Thank goodness for Julia, Margaret thought. She found Dr. Halsey a little intimidating, although it was clear that he had a warm heart under the professional veneer. He'd been so kind to her.

Margaret shook hands with Dr. Halsey and was hugged by the exuberant Julia. "This is my mother, Mrs. Atkins," said Margaret. "Mother, this is Dr. Halsey and Miss Julia Halsey."

"Oh, I'm supposed to tell them that we're all here," cried Julia after the introductions were finished. She darted off to the reception desk and returned in a flash. "Dr. D'Milano will be coming to get us and take us upstairs," she said breathlessly.

The ladies perched on the edge of the bench while Edwin remained on his feet.

"Oh, Father, do sit down," Julia urged, patting the seat next to her.

"I prefer to stand," he replied.

Julia leaned forward toward Margaret's mother and said lightly, "Father can be a little stubborn. He doesn't like to do what I ask."

Margaret's mother smiled. "I understand completely," she said.

A handsome, dark-haired man wearing a crisp doctor's coat suddenly appeared at Edwin's elbow. "Would you be Dr. Edwin Halsey from Monmouth Memorial Hospital?" he asked. When Edwin answered in the affirmative, the man replied, "I am Dr. Vincent D'Milano, and I am at your service. I am honored to meet you. I have read about you in the newspapers."

Another round of introductions followed, and Dr. D'Milano, who was, in Margaret's estimation, in his early thirties, led them toward the elevator.

"Fifth floor, please," Dr. D'Milano instructed the operator.

Julia either lost her balance—or pretended to—and ended up on the arm of the handsome young doctor. For the first time in weeks, Margaret had the urge to grin.

As the elevator rose, so did Margaret's curiosity. A week had passed since the Halseys had visited her. Still circling through her mind like a pinwheel were the last words spoken by Stanley.

The only thing that dislodged them, even for a moment, were the plans to meet Joey Dunn, the boy who had faced the same danger as Stanley but had somehow survived.

Margaret had always been a "born teacher." She simply liked children and found them endlessly intriguing. While some adults were worn down by being in proximity to children, Margaret bloomed.

At first, Margaret's mother had balked at the idea of her visiting little Joey Dunn, insisting that it would stir up awful memories of the shark. "Margaret, you're not thinking straight," she had said. "When you see this boy in a hospital bed, with his leg all bandaged up, I fear it will be too much for you."

"It is but one meeting, one little visit," Margaret had replied. "I am going, and that's that. I would like it very much if you came with me."

The elevator operator released the outer door with the push of a button. As they waited for him to manually open the inner, accordion-like metal gate, Margaret's throat tightened.

"Follow me, I would like to speak to you all before we meet the boy, the most fabulous patient I have ever had the privilege of treating," said Dr. D'Milano.

In an alcove with a large window overlooking New Brunswick, he informed them of the status of his patient. "Master Joey is doing remarkably well. He is a delight! We all love him. But you must be aware, we still do not know if we can save the leg. We are doing everything possible, but it is a grievous wound."

"I don't understand how he survived the blood loss," said Edwin.

"Ah, he did have blood loss," said Dr. D'Milano. "But despite all the damage, the disgusting creature did not rupture any major arteries in the leg."

"Remarkable," said Edwin. "Is he in a lot of pain?"

"At first, no," replied Dr. D'Milano. "Then, for about two weeks, he had a good deal of pain, and we had to medicate him when we cleaned the wound and changed the bandages. In the weeks since then, it seems to be tolerable. He has not complained, and we give him plenty of opportunity to do so. His attitude in general is excellent, and he is a joy."

"Extraordinary," said Edwin.

"Does he know we are coming to see him?" asked Margaret.

"Yes, absolutely, and he is looking forward to it. He knows who all of you are. He has read the newspapers."

"We were most surprised to hear from him," said Margaret's mother.

"Yes, this has been one of his little projects. One of the nurses assists him because she believes it is good for his morale. He writes the letters, and she mails them."

"Does he get many visitors?" asked Julia. Margaret noted she had finally let go of the young doctor's arm.

"It is difficult for his family to visit because they live in the Bronx. His mother comes every Sunday afternoon. She is a widow who works in a laundry. There are seven children in all. It amazes me that she can get here once a week, frankly. His older brother—the one who saved him—comes with the mother. There is an aunt who lives in Cliffwood Beach, but she works long hours. We have had him on the ward with the other children, and he loves that. However, two days ago, we moved him to a private room because we are worried about infection. He has done so well, but he is at a pivotal point. So we are keeping him away from the other children right now. It's hard on him because he has a long way to go. He was a big celebrity when he first arrived. That has all stopped."

"Oh, the poor little thing," said Margaret. "I have gifts for him. Is that all right?"

"I shall look the other way," Dr. D'Milano said grandly. "All right now, he is just down the other end of the hall."

They followed and soon arrived at a closed door with a hand-made poster with the words *Joey's Room* in sprawling, colorful lettering. Underneath, there was a child's illustration of a shark.

Margaret shrank back for a second. The others noticed the drawing too.

"Oh, that is just Joey," Dr. D'Milano said. "He has accepted what happened to him. Sometimes he even brags about it. He is a child, you must remember."

Margaret's mother shot her a warning look.

Perhaps she's right, Margaret thought, panicking. *Maybe this is a mistake.*

Dr. D'Milano rapped his knuckles lightly on the door, and a child's voice with a distinct New York accent responded, "Yeah! Come on in!"

He was lying flat, except for one leg that was elevated, but pulled himself up on his elbows as they entered the room.

"Hello, hello, hello!" he sang out cheerfully. He looked from one face to the next, smiling eagerly, missing nothing, a pair of startling blue eyes surrounded by improbably thick eyelashes, taking it all in. His skin was alabaster—perhaps a sign of fragile health or from being indoors for weeks at a time. His hair was deep brown with a wave near the front. He was in need of a good barber.

"I have four visitors—all at the same time!?" he exclaimed, adding, "THIS IS THE BEST DAY OF MY LIFE!"

The adults chuckled. Dr. D'Milano made the introductions, and Margaret was struck by the boy's focus and intensity as he insisted on leaning forward and shaking everyone's hand. He was not shy in the slightest.

"Joey, I have a telephone call I must make," Dr. D'Milano

said. To the others, he added, "I shall leave you to enjoy my favorite patient."

"Aw, I bet you say that to all your patients," Joey joked.

Dr. D'Milano laughed and shook his head. "Now, I will be back shortly to make sure you don't wear yourself out. I know how you love company, Master Joey."

There were two chairs by the bed already, one on each side. Edwin spotted two by the window and collected them.

"I would help you with the chairs, but I'm stuck here on account of my leg," said Joey apologetically, as if that weren't apparent.

"That's quite all right," remarked Edwin, the last to sit down. "Now tell us how you are feeling."

"Pretty good for a kid who got bit twice by a mean old shark!" replied Joey.

"Twice?" asked Edwin.

"Well, the first time, it grabbed me from my foot all the way up to my knee. And then the second time, it tried to take more of me—all the way up here," he said, touching his thigh. "I thought it was going to swallow me whole!"

Margaret's mother reached over and squeezed Margaret's hand, and Joey noticed.

"Oh, I'm sorry, Miss Atkins! I shouldn't of said that!"

"You shouldn't *have* said that," Margaret correctly him gently. "I don't know if you realized this, Joey, but I'm a school-teacher."

"Oh, I know all about you," said Joey. "Well, a little. You were in a story in the *Daily News*."

"I was?" asked Margaret. She looked at her mother.

"Yes, you were in one of the stories in the *Daily News*," her mother replied. "We never told you. You didn't want to see any of the papers."

"I've been in all the papers!" cried Joey. "It's the most exciting thing that's ever happened to me." Then he added, "Oh, but I
forgot. I'm really sorry, Miss Atkins, about your friend, Mr. . . ."

"Mr. Fisher," she said. "Stanley."

Then Joey turned to Edwin. "I want to thank you, Dr.
Halsey, for killing the monster. I'm glad someone did! I'm sorry
it was awfully close, from what I read in the papers."

Edwin smiled wanly.

"Do you know how much longer you'll be in the hospital?" asked Julia.

"Well, I think it will be a long, long time," replied Joey. "It
depends on whether they have to cut off my leg or not."

"Oh!" squeaked Margaret's mother.

"If they cut off my leg, I want one of those peg legs like a
pirate has," said Joey.

"Maybe you can wear an eye patch too, even though you
don't need one," said Margaret.

"Oh golly, I might do that. Whatever happens, I know I'll be
using crutches for years," he added without a pinch of self-pity.

"You certainly do have a good attitude, young man," Margaret's mother said.

"The doctors and nurses are working very hard to help you,"
said Edwin.

"Yes, everyone here has been stupendous," said Joey. "That's
my new favorite word. *Stupendous.*"

"That is a wonderful word," said Margaret. "Do you want
me to teach you how to spell it?"

I already know how to spell it," Joey announced proudly.
"S-T-U-P-E-N-D-O-U-S. I was in my school's spelling bee last
spring. I came in second. I would have gotten first place but I
got *geriatric* wrong. I don't even know what that means!"

"It means old," said Julia.

"Then why don't they just say old?"

"Well, since you like words, it seems I guessed right," said Margaret. "I brought you some crossword puzzles and books."

His eyes widened. "I never had my own puzzles or books before. Are they new?"

Margaret chuckled. "Yes, Joey," she said. "They're new. I also brought you some Oreos. I thought you might share them with the other children after you've all had your supper."

"Oh, do I have to share?"

"Yes," replied Margaret.

"Okay," he said reluctantly.

"And I brought you some clothes," said Julia. "New clothes. Dr. D'Milano told me on the telephone that you will be needing something to wear once you're walking around. He said you were buck naked when you arrived here, except for being wrapped in a blanket."

"Well, that's true! Ha ha ha! My brother and me and my brother's friend were skinny-dipping in the creek. It was so hot, remember? We're allowed to take the train from home to see Aunt Clovis in Cliffwood Beach, but—oh, don't tell anybody!— we like to take a detour from the train station and go swimming in the creek before we go to her house. Only this time, I got bit by the monster. And some old guy came along and wrapped me up and put me in his boat, along with my brother and his pal, and brought us closer to town. And then a fellow drove us all the way here to the hospital. I was hoping to go in an ambulance, like we have in New York City, with a siren. But we went in some nice man's auto. I found out his name and wrote a letter thanking him. I also apologized 'cause I got blood all over his automobile. My brother offered to clean it up, but the man said not to worry about it. How do you like that?"

"That was very nice," said Margaret.

"Yes, I've been very lucky," said Joey. "Each night when I say my prayers, I always say thank you for all the people who helped me, starting with my brother. We don't always get along; he picks on me! He's older. But he did pull me right out of the shark's mouth. So I start by thanking him in my prayers, and then I have a long list. It's getting longer and longer, but I've memorized it. Maybe now I should add the four of you to my list."

Dr. D'Milano returned and announced, "It is time for your visitors to let you rest, Master Joey," and the foursome rose to their feet. "Dr. Halsey," Dr. D'Milano added, "we will be changing the bandages and cleaning Joey's wound. Perhaps you would like to assist us? Maybe you have some knowledge that we don't. I know you are an expert on sharks."

"Oh, I'm not an expert," Edwin said quickly. "But I am happy to help."

"Father, I will wait for you in the lobby," said Julia.

"And I guess Mother and I will head home to Matawan," added Margaret.

"Oh, goodbye, and thank you so much for coming. And for the presents!" said Joey. "Please come again if you can spare the time. But you don't have to bring presents. I didn't mean I want more presents."

"Perhaps we will come again," Margaret said, glancing at her mother.

"Whatever you wish, Margaret. It's so nice to see you acting like your old self."

"Well, if you don't visit again, I will always remember meeting you, especially you, Miss Atkins, and you, Dr. Halsey. Now I've met two other people besides me who saw the horrible monster! We're like the Three Musketeers."

"Why, yes," said Margaret. "I guess you could say we're in this together."

"I loved *The Three Musketeers*," said Edwin. "That was my favorite book when I was growing up."

"My brother is jealous because he didn't get a good look at the shark's face," Joey said.

"Well, over the long run, he may be glad of that," said Edwin.

"But he doesn't get to be one of the Three Musketeers!" cried Joey. "And we do!"

As they filed out the door, Margaret lagged behind. "Thank you, Joey."

"For what, Miss Atkins?" he asked.

"I'm not sure how to explain it to you," she said. "But I like you, and I'm very glad we met. Oh, and you may call me Miss Margaret. All my pupils call me that."

CHRISTMASTIME 1916

CHAPTER 39

"Christmas is going to be stupendous this year," said Joey. He was seated on the sofa, his damaged leg elevated on a hassock. Margaret was decorating the tree with a string of popcorn and dried cranberries that she and Joey had made the previous evening. She couldn't believe he'd only been here two months. He had settled in so quickly.

As she draped the homemade garland on the branches of the tree, Margaret reminisced about how it came to be that Joey moved in. They found out in September that he would be discharged from the hospital in October. His leg continued to heal, and amputation had been avoided. He could even get around a bit on crutches.

The problem was that he had nowhere to go. Not that his mother didn't want him back. She had continued to visit him weekly. Margaret and her mother did as well, and the women had met several times.

But his family's apartment in the Bronx was a fifth-floor walk-up. Joey had progressed to the point where he could leave the hospital, but not enough to live in a building without an elevator.

At first, it was assumed he would live with his aunt in Cliffwood Beach. Dr. D'Milano objected, however, when he learned that the aunt worked very long shifts in a factory, and Joey would be alone all day with no one to change his bandages, cook for him, or assist him in any other way.

When it seemed Joey might be leaving the hospital only to end up as a temporary ward of the state, Margaret talked to her parents. "I can't bear it," she had said. "We have a bathroom on the ground floor. It's large enough to add a bathtub. He could live here for a while, and I could be his tutor."

"But, Margaret," her mother had protested, "his bandages need to be changed at least twice a day. I'm not able to do that, and neither are you since you're teaching all day."

This was true. Margaret was back to her old schedule, leaving the house at half past seven and returning around a quarter to four, when she began grading papers and planning lessons.

"What if we hired a nurse to come and look after his leg twice a day?" asked Margaret. "Surely, there is a way. I don't make much of a salary, but I would give every penny of it to have Joey here rather than an institution."

"I would need Sally for a few extra hours a week," said her mother. "There would be more laundry, shopping, and cooking to do."

"What do you think, Father?" asked Margaret, trying to hide how desperately she wanted to make this happen. Her hands trembled. She folded them on her lap so that her parents wouldn't notice.

"If we stick to a budget, yes," he said.

And so it happened. Joey's mother agreed, Joey was elated, and Dr. D'Milano went along with it, especially after Dr. Halsey, still on leave from Monmouth Memorial Hospital after his hospitalization in New York, agreed to come to Matawan weekly to examine Joey, working in conjunction with Dr. Brewster.

Two months had passed since the day Joey arrived by train and was greeted by Margaret and her mother. At first, it was shocking to have an inquisitive, talkative nine-year-old boy in the house. He was loud at times and uncouth. He got on her mother's nerves. Once, he ate all the pudding meant for dessert. Another time, late at night, he ate half a pie. He was in the habit of leaving his clothes in heaps on the floor. All was forgiven eventually, for his cheerful, guileless personality made it difficult to stay mad at him. With his presence in the house, Margaret began to heal. Seeing the world through the eyes of a child shifted her perspective away from the past and what had been lost toward the future and what it might bring.

What the boy understood instinctively, and accepted readily, was that they would never be free of the shark and, therefore, they had to make peace with it. For him, of course, the reminder would be physical. There were literally teeth marks on his leg. And most likely, he would never walk normally again. Only once, in Margaret's presence, did he question what had happened to him.

"Why do you suppose the shark bit me and not someone else?" he had asked one day, his brows knit together. "I mean, why did God let this happen to me—to my leg?"

"Nature did this, not God," replied Margaret.

"But didn't God create nature?"

Margaret sighed and looked Joey in the eyes. "There are things we aren't meant to know or understand."

He nodded. That was all.

Margaret, meanwhile, had not suffered the physical alteration and pain that Joey had, but the shark, she had come to realize, would be a part of her life forever too. Its shadow followed her everywhere. It was present whenever she sat on the front porch alone, without Stanley. It stalked her each time she passed Stanley's shop, where a new tenant had moved in. It lingered beside her at church when, each Sunday, she was confronted by the empty spot in the choir loft where Stanley had stood and sung so beautifully.

Stanley was gone from this world. So was Lester, the boy he had tried to rescue. There were two others as well—Charles Vansant from Philadelphia and the Swiss bell captain, Charles Bruder. Such suffering the monster had caused. Such grief it had left in its wake.

In Matawan, the group of boys did not return to swim in the creek. Their mothers forbade it, but that wasn't why they stayed away. Even when a rebellious lad occasionally worked up the nerve, he quickly learned that the experience wasn't the same. The blood had washed away, but the memory of it remained.

Blue herons and snowy egrets, meanwhile, still waded in the shallows. The tide rose and fell, then rose and fell again, subject to the pull of the moon and sun.

This was what Margaret came to see, and feel, a few days after Christmas, nearly six months after Stanley died. She did not go to the spot where the tragedy took place. Instead, she walked alone along the path to the site where, in a small, borrowed canoe, Stanley had asked her to marry him.

This is how I want to remember the creek, she thought. *This is how I want to remember Stanley.*

She memorized every detail. She closed her eyes and listened. Here, standing among the sea oats which fluttered and shifted in the cold winter breeze, she could almost hear his voice.

EPILOGUE

JULY 12, 1918

Edwin sat at the kitchen table alone. He washed his dinner plate and utensils, recalling the days when the kitchen bustled with life.

So much had changed.

The house was so empty now as 1918 was turning out to be a very difficult year. Spanish influenza had taken Hannah. She was buried in a Catholic cemetery beside her sister, who had perished three hours earlier, and her husband and children, who had died long ago. Since they had no living relatives in the US, Edwin had taken care of the arrangements.

Julia had joined the Red Cross and gone to Europe to help the war effort. Edwin was enormously proud but terrified at the same time. Mortimer had been opposed to her going and had yet to join up himself. She'd broken off the relationship and gone anyway.

Julia's most recent letter had just arrived. She was working very hard, she wrote. Even though she had not quite finished nursing school, they were happy to have her and even increased her responsibilities. Oh, and she had met a Scottish surgeon she liked a lot.

In the same letter, she mentioned a new interest, the Women's Suffrage Movement, and how volunteers were needed in Washington, DC. *It is ghastly,* she wrote, *that American women are not allowed to vote, don't you agree, Father? When I come back to the States, I intend to get involved.*

But what if she doesn't come back? Edwin thought helplessly. He shuddered, and a small groan escaped his lips. He so badly wanted her home and out of the war, yet he understood why she was there. At the train station when she departed, she had told him, "It's the right thing to do, Father." He knew this was true, but that didn't make it any easier to let her go.

Two years had passed since his hospitalization, but Edwin had not fully regained his strength. He had closed his full-time prac- tice but still saw a few patients at his home office. At the hospital, he had accepted a new role as a professor of surgery. While he no longer wielded a scalpel, he oversaw those who did and was content with passing along his knowledge to the next generation.

President Wilson had been reelected in November 1916 with his anti-war platform, but the country joined the war effort in April 1917, after an escalation of submarine warfare by Germany. Edwin eagerly volunteered to organize and launch a surgical tent, staffed with Monmouth Memorial doctors and nurses, to be sent to the war zone in France.

At first, Edwin had clung to the idea of going along. Julia convinced him in a series of letters that he was more useful stateside, however, as someone needed to keep collecting medi- cal supplies, raising funds, and recruiting additional volunteers. Edwin knew she was right, although it was disappointing.

A bright spot in his life was his friendship with Alice Munroe, the nurse who had looked after him at the hospital in New York. She left her home in New York City in January 1917 and moved to Ocean Grove, where she now lived with her sister. When she arrived, she sent him a note, and he'd called her. They had been seeing each other ever since.

Romance was also blooming in Matawan. Margaret Atkins had married Rusty Conover, Stanley Fisher's friend. Everyone had seen this development coming except, apparently, Margaret and Rusty.

Joey Dunn, the boy from the Bronx whose leg was mangled by the shark, continued to live with Margaret Atkins's parents, even after Margaret's marriage to Rusty. His leg had healed better than anyone could have hoped, but he continued to have difficulty with stairs and probably always would. He had told Edwin, who visited regularly to examine the wound, that his mother and siblings had grown attached to Matawan during their visits to the small town and were considering relocating from the Bronx.

The epidemic of infantile paralysis had peaked in August and lasted through October 1916, claiming the lives of six thousand Americans, the vast majority of whom were very young children. Of those who survived, at least twenty-seven thousand were paralyzed. The arrival of summer in 1917 was greatly feared, but an epidemic did not materialize, nor had there been any sign, so far, in 1918.

There had also been no more shark attacks. Schleisser sent Edwin a postcard from somewhere along the Nile River after the first anniversary of their close encounter, saying, *I guess we got him! I've heard no more attacks! Hope all is well.*

Edwin shook his head in wonder at Schleisser's astonishing resilience and derring-do. What he wished he could tell Schleisser was that the shark was gone but in its place was a newfound, almost universal fear of the water and what might be in it. One rogue shark wreaked havoc, and now no one seemed to think of the seashore in the same way. *It is humbling*, Edwin mused. His generation tended to believe that humans were superior to all creatures. During the summer of 1916, in just twelve days, along the golden East Coast of America, came a stark reminder that nature plays by its own rules.

Edwin didn't like it when people asked about his experiences with the shark, but he realized he couldn't get away from the topic entirely. It simply could not be avoided. He often overheard people discussing it, even though two years had gone by, the war raged in Europe, and millions were dying of influenza.

Those who weren't humbled by the shark were resentful, as if the creature had been a willful intruder intent on destroying their innocent vision of the seashore. Nowhere, they now understood, was safe, and the knowledge made them angry. *They aren't angry at the shark for killing people*, he realized. *They're angry that it ruined their summer, and all the summers to come, as long as people remember*—which, Edwin was beginning to think, might be a very long time.

Gradually, Edwin acknowledged a little recognition for his role in alerting the public about the shark, as well as its demise. He would not, however, talk about the latter. He accepted two speaking engagements: The first, a meeting of public health officials with the topic, "When No One Listens to You," in which he compared the public reaction to the shark attacks of 1916 to epidemics of disease. He told the audience that he wished he had a dollar for every time someone had said to him:

"But we don't have sharks like that."

"That can't happen here."

"It's impossible!"

"It won't happen to me."

"Everyone is hysterical over nothing."

"I'm not going to live my life in fear."

The second time, he spoke to a gathering of state health officials in Trenton with a talk entitled, "Rescuers: The True Heroes of 1916," in which he focused on the heroic lifeguards and ordinary citizens, especially Stanley Fisher, who gave his life in an attempt to rescue Lester Stilwell.

For a while, conspiracy theorists continued to express their belief that the shark attacks were in some way associated with the war. Many still insisted that the German U-boat was the culprit, noting a peculiar coincidence of timing: there were no more shark attacks after the *Deutschland* left the area.

As the days ticked by and nothing happened, Edwin grew more confident that he and Schleisser had killed *the* shark.

It's in the past, he told himself often. *The horrible monster is no longer.* The fear he had carried within him since he was thirteen and encountered the shark for the first time was wearing down, like shards from a broken bottle that turned into smooth-edged pieces of sea glass.

Other than Joey Dunn, Margaret Atkins, and Alice Munroe, the people Edwin met in the summer of 1916 had faded from his life. Then, in the same mail delivery that included the letter from Julia, he noticed an envelope postmarked in Point Pleasant but with no return address.

Not doing well and would like to see you. Always at Bill's Tavern after four for supper. It was signed, *Old Timer.*

Good Lord, he's still alive? Edwin thought. *Why, he was in poor condition two years ago!* But Edwin was pleased that the old fisherman had asked for his medical expertise. He looked at the grandfather clock. It was a quarter to four. He had no plans whatsoever. Why not go now? He packed his doctor bag and supplies and put them on the passenger seat of the new Model T that he'd purchased to replace the one he'd badly damaged in the Manhattan accident.

Secretly, Edwin was delighted to be called away from home by a sick patient, just like in the old days. *Oh, the joy of getting behind the wheel and responding to a call for help,* he thought, permitting himself a small smile.

As he drove, he tried to recall Old Timer's medical condition. The man, who might have been about sixty-five—although that was only a guess—suffered from a palsy of some sort. Edwin had noticed it twice, first when Old Timer lifted a beer glass to his mouth and again when he picked up Edwin's business card and put it in his pocket. How might his condition have deteriorated in two years? The man must be suffering from poor health indeed if he had finally summoned a doctor.

Lost in these thoughts, the drive passed quickly. As he parked near the bar, Edwin could hardly contain his joy. *I'm going on a house call!* he thought. *Well, a bar call.* He laughed to himself, then he tamped down the giddiness, realizing how inappropriate it would seem to his patient.

Inside, the bar was just as Edwin remembered. The Fisherman's Prayer still hung over the bar. The shadowy outline of Old Timer could be discerned in the same chair at the same table against the far wall.

Edwin anticipated that he might need to convince Old Timer to go with him to the hospital. *He is very unlikely to agree,* Edwin reminded himself, *unless he is at death's door.* Such was the case, nearly always, with stubborn old men.

As he pulled up a chair, Edwin's eyes slowly grew accustomed to the dim light. Old Timer did indeed look worse.

"It does my heart good that you got in touch," said Edwin. "What is the matter? What are your symptoms? Is there someplace we can go where I can examine you?"

Old Timer coughed horribly. When Edwin started to ask another question, the old man held up his hand. "That's not why I contacted you," he said.

"But you wrote that you're not doing well and would like to see me," said Edwin. "And frankly, you do look quite poorly."

"You don't understand," Old Timer muttered. "It's true I'm

not doing well—in fact, I think I'm going to die soon. What I meant is that, before I'm dead and buried, there's something I want to tell you."

"What's that?"

"I saw it again," replied Old Timer. He took a mouthful of beer.

"Saw what?" asked Edwin slowly.

"The beast."

Edwin stared. "No, you didn't!" he cried. He folded his arms tightly across his chest and sat back in his chair. "That's impossible! It's dead!"

"It is not dead."

"What are you talking about?" Edwin demanded.

"Last week, I went out in Bobby Truax's boat, and I saw it," said Old Timer. "Right here off Point Pleasant, about two hundred yards from the beach. Damn thing swam right past me like it was playing a game. 'Twas going faster than me. When it was ahead, it turned and looked right at me. Lifted its damn head right out of the water. Trying to decide if I was worth the trouble of going after, I guess. Decided I was a skinny old turnip and went on its way." He laughed hard, which led to a coughing spasm.

Edwin had brought something with him to treat a bad cough, but his doctor bag seemed impossible to reach, even though it was sitting right at his feet.

"Look at you, Doc, you're speechless!" Old Timer chortled. "Cat got your tongue, eh?"

"But we killed it in Raritan Bay! Schleisser and me. Two years ago!"

"Yeah, I heard all about that. Everyone was talking about it. Look, I don't know what you killed. But it wasn't the beast. Or maybe it was the beast playing some kind of trick on you. Made a copy of itself, just to fool you."

"Why would you say that?"

"Because you can't kill the beast," he replied, then added, "Why is everybody trying to kill it, anyway? It has just as much a right to be here as we do."

"Schleisser and I didn't have any choice!" said Edwin. "I'd rather not relive the details, but it was either the shark or us! And despite what you think you saw, I can assure you, we killed it!"

"You still don't understand," Old Timer said, groaning. "Your kind of people think human beings are the masters of everything. Well, that's hogwash. I thought people like you might have finally learned your lesson when the *Titanic* went down. They said it was 'the ship that could not sink.' Ha! Then it hit an iceberg and went straight to the bottom of the sea."

"So this is why you wanted to see me? To tell me that I'm a fool?"

"I just figured you'd want to know."

"I have to think about this," said Edwin.

"What's to think about?"

Edwin studied Old Timer's face in the dim light. The man looked terrible, like he truly was at death's door, and in Edwin's experience, people who were dying didn't make things up. No, the opposite was true. They had nothing to lose, so they spoke the truth.

"You have to understand," said Edwin. "I rather prefer the idea that it's dead. And I am not alone in this! Why, everyone is quite happy that the shark lives no more."

"Well, everybody's happy that the war is probably going to end soon, but I don't think that'll ever really be over either," said Old Timer.

"So either Schleisser and I encountered some kind of mythical beast, as you say, or there's more than one," said Edwin. "If there's more than one, then there could be hundreds of them for all I know. What a nightmare. And how will we ever figure it out?"

"Why are you so hell-bent on 'figuring it out'?" asked Old
Timer. "Why can't there be mysteries?"

"Someday, science will solve *all* of the mysteries."

"No," said Old Timer. "That day will never come."

"I think it will," Edwin countered.

"You'd better hope you're wrong," Old Timer mumbled.
"Mark my words, Doc. If the day ever comes when there are
no more mysteries, life won't be worth living."

Edwin pushed back his chair and stood up slowly. He patted
the old man on the shoulder and left.

He expected to go straight home, but instead he drove to
a place he had avoided for many years, Sea Bright. The town
had changed. New homes had been built. Unfamiliar shops and
businesses lined the main street. He parked at the town beach.

A few people were milling around, but it was dinnertime,
so he had the beach mostly to himself. He walked to the water's
edge and looked out to sea, so peaceful and sanguine. This was
where it all started when he was thirteen—right out there, just
off Sea Bright Beach. He hadn't returned even once, although
it was but a few miles from his home in Red Bank.

"I give up," he said aloud to the sea. "I know you're out
there somewhere, whatever you are. You win."

Edwin started to walk back to his Model T, his shoes full
of sand, when he stopped abruptly, almost tripping over his
own feet. *Wait a minute*, he thought. He turned to face the sea
again. *Maybe you really are the beast*, he mused. *Maybe you have
survived. Maybe the Death Spirit, Matanto, arrives with you or
maybe it doesn't. But guess what—I survived too!*

For so long, Edwin had been fighting the image of himself as
an incredibly unlucky man—a guy who went out in a boat just
twice in his life and was attacked by a vicious shark both times.

Suddenly, he realized he'd been looking at his situation

completely wrong. He was the incredibly *lucky* guy who got away—twice.

He thought about the other traumas of his life, as he always did after ruminating about the shark. *I survived the Spanish-American War in my younger days,* he thought. *The disease that took my wife and children, all except Julia, I survived that too, along with the Spanish flu that killed Hannah. I do not know why I am here, but I am.*

He was, he realized, speaking to the universe as much as to his old nemesis, the beast. Dr. Edwin Halsey, eminent physician, did not have all the answers. He was not likely to ever find satisfactory explanations. And yet, to his surprise, he was undisturbed by the notion. Letting go of the need for certainty had freed him.

The drive back to Red Bank was unremarkable, yet as he pulled into town, he had the oddest sensation that the familiar now felt new. He saw beauty in the simplest, most ordinary things. A tiny boy in a sailor outfit running clumsily along the sidewalk, his mother in pursuit. A small white dog trotting behind a man on a bicycle. The symmetry in a row of small pine trees.

Home beckoned. He could hardly wait. He would no longer take the old house for granted. He would have the broken shutter replaced and the slate roof repaired. He would invite Alice for dinner and ask her advice on redecorating the parlor. But first, there were more important things. He would sit in his favorite chair and sip some whiskey, celebrating his newfound peace. No, that's not what he would do. He would go straight to his study. He would craft a letter.

Dear Daughter, he would write. *I miss you. Please come home.*

AUTHOR'S NOTE

This is the first novel about these historical events. Several nonfiction books have addressed the topic, but as a fiction writer and longtime resident of the Jersey Shore, and a descendant of people who lived here for generations, I envisioned the story being told differently.

I wanted to write from the perspective of the people who experienced the tragedy as it unfolded, without any of the knowledge of ocean creatures we have now. I saw the subject as a springboard or creative opportunity to explore the varied human reactions to what felt like an invasion by a new and unforeseen enemy.

These reactions, as reported in the many newspapers that covered the events, ranged from fear and confusion to conspiracy theories and denial.

At the same time, the tale as I imagined it, is one of resilience, love, grief, and courage.

I created the main character, Dr. Edwin Halsey. He is loosely inspired by a surgeon who tried to save Stanley Fisher's life at

Monmouth Memorial Hospital, as it was then called, and signed the death certificate.

Margaret Atkins, also a significant character, is loosely inspired by Stanley Fisher's real-life girlfriend, who was reported to have been present when he was attacked by the shark in Matawan Creek.

Invented characters include the free-spirited Julia Halsey and her irresponsible boyfriend, Mortimer Weeks. The pivotal character called Old Timer is a composite of seafarers I have known during my twenty-seven years here at the shore, including at marinas and boatyards during my summers as a boater.

As much as I could, I maintained the actual timeline of the shark attacks as well as details from witnesses and locations. In some cases, I changed the names of those involved.

Newspapers sometimes provided conflicting information, leaving me to make a choice or educated guess.

At the time, little was known about sharks. In more recent years, there has been an ongoing argument about which type of shark—generally narrowed down to bull shark or great white—caused the mayhem in 1916. Those who support the theory of a bull shark note that particular species tolerates brackish water, such as the briny mix in Matawan Creek, while the great white does not. I favored the bull shark theory until I read that the extreme high tide would have greatly increased the amount of saltwater in the creek, making it possible for a great white to survive.

Also challenging was the size of the killer shark, the estimates of which varied. Finally, I decided to model the famed shark after a present-day great white called Breton who is the subject of scientific studies and is known to roam up and down the East Coast. On July 12, 2021, Breton's transmitter pinged several miles off Long Beach Island at the Jersey Shore, and I realized that Breton, who weighs 1,400 pounds and is thirteen feet, three inches in length, could be the perfect stand-in for the 1916 shark. For all we know, Breton may even be descended from or related in some other way to the original beast.

The real events are widely believed to have launched a national obsession with sharks—a fascination that spawned *Jaws* and, more recently, Shark Week.

In twelve short days during the summer of 1916, however, a real shark changed history. Four persons were killed, and a fifth was seriously injured at the Jersey Shore. Lives were ended, ruined, and altered, and millions were frightened half to death by a lone rogue shark that reminded America that nature plays by its own rules.

A note about the Native American references in this book: The information was shared with me by the late Marion "Strong Medicine" Gould (1922–2016), a matriarch and mother of the longtime chief of the Nanticoke Lenni-Lenape Tribal Nation of Bridgeton, NJ. They are the largest Lenni-Lenape group still living on ancestral lands, not on a reservation, a fact I learned while helping my father research our family tree, which includes long-ago Lenape ancestry. In 2010, in honor of my book, *"Strong Medicine" Speaks: A Native American Elder Has Her Say* (Atria Books/Simon & Schuster, 2007), I was given the name Smiling Songbird Woman by the tribe in a formal ceremony on private tribal land in Cumberland County, New Jersey, near Delaware Bay.

ACKNOWLEDGMENTS

I owe a very heartfelt thank-you to my literary agent, Mel Berger, at William Morris Endeavor in New York, for supporting my interest in trying my hand at writing a thriller; Blackstone Publishing, especially Rick Bleiweiss for believing wholeheartedly in this project from day one, and Anthony Goff for his cheerful enthusiasm and support; my extraordinary husband and love of my life, Blair, whose experiences long ago as a scuba diver, life guard, and Civil Air Patrol pilot and observer provided additional, fascinating background; my dear friend and fellow writer Audrey Glassman Vernick, who read an early draft and may never forgive me for her newfound fear of the ocean and tidal streams; my longtime friend and trusted attorney, John Firestone; and last but definitely not least, my brilliant editor, Madeline Hopkins, who gave me the nudge I needed to return to my writing desk, face this challenging topic one more time, and do the final polish on this book.

As a twenty-seven-year homeowner at the Jersey Shore who loves boating, I've had many discussions about the 1916 shark attacks at Monmouth County marinas and boatyards, providing me with extraordinary insight into the events and the trauma that afflicted the unsuspecting people of the shore. So many people have contributed to my knowledge that I can't mention them all. I would be remiss, however, not to mention the late George Moss of Rumson, NJ—a historian of the Jersey Shore with whom I discussed the attacks and many other topics over the years. His knowledge and generosity will always be remembered.

SOURCES AND
SELECTED BIBLIOGRAPHY

My primary sources were vintage newspapers, some of them now defunct but available online or at libraries. They include the following:

Asbury Park (NJ) Press
Baltimore Sun
Boston Globe
Brooklyn (NY) Times-Union
Chicago Tribune
Daily News (New York, NY)
Evening Public Ledger (Philadelphia, PA)
Evening World (New York, NY)
Home News (Bronx, NY)
Keyport (NJ) Weekly
Matawan (NJ) Journal
New York Times
New-York Tribune
Passaic (NJ) Daily News
Perth Amboy (NJ) Evening News

Philadelphia Inquirer
Pittsburgh Daily Post
Press of Atlantic City
Red Bank (NJ) Register
San Francisco Examiner
Times (London)
Washington Post

Other primary sources:
Bureau of Vital Statistics (Death Records), a division of the
   New Jersey Department of Health
Library of Congress
United States Census 1910
National Oceanic and Atmospheric Administration
   (NOAH)
Monmouth County (NJ) Library
Rutgers University Library
Ocean County Historical Society
Monmouth County Historical Society

Books:
Berg, A. Scott. Wilson. New York: G. P. Putnam's Sons,
   2013.
Bucco, Gloria. Precious Cargo: A Collection of Stories
   from the Italian Immigrants of Matawan, New Jersey.
   Lincoln, Nebraska: Gloria Bucco: 2015.
Capuzzo, Michael. Close to Shore: The Terrifying Shark
   Attacks of 1916. New York: Broadway Books, 2001.
Fernicola, Richard G. Twelve Days of Terror. Guilford,
   Conn.: Rowman & Littlefield, 2001.
Henderson, Helen B. From the Back Street to Main Street
   and Beyond, a History of the Society of Methodists of

Middletown Point. Matawan, N.J.: Helen B. Hender-
son, 2015.

————. *Matawan and Aberdeen: Of Town and Field.*
Matawan, NJ: Matawan Historical Society, 2003.

Koerver, Hans Joachim. *The Kaiser's U-Boat Assault on*
America: Germany's Great War Gamble in the First
World War. South Yorkshire, England: Pen & Sword
Books Limited, 2020.

Lloyd, John Bailey. *Eighteen Miles of History on Long Beach*
Island. West Creek, NJ: Down the Shore Publishing,
1994.

Van Hemmen, Hendrik F. *A Chronology of Boating on*
the Navesink River. 2nd ed. Red Bank, NJ: Navesink
Maritime Heritage Association, 2015.

Websites (accessed and accurate as of November 3, 2022):

"International Shark Attack File," Florida Museum,
updated May 17, 2022, https://www.floridamuseum.
ufl.edu/shark-attacks/.

"New Jersey Transportation Chronology," Liberty Historic
Railway (LHRy) of New Jersey, posted March 21, 2018,
https://www.lhry.org/nj-transportation-chronology.

"Breaking the Back of Polio," Yale Medicine Magazine,
Autumn 2005, https://medicine.yale.edu/news/
yale-medicine-magazine/article/breaking-the-back-of
-polio/.

"Photos of Lehigh Valley Barges at Work in the NY Harbor,"
Waterfront Museum, https://www.waterfrontmuseum.
org/lehigh-valley/photos-lehigh-valley-barges-work
-ny-harbor.

"Train Ferries: The Hudson River's Most Unusual
Steamers," New York Almanack, April 7, 2021,

https://www.newyorkalmanack.com/2021/04/train
-ferries-the-hudson-rivers-most-unusual-steamers/.

*"Infrastructure, New Yor k City (NYC) Holland Tunnel
(1927)," NYCdata, Weissman Center for International
Business, Baruch College, City University of New York,*
https://www.baruch.cuny.edu/nycdata/infrastructure/
holland_tunnel.html.